THE ISOLATOR

realization of absolute solitude

Sect.001
The Biter

REKI KAWAHARA
ILLUSTRATION BY SHIMEJI
CHARACTER DESIGN BY BEE-PEE

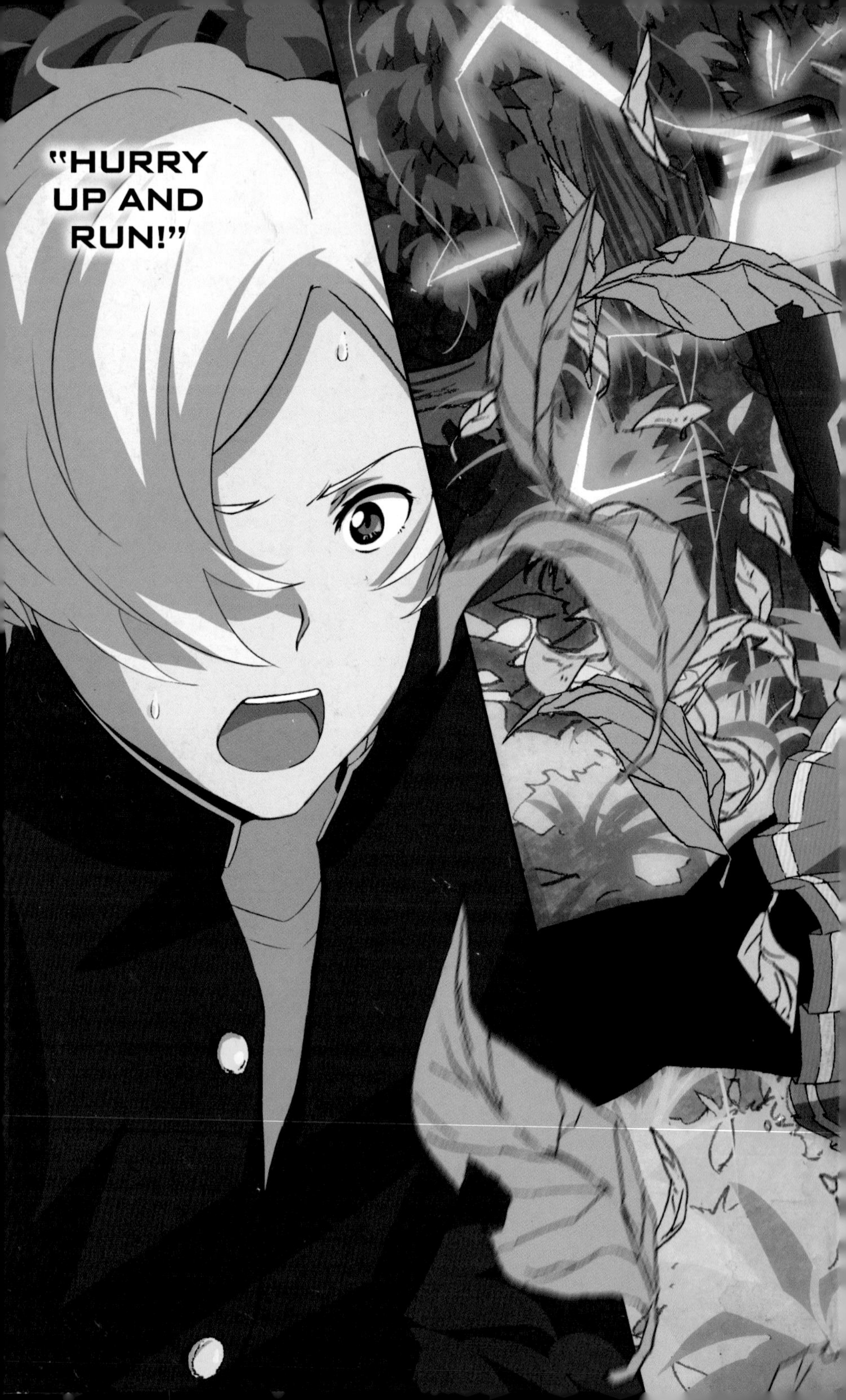
"HURRY UP AND RUN!"

"MOVE NOW!!"

>> YUMIKO AZU
THE GIRL WHO RUSHES IN DURING A BATTLE WITH THE MYSTERIOUS ATTACKER "THE BITER." BELONGS TO A CERTAIN ORGANIZATION THAT SPECIALIZES IN DEALING WITH THOSE WHO POSSESS MURDEROUS THIRD EYES.

"MORNIN', UTSUGI!"

>> **TOMOMI MINOWA**
A HIGH SCHOOL GIRL WHO WENT TO
THE SAME MIDDLE SCHOOL AS MINORU.
A RELATIONSHIP DEVELOPS BETWEEN
THEM AFTER A CHANCE MEETING ON
AN EARLY MORNING JOG. A LIVELY GIRL
WITH A BRIGHT PERSONALITY.

"...GOOD MORNING, MINOWA."

>> **MINORU UTSUGI**
AN ORDINARY BOY WHO LIVES WITH HIS ADOPTIVE SISTER, NORIE. LOVES SOLITUDE AND HATES BEING REMEMBERED BY OTHER PEOPLE. BECOMES AWARE OF A UNIQUE ABILITY GIVEN TO HIM BY A MYSTERIOUS ORB FROM SPACE CALLED A "THIRD EYE."

NORIE YOSHIMIZU
THE WOMAN WHO TOOK MINORU IN
AFTER HE LOST BOTH HIS PARENTS.
HAS A BRIGHT AND CHEERFUL
PERSONALITY, AND IS ALWAYS LOOKING
OUT FOR MINORU.

"..."

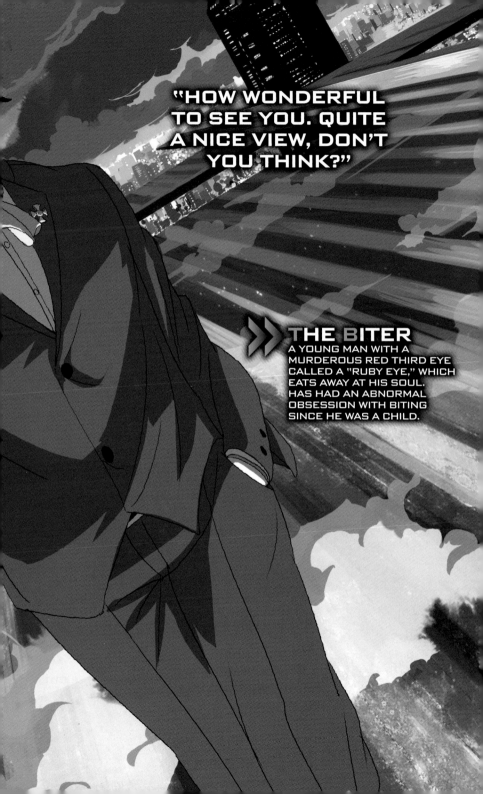

"HOW WONDERFUL TO SEE YOU. QUITE A NICE VIEW, DON'T YOU THINK?"

THE BITER

A YOUNG MAN WITH A MURDEROUS RED THIRD EYE CALLED A "RUBY EYE," WHICH EATS AWAY AT HIS SOUL. HAS HAD AN ABNORMAL OBSESSION WITH BITING SINCE HE WAS A CHILD.

THE ISOLATOR
realization of absolute solitude ≪◎≫ CONTENTS

THE ISOLATOR
realization of absolute solitude

Sect.001 The Biter

"I'M LOOKING FOR ABSOLUTE SOLITUDE... THAT'S WHY MY CODE NAME IS ISOLATOR."

REKI KAWAHARA
ILLUSTRATIONS BY SHIMEJI
CHARACTER DESIGN BY BEE-PEE

YEN ON
NEW YORK

ISOLATOR Volume 1
© REKI KAWAHARA

Translation by Adair Trask

ZETTAI NARU ISOLATOR
© REKI KAWAHARA 2014
All rights reserved.
Edited by ASCII MEDIA WORKS
First published in Japan in 2014 by
KADOKAWA CORPORATION, Tokyo.
English translation rights arranged with
KADOKAWA CORPORATION, Tokyo,
through Tuttle-Mori Agency, Inc., Tokyo.

English translation © 2015
by Hachette Book Group, Inc.

Yen On
Hachette Book Group
1290 Avenue of the Americas
New York, NY 10104
www.hachettebookgroup.com
www.yenpress.com

Yen On is an imprint of Hachette Book Group, Inc.
The Yen On name and logo are trademarks of
Hachette Book Group, Inc.

First Yen On edition: June 2015

ISBN: 978-0-316-26059-6

10 9 8 7 6 5 4 3 2 1

RRD-C

Printed in the United States of America

FRAGMENT 01

Memories?
What are memories?

At Minoru's question, his older sister Wakaba's hand went still as it was scooping up the custard caramel they were having for a snack. She thought a bit before answering.

"Mii, do you remember what snack we had yesterday?"

"Um…"

Minoru shifted his gaze from Wakaba sitting right next to him to his mother in the kitchen, who was humming as she did the dishes. The snacks they had on Saturdays and Sundays were always ones their mother made herself. When three o'clock rolled around, she would produce custard caramel or cookies or pie from the pantry adjoining the kitchen, just like magic. Minoru and his sister called the pantry Mama's Secret Room.

What appeared from the Secret Room yesterday was…

"Um, oh yeah, barbarian cream."

"Uh-huh. It was Bavarian cream."

Grinning, Wakaba wiped some caramel sauce from the corner of Minoru's mouth with a napkin on the table and continued on.

"So, Mii. Which do you like better, the Bavarian cream from yesterday or the custard caramel from today?"

Minoru thought about this new question as he gazed at the custard caramel in front of him, which was already half-eaten. He loved the custard caramel that his mother made for him. Unlike the ones sold in stores, the caramel wasn't bitter at all and the custard actually tasted of eggs like it should.

But he liked the Bavarian cream about the same. Anyway, the Bavarian cream he ate yesterday was strawberry. It melted lightly in his mouth like snow.

"…But I like both…"

Unable to choose, Minoru felt his eyes begin to tear up and Wakaba patted his head gently, smiling.

"Yeah, I like both, too. Hey, Mii, do you remember what flavor the Bavarian cream was yesterday?"

"I remember! Strawberry!" Minoru shouted, instantly forgetting his tears.

From the kitchen, their mother turned her gaze to the living room, breaking into a smile at the sight of her children.

"Yeah, it was strawberry. The reason you can remember what flavor the Bavarian cream was now is because the memory of it is inside you, Mii. Memories are remembering."

"Huh…"

It was a little difficult for Minoru, but he thought as hard as he could about the meaning of what his sister had said and came to one conclusion.

"…Well, then I'm going to memorize all the snacks we have from now on!"

"Why?"

"Because if I memorize them, I can remember the snacks even after I eat them! I'll memorize the custard caramels, the barbarian creams, the cream stuffs, everything!"

"Huh."

Peering at Minoru's face, Wakaba smiled again.

"Well, then we'll have to really enjoy eating everything. When we're done eating, let's draw a picture of the custard caramel together. Then I'm sure we can always remember it."

"I'll remember it forever and ever! And then when I grow up, I'll make custard caramel for you and Mama, Waka!"

"Thanks. I can't wait. It's a promise."

—A memory, Minoru four years old and Wakaba seven.

* * *

Hey, Waka.
What is memory made of?

At Minoru's question, his older sister Wakaba's hand went still as she did her elementary school homework. She cocked her head with a bemused look on her face.

"…What do you mean, what is it made of?"

"So…memories build up inside your head, right? So when you remember playing or singing, some new things pile up, and when you forget them, some things go away, right? So what are those things that pile up or go away? Are they words?"

"Wow, Mii, you've started thinking about some pretty difficult things," Wakaba said with a grin.

No matter how many books he read at home and at kindergarten or how many different things he learned, he was never even close to catching up to the knowledge of his sister, who was three years older than him. When Minoru asked her about something that mystified him, she would almost always explain it to him right away in a way that was easy to understand.

But there were occasionally times even Wakaba couldn't answer right away, and Minoru loved the look on her face at those times. It was a grown-up look, an ever so slightly bitter smile mixed in with her gentle one.

"The medium for memories…hmm. Hmmm… Okay, so in a person's head…"

Speaking slowly, Wakaba reached out her right hand and ruffled Minoru's hair.

"…There is a brain. The brain is made of things called neurons, and those neurons are connected by synapses."

"Neurons… Sap…nypses?"

"They're 'synapses.' People say that our memories are stored in those synapses, but they don't know what the memories are made of yet. Right now scientists all over the world are working hard to figure that out."

"Huh… So…those synapse things, about how many are there inside our heads?"

At this, Wakaba's wry smile intensified.

"Hey… What number can you count up to, Mii?"

"A hundred!"

He energetically shouted out this number, which he had finally learned how to count to just recently, and Wakaba responded, "That's amazing," patting him on the head again.

"…So, the whole brain is said to have about a hundred billion neurons. A hundred billion means ten times a hundred, times a hundred, times a hundred, times a hundred, and times another hundred."

"Times a hundred…times a hundred, times a hundred…?"

Minoru couldn't even understand the concept of multiplying by a hundred, and he scowled.

"…So which is bigger, that or the number of books in Papa's room?"

Their father's study had a bookshelf built into one of the walls, and it was crammed full of rows of books old and new. Minoru had once tried to count them starting from the end, but even when he made it to fifty, he had only gone through a fraction of them, and he ended up losing count.

Wakaba giggled and nodded.

"Papa does have a ton of books. Maybe around a thousand…but a hundred billion is *much, much* more. And you know…I guess there are about ten thousand synapses for each of those one hundred billion neurons."

"…?"

Unable to imagine the enormity of the numbers his sister was talking about, Minoru's mouth hung open.

Pulling her little brother to her in a hug, Wakaba turned her gaze to the blue sky outside the window.

"A hundred billion times ten thousand is a quadrillion… The number of stars in our galaxy, the Milky Way, is a hundred billion, too, so the number of synapses inside my brain and your brain is the same as the number of stars in ten thousand galaxies put together. Someday you'll be able to count… No, you'll be able to imagine that, too, Mii."

Wakaba paused there for a moment, holding Minoru to her tightly, and then whispered, "When you get to that point, tell me about it, too. Tell me what you felt with a quadrillion synapses, Mii. … Promise?"

Out of all the things his sister had said, Minoru could only understand the last one. So, looking up at his sister's face, Minoru nodded vigorously.

"Yeah, I promise! Once I get to elementary school, I'll be able to count to a quadrillion!"

A memory, Minoru six years old and Wakaba nine.

* * *

Waka…
I'm scared, Waka.

Wakaba crushed her little brother in a hug as if to be sure no one would be able to hear Minoru's weak wail.

Her arms loosened around him immediately, though, allowing Minoru to crouch down. Another wail threatened to surge up in him, but Wakaba pressed a finger to her lips, so he held it in somehow.

The two of them were in Mama's Secret Room, at the back of the small pantry connected to the kitchen. Pulling a large basket out from the bottom row of shelves, Wakaba quickly opened the hatch of a storage compartment under the floor that was hidden there. Two ten-kilogram bags of rice were stored inside, but Wakaba pulled them out with a force that would make a person wonder where in her slender arms she kept so much power. She pushed Minoru inside in place of the bags.

Minoru desperately gripped his sister's hand as she tried to stand.

"…Waka, where're you going…?" he asked her in a shaking voice.

Wakaba answered this with a smile that was gentle despite its stiffness.

"Your big sister is going to go call the police, so you're going to sit tight in there."

"No… Waka, let's stay…!"

Wakaba interrupted Minoru with a voice full of certainty and determination.

"It'll be okay."

"…But…"

"It's okay. I'll protect you, Mii. Trust me and just count silently to yourself in there, okay? If you count up to a thousand, I'll make custard caramel for you."

"…Really? You promise?" Minoru asked with tears in his eyes.

With a smile on her face, Wakaba nodded firmly.

"Yeah, promise. So you absolutely can't come out of there."

The hatch closed above his head, and the storage compartment was enveloped in darkness. He heard two heavy sounds in succession.

Then came the sound of a large object being dragged. Wakaba placed the two rice bags in the basket and put them back on top of the hatch.

The faint sound of footsteps receded and disappeared in no time. Suppressing his rising sobs, Minoru began to count inside his head in earnest.

One, two, three, four, five, six, seven…

From somewhere far off, there was a heavy *thud, thud* sound. Wild, rough footsteps that didn't belong to anyone in his family.

Fifty-two, fifty-three, fifty-four, fifty-five…

The footsteps were coming closer. Something big had broken and fallen to the floor in the living room. A dining room chair fell over next. Someone was coming into the kitchen. He heard someone violently opening and closing the doors to the refrigerator and the cupboards. Dishes and glasses were being knocked down forcefully, shattering.

One hundred twenty-nine, one hundred thirty, one hundred thirty-one, one hundred thirty-two…

At last, the owner of the footsteps stepped into the pantry. The spice collection that his mother was so proud of fell down and scattered. Pots and frying pans joined the spices on the floor. Although he couldn't see a thing, he had a clear picture of the scene. *Thud, thud.* The footsteps marched in place over and over just like they were checking under the floor.

One hundred fifty-five, one hundred fifty-six, one hundred fifty-seven…

Something heavy was scraping along right above Minoru. It was the sound of someone moving the basket where the two ten-kilo rice bags were stored.

One hundred fifty-nine, one hundred sixty…

But when the basket was pulled only about halfway out, the movement stopped.

One hundred sixty-one, one hundred sixty-two…

The footsteps slowly receded. Sounds of destruction came from the kitchen and the living room again.

One hundred eighty, one hundred eighty-one, one hundred eighty-two…

The footsteps disappeared. A long, long silence stretched out.

Minoru continued to count. Just as his sister had told him, he counted with all his might.

Finally, sirens approached. They stopped near his house. A herd of footsteps was coming inside. He heard several strained adult voices shouting.

Count. Count.

When he had counted up to 3,617, the basket directly above him was finally pulled out completely, and the hatch to the storage compartment was opened.

Squinting his eyes from the brightness, Minoru looked up.

But what he saw there was the face of an unknown man wearing a navy blue suit and a hat with a gold badge attached to it.

The face of someone who was not Wakaba.

Minoru once again curled into a little ball and began counting.

Three thousand six hundred eighteen.

Three thousand six hundred nineteen.

Three thousand six hundred twenty—

A memory, Minoru eight years old and Wakaba eleven.

For all eternity, these three promises would remain unfulfilled.

FRAGMENT 02

July 2019.

Dryden I, the large-scale radio telescope built inside the Dryden crater on the far side of the moon, picked up a radio wave burst that was faint but fraught with meaning. It was a very short signal with a center frequency of 1420.406 megahertz, and over and over again it repeated twice, thrice, five times, seven times, eleven times, thirteen times, and seventeen times with small intervals in between.

Two, three, five, seven, eleven, thirteen, seventeen. Those are the first seven prime numbers, a fact that even elementary school students could understand. The news surged around the world, and scholars, experts, and amateur enthusiasts from every conceivable field threw themselves into analyzing the signal itself.

Taking the first letters of the words "seven prime numbers," the signal was named the SPN Signal. Within one short week, this "message from space" had been translated in every conceivable way and presented on the Internet. But no one argument was strong enough to convince people universally.

It was only after everything had already begun and ended that it became clear that the SPN Signal had been a warning for a certain disaster.

September 2019.

In a number of energy-dense regions on Earth, the first organic extraterrestrial life-forms that the human race would encounter descended. But because they were so very small and couldn't be called intelligent life-forms, knowledge of that fact was mostly limited to people involved in the encounters.

Sect. 001
THE BITER

Had it been a coincidence? Or was there something inside him that had summoned it?

After the encounter, Minoru Utsugi had wondered that many times. He didn't know the truth. But there was just one thing he was certain of: That black orb had misunderstood Minoru's wish.

Even with the supernatural power the orb had given him, the solitude Minoru sought would never be his. That was because he still hadn't been able to find it on his own.

Just what was the ultimate, perfect, absolute solitude he'd been searching for ever since that day?

1

Passing through the morning fog, the long, narrow black asphalt stretched on and on.

The thin soles of his running shoes gripped the damp surface of the road, and he pushed off. He inhaled twice through his nose in time with his pace and exhaled two white puffs of breath through his mouth. His heart pulsed rhythmically, circulating blood throughout his body.

His breathing, his pulse, and the expanding and contracting of his muscles. Those were the only things Minoru felt as he ran on.

His body mass index was far below the average, and he wasn't on the track team at his high school or anything, so his goal wasn't fitness or training. He didn't even know if he'd always had a fondness for running.

The reason Minoru had a habit of running ten kilometers every morning was that, just while he was running, he didn't have to think about anything. He also got the feeling that his breathing and the pumping of his blood washed away useless memories.

That was why, truthfully, he wanted to run late at night instead of early in the morning. At the end of the day, running down the recreation trail on the embankment guided only by moonlight and the light of the far-off city, he wanted to take the memories that had accumulated throughout the day and wash them away completely with his sweat.

But once, when he had actually tried to go out running around ten o'clock at night, his adoptive sister, Norie Yoshimizu, had gently forbade him in a way that left no room for discussion.

At night, the riverbed of the Arakawa River really was filled with the roars of modified motorcycles. It was also unthinkable for him to disobey Norie; he was just a high school sophomore who was completely dependent on her for everything in his daily life.

That's why Minoru had kept up this habit every morning since he started five years ago until today, December 3, 2019.

His feet kicked. His chest swelled. He inhaled and he exhaled. It was quite humid for an early December morning, and with the zipper of his Windbreaker pulled halfway down, the air felt good on his chest. According to the forecast, it would be rainy for a while starting next week, so he only had a few days left to dress light on his runs. The advantage of running in the rain wearing a rain jacket in the middle of winter was that he could have the ten-kilometer course almost entirely to himself, but he was in danger of overdoing it before going to school, exhausting his mental and physical energy.

Of course, to a certain extent, it was pointless to run if it wasn't a challenge, but his priorities needed fixing if he was willing to end up sleeping at school and angering the teacher. Minoru ran to reset his memories, but if he earned his teacher's ire in the process, it would take him any number of weeks to forget it.

The last time he'd been reprimanded by a teacher was two years ago in the second semester of eighth grade. His homeroom teacher had announced that the homemade cherry pie from Norie in Minoru's lunch box fell into the "sweets" category, which was banned by the school. Once he'd received a thorough scolding, his pie was confiscated.

At the time, his teacher had gone so far as to speak ill of Minoru's adoptive sister. As he desperately suppressed the urge to talk back, he ended up letting just a few tears slip out. An unkind classmate saw and jeered at him; that time, he couldn't hold back…

"…!!"

He gritted his teeth and picked up his pace. Blasting through the course at almost the same speed as a sprint, he spat out the fragments of a sentence.

"Why…did I…remember that…?!"

Forget. He needed to forget. He had to forget all the memories, including the ones of his stupidity.

That's because they would surely connect everything together. With that day eight years ago. The memory of that day when Minoru's world was completely destroyed—that day when he counted with all his might in a dark hole.

He kicked the asphalt as hard as he could. His breathing became ragged and his pulse quickened. But still, it wasn't enough. He needed to struggle much more or he wouldn't be able to reset his mind, which was immersed in memories like black water.

Run. Run.

If only he could go on running like this until his heart or his lungs were ragged. If he could do that, he could leave behind all those memories and go to someplace other than here…

But a few seconds later, silver poles emerged from the morning fog. They blocked cars from entering the trail, and he used them as markers for the start and finish line of his jogging route.

He suppressed his reckless urges and slowed his pace a little at a time. Once the passing breeze that had cooled his chest died down, sweat came pouring out from the bottom of his Windbreaker. His breathing and his pulse returned to normal immediately.

After wiping the sweat from his brow with his wristband, he pressed the stop button of the sports watch on his left wrist. Once he heard an electronic *beep, beep*, he peered down at the LCD screen apprehensively. Looking at the digital numbers that were displayed, he frowned without realizing it. He had anticipated this, but today he really was still—

"…Too fast…," he whispered, the words spilling out of his mouth. He blew them away with a deep sigh.

Because he'd been doing his early morning ten-kilometer run for five years straight, he'd developed confidence in his long-distance running skills, humble though they were. But that's exactly why he could declare his time to be too fast. A person's time wasn't something that could be so easily improved. While times can rise and fall daily depending on conditions like physical state and weather, people get faster little by little over a span of months—no, they realize they got faster after the fact. At least that's how it had been up until now.

Despite that, the number now displayed on Minoru's watch had gotten almost three times smaller compared to the number just three months ago.

Even though he had sprinted a little at the end, he'd actually intended to hold back overall during the run.

His right hand was still on his watch, and he brought it back down to chest level. He lightly pressed the center of his sternum with a fingertip. It didn't feel painful or strange. But still, he could definitely feel it. A faint hint of something quietly breathing directly above his heart.

"...Is it because of you?" he whispered to it, receiving no answer.

But at this point, that was the only explanation.

What happened three months ago wasn't a dream. Something had come down from the sky, slipped inside his body through his chest, and disappeared. No, it had assimilated with his tissue.

Because of that something, his running time had improved abnormally. That wasn't all. He also had the feeling that his hearing and his eyesight were better than before.

There's no way. It's just nonsense.

In his heart he denied it, but at the same time another version of himself whispered to him, *Common sense is nothing but an illusion.*

Every event that can possibly happen will happen, no matter how abnormal or frightening or sad it may be.

Take what had happened to his family. The four of them had lived a happy life together, but on that day, everything was suddenly destroyed without a trace of it left.

"...What does it even matter?" he spat in a low voice, lowering his right hand.

What did it matter what the thing was that had entered his body, and what did it matter if it increased or decreased the time it took him to run ten kilometers? It wasn't like he was running to prepare for a competition.

What he wanted was for the days to pass him by, clear and colorless.

He wanted to live a quiet life just like a ghost, not creating extra memories and not sticking in the memories of anyone else.

Yeah, I'm just like a ghost now. The truth is, I was supposed to die on that day with my father, my mother, and...my sister.

Talking to himself silently, Minoru turned to face in a different direction. A little way ahead, he could see the stairs leading down from the embankment. From there, it was about a kilometer to his house.

He switched his watch from stopwatch mode back to time display mode, confirming that he still had enough time until school began. Raising his head, he took in the sight of the reddening sky. Another day was beginning now, no different from the day before it.

As he turned to head to the stairs while going over his schedule in his head...

...He heard rhythmic footsteps coming from behind him. He was being overtaken by another jogger running the same course.

Minoru moved down to the left edge of the trail for a moment. In that area people could only run in the center of the path because of the poles that kept out cars, and if he blocked that part, he'd be in the way of a runner trying to pass. A runner might click his tongue at him in irritation, and then Minoru would already be stuck with a bunch of those nasty memories that he'd worked hard to clear from his head.

As he waited for the runner to pass by, he gazed at the block of skyscrapers in Saitama's new urban center, which glinted in the distance as they were hit by the midwinter morning sun. Then—

The footsteps slowed little by little, coming to a stop right behind Minoru. He heard roughly panting breaths and smelled a faint scent. He couldn't see her, but it was probably a female runner. It seemed that, like Minoru, she also used this point as her finish line.

If so, there was no reason for him to go on standing here until who knows when. Keeping his face averted, Minoru set off for the stairs, but he couldn't help coming to a halt again. From diagonally behind him on his right, she had suddenly called out to him.

"Oh, wait... You're...Utsugi, right?" she said between breaths.

At this, he stopped with a start. Her voice didn't sound familiar. He didn't have any memory of an acquaintance running this course at

this time, either. If he had, he would've changed to a different location or time.

For just a moment, he considered saying she was wrong and running off, but through several previous failures, he had learned that this impulsive, escapist response was not the optimal choice. He gave up on breaking away and turned around in an awkward motion.

About two meters away from him, a petite woman—no, a girl—was standing with both hands on her knees, exhaling big white breaths. She seemed to be the same age as him or a little younger and was small-framed with short hair. She seemed delicate at first glance, but the arms and legs that stuck out of her pastel green running outfit were solidly muscled, and it was obvious that she ran regularly.

And yeah, he had an inkling that he might remember that face, which was looking up at him.

"...Uh...so..."

He trailed off, unable to say, "Who are you again?" Her slight smile disappeared and her mouth bent into a tremendous frown. Inhaling deeply as if she had finally caught her breath, she righted herself, planted both hands near the back of her hips, and—

"Minowa."

"Wh-what?"

"Tomomi Minowa. I'm a sophomore at Yoshiki High in Class Eight."

"...O-oh..."

He couldn't decide how to respond, so for the moment he just nodded with his head inclined slightly.

Minoru did go to Yoshiki High, a public high school in Saitama Prefecture, and he was in the same year, but their classes were different. Minoru was in Class One, which was on the opposite side of the school grounds, and having only been at that school for eight months, it was understandable that he wouldn't remember the face of some girl named Tomomi Minowa.

He had only thought things through that far when Tomomi opened her mouth again.

"...And I was in Class Two at Hachi Middle in eighth grade."

"...O-oh..."

This time, he nodded a little more deeply than before.

Hachiou Middle School was another school Minoru had attended. He also remembered being in Class Two when he was an eighth grader. That meant that just two years ago—no, technically one year and nine months ago—the girl Minoru saw before him had been his classmate.

Remembering people's faces was not his strong point. He didn't look at them properly during conversation, so one could say it was to be expected. Even so, he should have spoken to her at least once or twice if they had studied in the same class for a year. Did his inability to remember this mean that his daily memory-reset run was more effective than he thought...?

As he considered these things, the faint memory of a face overlapped with the sullen one before him. Brow furrowed, he worked to pull up the far-off memory.

"Um... Minowa... Minowa... Oh...I feel like you used to have longer hair...," Minoru muttered.

In a flash, the smile returned to Tomomi's sullen face. She nodded, her short hair swinging around vigorously.

"That's right! I chopped it off before I moved up to high school."

"...Huh..."

Was this the point where he was supposed to ask why she chopped it off or not?

Luckily, there was no need to worry about that; Tomomi came right out with the answer as she grabbed the ends of her hair, which was cut about three centimeters above her shoulders.

"Long hair isn't allowed for new members on our track team. In middle school it was okay as long as you put it up, though."

"Oh, so that's why," Minoru said, giving the most neutral response.

Minoru ended up thinking that, if she found the team rules unreasonable, she should just push to get them fixed or quit the team, but he didn't say so. He heard that clubs, and sports teams in particular, weren't that easy to quit, and if new members complained about old rules, that would create other annoyances in and of itself.

No, that's beside the point.

Simply put, this girl Tomomi Minowa probably liked track... liked running. For that, she was probably willing to at least chop off her hair.

Those thoughts called back another flash of memory: a girl onstage at the school-wide morning assembly doing a quick bow as the principal passed her a certificate of achievement, her ponytail swinging happily on the back of her head.

"Oh...Minowa, did you by chance compete in nationals in the last year of middle school...?"

"It took you long enough to remember!" Tomomi shouted with a displeased expression before popping right back into a smile. "But that's how things always go when you're talking about someone else's extracurriculars, right? And even though I went to nationals for middle school, I was only tenth place... And this year, I didn't make it past the prefectural qualifiers..."

"W-well, I think that's great. It's not that easy to be tenth in the country."

A flustered Minoru had been trying to smooth things over, but for some reason Tomomi's mouth once again turned to a pout.

"...You say that, but Utsugi, I couldn't come close to catching up with you."

"Huh?"

"I took off after you when I saw you at Hanekura Bridge, but until I got here, I couldn't come close to catching up with you!"

"...I-I didn't realize..."

"From what I can see, you're not even that sweaty."

"...I-it's really cold today...," he said, making excuses as he panicked internally.

He hadn't at all realized that a student at the same school as him had discovered him running or that she'd been following him. Worse, his pace had been so— He had never dreamed that he would rise to the same level as a member of the girls' track team who'd gone to nationals.

Tomomi's big brown eyes fixed Minoru with a stare when he lapsed into silence.

"Utsugi, you didn't run track in middle school or high school, did you?"

"...No."

"Do you run here every day? Since when? How far?"

"Um..."

He didn't know what he should exaggerate or what he should downplay to fool her, so he answered honestly.

"About ten kilometers for five years."

"Whoa—! That's amazing! There aren't many people who practice every morning independently like that, even on our team," Tomomi said loudly, giving her interpretation of Minoru's response with another smile on her face. Then she came right out and said the words that Minoru had been fearing. "You're so fast you should just join the track team!"

"Um... Uh..."

It wasn't like he could just answer "uh-huh" to all these things.

He'd probably build up many times more useless memories than he did now if he belonged to any club, not just track. Besides, the speed that had piqued Tomomi's interest in the first place wasn't something he'd gained from five years of running. He could only think it was caused by that *something* that had entered his body three months ago.

There was no way he could compete with the members of the track team—who were sincerely putting in the work—with what could be called a borrowed ability. There was also the possibility that he could suddenly lose his speed in the same way he'd gained it. If he joined the track team on her invitation and then suddenly got slower... Just thinking about it made him break out in a cold sweat.

"...Well..."

It's not like I'm running to get faster.

Minoru kept racking his brain for a nice way to say that, but before he could put the words together...

"...!"

His ears—which he felt had gotten incredibly sensitive lately—picked up on something like a light whirring sound. Looking reflexively to his right, he saw a shadow speeding toward them through the dense morning fog.

A bicycle—a racing bike. It was going to plunge through the gap in the poles without slowing down. And on top of that path stood Tomomi Minowa. It wasn't clear if the rider was aware of the figures in front of him, but Tomomi had obviously not noticed.

At this rate, they would touch—no, collide—in less than three seconds. If they were hit by a bike that looked to be going thirty kilometers per hour, they wouldn't get away with just scratches.

Finally seeming to spot Tomomi, the rider yelled, "Hey!"

At his shout, Minoru finally moved. Taking a step forward, reaching out his right hand, and wrapping it around Tomomi's back, he wrenched her over to the left. The thin tires of the racing bike locked up as the rider slammed on the brakes, sliding across the road dampened by the morning fog.

Minoru had pushed Tomomi out of the bike's path, and as a reaction, he fell forward. The bike closed in from the right, unable to stop.

It would hit him.

Minoru held his breath. His heart pounded.

Then—

Something happened.

All sound died away. His whole field of vision took on a slightly blue cast.

The soles of his shoes left the ground, his body rising a few centimeters.

The brake levers, sticking out like horns from the racing bike's handles, made contact with Minoru's right arm. Or that's what should have happened.

But Minoru didn't feel anything. There was no pain, no impact, not even the sensation of touching something.

Although the bike veered right like it had been deflected and then swayed around, the rider just barely regained his balance and returned to the center of the trail. At about the same time, the *something* that had visited Minoru left him.

The color of the world went back to normal, and his floating feet touched the ground. The peculiar silence vanished and ambient sound rushed in.

"Watch out!" the rider roared.

He turned to glower at them through his sunglasses as he rode on slowly, then sped up to ride away to the north.

Minoru had no time to be thankful that it hadn't been a huge accident.

What was that just now?!

Still in an unstable position, he drew in a sharp breath. He moved his rigid right hand up in front of his eyes.

The bike definitely should have connected with his hand. This wasn't a graze. The impact had been enough to change the bike's course, so it was strange that he, too, hadn't been sent flying or at least been given a bruise.

But no matter how much he scrutinized his right hand, he couldn't find any bruises or cuts. Of course, he wasn't in any pain, either.

"U...Utsugi! Are you okay?!"

At her hoarse voice, he dropped his right hand and turned his face to the left.

There was Tomomi Minowa, both hands clasped in front of her chest. Her eyebrows, which were quite defined for a girl these days, were knitted impressively. Tears threatened to spill from her wide-open eyes, and her mouth was a stiff oval. Looking at this overly rich display of expression—

A little laugh burst out of him. Flustered, Minoru covered his mouth and apologized.

"S-sorry. You were just making this crazy face, Minowa."

Tomomi blinked at this in bewilderment, and then her cheeks reddened.

"S-so what, I was concerned! Things have always shown too much on my face! More importantly, are you hurt?! The bike hit you just now!"

"...Yeah, but..."

Minoru adjusted his expression and showed Tomomi his right hand.

"It seems okay. I didn't get hurt anywhere."

"R-really? ...I'm glad...," she said, looking as relieved as possible. Then she bit her lip and her head sank down suddenly. "I'm sorry I was zoning out! And thanks for protecting me!"

"I-it's fine... I'm glad you weren't hurt, either."

Even at this reply from Minoru, the petite track runner kept her head down for another five seconds or so, then raised it timidly.

"...I was almost hit by a bike here before. That's why I've always done my road training at Akigase, but..."

The place Tomomi mentioned was a large park built on the embankment along the main course of the Arakawa River in the southwestern

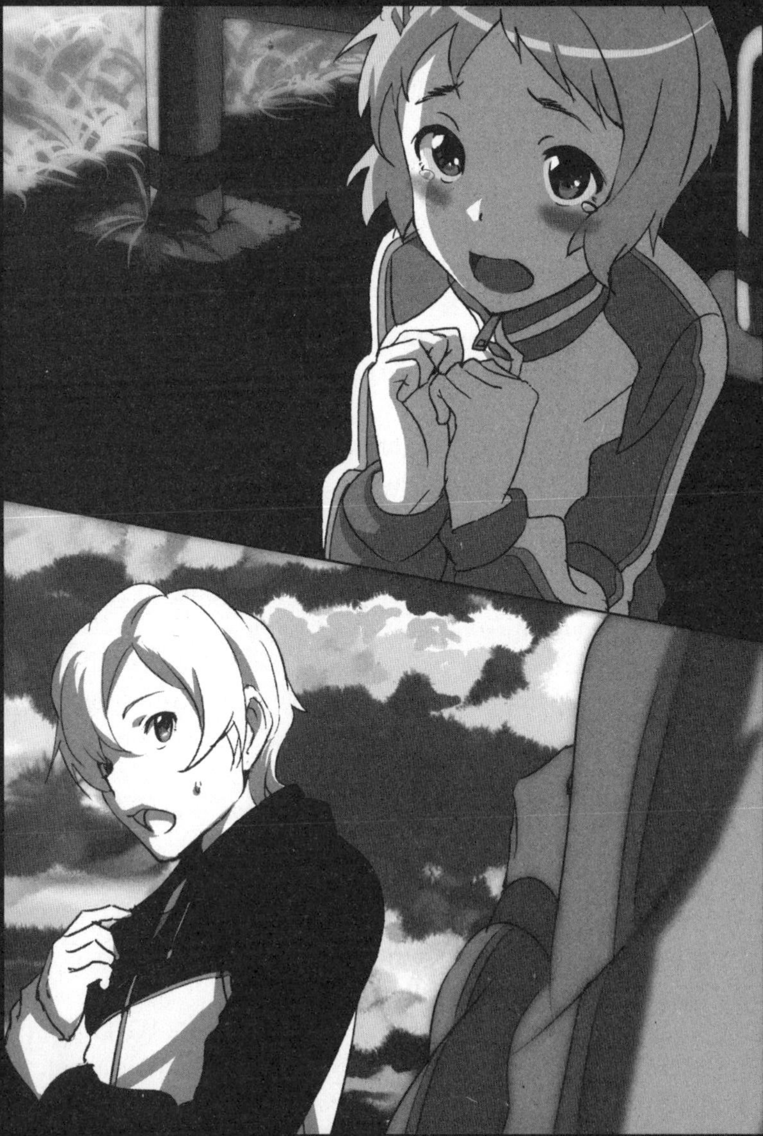

Sakura district of the city of Saitama, Saitama Prefecture. It was a popular spot with joggers, but Minoru didn't make his way there much. When he went into any big park, not just Akigase, it stirred up old, old memories.

"…Bikes get going really fast on this path, huh? But I'm glad nothing happened."

When Minoru got his thoughts in check and repeated what she had said, Tomomi finally gave him a smile.

"Yeah. Thanks, Utsugi, really. We've got a training retreat with other teams coming up really soon, so it would've been terrible if I'd gotten hurt. Utsugi, you've really always been…"

She paused there, and Minoru inclined his head slightly.

At this, Tomomi's expression grew a bit hesitant. Then she went on speaking.

"…So, there was one time in eighth grade where you really raised your voice in class—which was unusual for you, right, Utsugi? I remember it really well. You got angry because the teacher was saying bad things about your sister. I was really mad, too, and I wanted to talk back to the teacher, but I was too scared. That's when I thought, *Utsugi's got some courage…and he's a nice person…*"

Those words of Tomomi's—

Minoru had mostly stopped listening to them halfway through. He couldn't breathe. His core temperature climbed, yet his limbs grew as cold as ice.

He had to forget—it was a memory he should have already forgotten. It was a memory that not a single one of those who had been there should remember.

He kept his eyes far down. He clenched his hands tightly. Somehow he managed to inhale and exhale through his closing throat.

"…Utsugi…?" Tomomi said doubtfully.

"I…I've got to get home soon or I'll be late for school. Well, then… see you," Minoru answered in a hoarse voice without looking at her.

Then he turned to face the other direction and ran at full speed toward the stairs a little way ahead. Tomomi Minowa would think he was strange running away like this. To be precise, being thought of as strange would give him more memories to hold on to that he couldn't easily erase.

Knowing this, he couldn't stand not running.

...And I've been working so hard to blend into the background, too. Why, then, do people still remember me? Why won't they just leave me alone?

Solitude. He wanted to have solitude. He wanted to stay curled up forever in a blank world where he didn't stick in anyone's memories and he didn't remember anyone else.

Even after dashing down the concrete steps and entering a residential street, Minoru kept running as hard as he could. That abnormal phenomenon that had invaded him—or protected him—earlier was almost entirely forgotten.

2

No good.

It was no good at all. It was trash that didn't deserve to be called food.

Hikaru Takaesu perfectly concealed his derision as he put down his knife and fork and wiped his mouth with a napkin.

When he lifted his wineglass and put it to his lips, he wanted to take the hard, smooth inorganic object and completely crush it in his mouth just to cleanse his palate—the urge welled up in him, but of course, he couldn't act on it.

After holding a mouthful of the white wine in his mouth and savoring it as if he were chewing, he swallowed. For how grandly the waiter had suggested it, both the flavor and the aroma of the wine were a bit lacking; still, it was much better than the food.

With the glass still in his right hand, he looked down at the plentiful amount of pasta left on the plate. He had heard that the handmade fettuccine was the standout menu item at this restaurant, but if this was the best they could do, using dried noodles probably would've been better and more edible. Unlike dried noodles, when it came to fresh pasta that wasn't prepared al dente because the core was left uncooked, if one didn't pay close attention to the ingredients, the dough making, and the adjustment of the boil, it was easy to lose the firmness, which was the soul of the pasta.

That was exactly the case with the fettuccine at this restaurant. The flour was bad, the way they kneaded it was bad, and the way they boiled it was bad.

As a result, it had no firmness when chewed and was reduced to a slimy, gummy, tangled mass.

Firmness. The factor that should be considered most important for all cuisine, not only the Italian food that Takaesu primarily critiqued, was not flavor or aroma or presentation, but firmness—the way it feels in the mouth.

Biting, tearing, crushing, mashing. These actions activate primal instincts in humans and create satisfaction in the act of eating. Anyone would prefer the taste of a three hundred yen beef bowl made with sinewy imported meat over a Kuroge wagyu steak turned into a syrupy liquid with a food processor.

Chefs who didn't have the instinct to use texture to their advantage ultimately lacked talent in other areas as well. At this rate, the *secondo piatto* being served next would likely be a letdown as well. He would rather have just gotten up and left, but he couldn't do that. He had come here at the suggestion of someone in the media who was a regular at this place, so he had no choice but to write an article that was flattering in its own way.

He picked up his fork grudgingly, and as he was forcing down another mouthful of the fettuccine that was worse than dog food, a man in a chef's coat walked out of the kitchen.

The smiling, unshaven man who gave no impression of cleanliness was the restaurant's chef and owner, if Takaesu remembered correctly.

"Welcome, Mr. Takaesu! And how is everything thus far?" the man called loudly to Takaesu, who returned his smile for the sake of appearances only.

"I'm quite enjoying myself, thank you."

"Well, that's great to hear. We'll be serving you more carefully crafted dishes tonight, and, oh, it will be on the house. This next dish will be just the thing!" the chef said, placing a full flute of *spumante rosso* wine on the table.

Really, what kind of sense could this chef have? He had actually poured Takaesu's wine—and sparkling wine at that—in the back of the restaurant without even showing him the bottle. Takaesu could feel his irritation rising again, but the chef gave no sign that he noticed and for some reason chose this time to go for a handshake.

With no other choice, Takaesu stood up, shook the man's hand in return with a smile, and—

...*Why don't you bite him?* something inside him whispered.

He lifted up a boorish, rough, tobacco-stained finger from a right hand that he couldn't believe belonged to a chef and...took a leisurely bite.

After splitting open the skin and flesh and reaching the middle phalanx, he slowly applied more pressure. All the textures were there: First, the outer bone membrane split open, the compact bone snapped, and the haversian canals popped. Then the inner bone membrane staged the final resistance. When Takaesu bit down hard, the incredibly juicy marrow burst. Al dente. Al dente. A pleasurable al dente.

"...Sir?" the chef questioned, a bit of confusion slipping into his voice.

Takaesu blinked. He realized he was still clutching the chef's right hand, and he let go with a smile still on his face.

"How rude of me. I was just thinking about how this hand created the wonderful food this evening, and it moved me."

At this, the chef gave him a stiff smile in return as he massaged the right hand with the left.

"Oh, ha-ha. I'm the one who's moved hearing that from someone of your stature, sir."

The reason the chef was a bit nervous was probably not because Takaesu had shaken his hand for about five seconds, but because he did not make the bulk of the dishes himself. Takaesu, however, was not inclined to complain about that. The day he ate fresh pasta kneaded by hands that stunk of tobacco was the day he would need to give someone a thorough tongue-lashing in his magazine, even if he had to burn a bridge or two.

Watching the chef as the man hastened back to the kitchen, Takaesu straightened the collar of his custom-made suit and took his seat. He took a mouthful of the sparkling wine in his mouth, cooling that *thing* that throbbed in the soft tissue of his lower jaw. *Thump. Thump.*

The source of this itchy, painful, uncomfortable, yet pleasant sensation was a lump with a diameter a little less than two centimeters. He hadn't been to a doctor, but he was convinced that it wasn't any type of tumor. He knew this because the red orb—just like the eye of a living creature—wasn't something that had been born inside Takaesu's body.

The eye had come from somewhere *outside*. Outside of Tokyo... Japan...and maybe even the Earth itself. And one night three months ago, it slipped into Takaesu's lower jaw and gave him two things.

The first was the urge to bite. The second was the power to do it.

From that point on, that thing—since it was already inside his body he should probably call it *this* thing—was constantly tempting Takaesu. Tempting him to take things in his mouth, bite them, chew them. Telling him that he was no longer human, that he was a predator swimming lithely along the bottom of the city hunting for prey.

But for as long as Takaesu was able to call himself a gourmet food critic, he had no intention of putting things in his mouth if there was no value in biting them. Things like the fingers of the owner-chef from earlier that stunk of tobacco, for example.

...Hold back just a little longer.

When he whispered this to the eye inside his mouth, the throbbing gradually eased. But it probably wouldn't be so well behaved for long. The last time he had bitten bone was one week ago today.

Just as Takaesu was starting to remember that ecstasy-filled banquet seven days ago, the waiter finally brought over the *secondo piatto*. A veal saltimbocca without a shred of originality sat on the plate. He could imagine what it tasted like with just one look. On top of that, it was overcooked.

If the meat had at least had bones... No, even if it had, he wouldn't be able to take an entire bone in his hand and gnaw at it.

Rather than sighing, Takaesu reached out a hand for his knife, forcing a smile that seemed to say he was enjoying everything tremendously.

Full of relief upon exiting the restaurant, he shook his head and started heading toward the paid lot where he'd parked his car.

The road was large, but for six o'clock at night there weren't many people around. Even in the skyscrapers that towered above his head, most of the windows were cloaked in darkness. The name "Saitama's new city center" sounded dynamic, but would there really come a day when it would take the place of Tokyo's city center, Shinjuku? It was at least certain that the Italian restaurant behind Takaesu would be closing its doors by then. It really irked him that he was forced to write a flattering article about the restaurant.

The slimy texture of the fresh pasta still clung to the inside of his mouth. If nothing else, he wanted to get back to his car quickly and brush his teeth. In his glove box, he had a bottle of mineral water and a travel toothbrush set on hand. He thought his mood would lighten a bit once he was able to scrub his teeth as hard as he could with a toothbrush slathered in toothpaste. Scrub, scrub. Now, even if Takaesu went on brushing his teeth for hours, it wouldn't hurt him at all. It didn't used to be like that.

When he got back to Tokyo, he would get ahold of his next bone and chew to his heart's content with his clean teeth. He had readied four targets. He needed to plan more carefully than before, but the time spent coming up with all the details of his dinner menu was another part of the fun.

He walked another twenty or thirty meters on the road that ran alongside Saitama Super Arena until he was back at the parking lot, the heels of his bespoke shoes clicking loudly. He stopped briefly at the entrance and gazed at his dark blue Maserati GranTurismo, which was parked in a space at the back. The glamorous body that overflowed with a sense of power. The oblong oval grille that glinted like a row of fangs. The three vents that were reminiscent of gills. This car was a shark. And what's more, it was a mako shark, the fastest swimming of all sharks. Takaesu's fourth favorite shark.

His mood would probably improve once he had settled in the cockpit, jumped on the freeway from the nearby ramp, and put his foot on the throttle. Before that, it was first time to brush his teeth.

When he stepped up to his car and was about to unlock the door—that's when it happened.

Takaesu abruptly stopped moving. Something smelled good. His nose twitched as he sniffed. Somewhere within the bone-chilling

December air was a faintly sweet smell. It wasn't flowers or perfume, either.

It was the smell of healthy, well-developed, tightly packed muscle and bone.

His sensitive hearing, second only to his sense of smell, picked up the *tap*, *tap* sound of nimble footsteps. Standing so he would be near his large car, Takaesu waited for the owner of the approaching footsteps.

The person who soon appeared in his field of vision was a young woman jogging on the sidewalk wearing workout clothes. A middle school student or high school student. Her short hair was undyed, and she didn't smell of cosmetics or any other chemical substances. The only smell coming from her sweat-dampened skin was the healthy scent of a person's body, reminiscent of milk.

It was a very good smell. He closed his eyes and focused his attention on the footsteps.

Amid the dry sound of shoes hitting the asphalt, he picked up on the echo of bone. Takaesu was most fond of the leg bones—the harmony played between the carefree tibia and the graceful fibula. How wonderful.

True to its name, the compact bone that made up the outer layer of bone was finely packed. She must have gotten plenty of high-quality calcium and vitamins ever since she was young. He felt as if he could see the outer bone membrane gleaming white like a pearl under her developed muscles.

When the footsteps passed in front of the parking lot, Takaesu opened his eyes and his tongue darted out to lick his lips.

Thump, thump. The red eye throbbed in the middle of his lower jaw.

Bite her, bite her, it invited him.

"...Don't be hasty, *compagno*," Takaesu whispered back to it.

After waiting a bit, he left the parking lot.

The girl's retreating figure had gotten quite a bit smaller. But as long as Takaesu had his sense of smell, honed like a shark's, tracking her would be no trouble even if he lost sight of her completely.

Turning up the collar of his coat, Takaesu started walking, a thin smile hidden behind the fabric.

3

The sky on Wednesday, December 4, was full of wispy clouds, heralding the low-pressure system that was approaching.

Minoru rode his bike the six kilometers it took to get to the high school from his house at the northern edge of the Sakura district in Saitama city, crossing the Metro Express Saitama Omiya line, the JR Saikyou line, and the Touhoku Main line. He had a common city bike, not a sporty bike like the one he had nearly collided with yesterday.

Six kilometers was a distance he would be able to run, but then he would have to change clothes at school. More importantly, Minoru would stand out if he imitated people on sports teams when he himself wasn't on one. How would he be able to ride out the slightly more than three weeks left in 2019 safely, without rocking the boat? At the moment, that was Minoru's biggest and sole concern.

In that sense, he regretted his blunder yesterday morning. It had been completely stupid of him to lose his head and run off when he was leaving Tomomi Minowa.

Even before that, if he had made a move right away after noticing the road bike coming toward them, he probably could have gotten Tomomi to take cover without having to protect her in that exaggerated way. From the beginning, a simple greeting would have been enough to finish things up without getting into a conversation that long.

He thought he had understood that carrying on a long conversation with someone would only increase the memories he wanted to erase.

But there was no use crying over spilled milk.

Even as he prayed Tomomi would forget yesterday's scene right away, there was probably nothing to do but avoid contact with her for a while. He had already changed his running route, starting this morning. Since they were in the same year, passing by each other on school grounds was unavoidable, but there was absolutely no reason Tomomi would strike up a conversation with a student of Minoru's status in a place where other people could see. Tomomi, after all, had competed in nationals and was the track team's best hope; in other words, she was on the highest rung of the school's hierarchy.

These thoughts flew around Minoru's head as he finished biking the full six kilometers to school. He stopped his bike at the edge of the bike parking area for students and locked it up tight. He wanted to do whatever he could to avoid the trouble of finding his bike gone when he wanted to go home, so he used a tough wire lock that required a key.

He put his water-resistant messenger bag back on, covered the bottom half of his face with his scarf, and walked toward the entrance, mixing in with the other students.

Retrieving his school slippers from his shoe locker, he put his sneakers in and closed the metal door, spinning the three-number combination lock at random. Truthfully, using a little padlock would keep his things safer here, but the risk of standing out in a bad way was bigger. Once you reached high school, it was hard to imagine people pulling pranks like hiding shoes. Most students didn't even use a combination lock, but that was Minoru's nature and he couldn't help it.

At the end of the day, I guess I don't trust people. It's too late to change that now, so I guess I'll just have to keep it from showing. Just keep quiet all day today without having unnecessary conversations with anyone. Anyway, I don't think there's anyone who'll be concerned about my attitude.

Minoru had spent the morning absorbed in this negative introspection.

Someone behind him gave him a pat on the back. At the same time, an energetic voice called out, "Mornin', Utsugi!"

His whole body went tense in an instant, and he turned around awkwardly.

Tomomi was standing there dressed in workout clothes from top to bottom, an innocent smile on her face. She was carrying a yellow day pack on her shoulders that seemed to have everything from notebooks to writing utensils to track equipment inside, and her forehead had a light sheen of sweat.

She won't strike up a conversation with me at school.

Shuddering at the fact that this prediction from a few minutes ago had been contradicted just like that, Minoru somehow managed to return her greeting.

"…Good morning, Minowa."

Since things had ended up like this, he knew he should get out in front of it and apologize for his sudden escape yesterday, but he didn't know how he should bring it up. Even so, how would it help things to fall silent when Tomomi was right here? Somehow, he had to handle this in a natural way that wouldn't cause offense…

What came out of his mouth as a result of this super-speed thinking was, "Do you run to school every day?"

At this, Tomomi nodded as she took off her running shoes and stepped onto the wood floor.

"Yeah, but just a light run. By the way…you've gone past me on your bike a bunch of times before, Utsugi."

"Oh…s-sorry, I never noticed…"

After apologizing, he asked another question about something that had him somehow concerned.

"Are there other people besides you who do the same thing, Minowa?"

"Hmm, as far as the track team goes, there are about three guys and girls other than me who do it. If you include all the sports teams, I think there are probably more? The sidewalks around here are wide so it's easy to run."

"Huh…is that so…?"

"Do you want to do it, too, Utsugi? Where was your house again?"

"Oh, it's near the water treatment plant in the Sakura district."

"Oh, over there? It's pretty far, huh? About six kilometers one way?"

"Yeah, something like that. How about you, Minowa?"

"'Bout four kilometers. It's pretty close to your place, Utsugi…but I guess that's no surprise, since we were at the same middle school."

The reason this exchange happened so naturally as they walked from the school entrance toward the classroom was because Minoru was halfway zoned out. He was using half of his mind to consider if it would be possible for him to run to school, too.

To avoid trouble, Minoru kept the things he carried around with him to an absolute minimum, so if he could get by without his bicycle, too, he couldn't do any better than that. Six months ago he got himself into a mess once when he got a flat tire and had to walk his bike to the nearest bike shop. It hadn't happened to him yet, but obviously the risk of running into a pedestrian or a car was higher than it would be if he walked.

But still, there were definitely people who would think Minoru, who wasn't involved in sports, was odd for running to school. He would also have to change bags and buy a backpack. He had enough savings for it, but his sister Norie had just this April bought the messenger bag he had now, so he would feel guilty if he stopped using it after just six months. The sales tax had just gone up to 12 percent, too…

"…gi. Hey, Utsugi."

"Huh…? Oh, s-sorry."

"We're at your classroom."

Hearing that, he realized that at some point they'd stopped in front of the door to Class One for the sophomores.

Tomomi giggled and said, "If you do want to jog to school, let's meet up somewhere in the morning and run together," giving a wave as she dashed off toward her own classroom.

Minoru groaned inwardly as he belatedly became aware that a lot of students had observed him having a long conversation with the star of the track team.

Running to school together every morning?

It was ridiculous, inconceivable, and just thinking about it was frightening.

Just rewind the clock five minutes. No, please, rewind it seventeen hours, until early yesterday morning. If that's impossible, just erase the memory of Minowa and me talking from everyone in school.

Minoru entered his classroom as he sent this prayer to the creator of the world.

Of course, time did not go backward. And the memories of the students who saw Minoru and Tomomi as they walked and chatted did not disappear.

School was out. When Minoru unlocked his shoe locker and opened the door, he noticed a small scrap of paper floating to the floor. It had probably been stuck between the door and the frame.

Despite a keen sense of foreboding, he picked up the scrap that had fallen to the wood floor. A row of words was scribbled on the paper, which seemed to have been torn from a notebook. It said, "Come to the back of the dojo."

"...Oh..."

Since this was the first time he'd received a summons like the one in his hand, the word had slipped out of his mouth involuntarily; he wasn't able to put up a carefree front.

He could either follow the instructions on the scrap of paper or ignore them. He had to think seriously about what choice would allow him to keep his life at school peaceful.

For now, he changed into his shoes, went outside, and came to a stop again, glancing in both directions. If he was going to the bike parking lot, it was on the left, and if he was heading to the dojo, it was on the right.

The air he sucked into his lungs changed into a long sigh and came out as a "hah." Minoru turned to face right.

The only reason that came to mind for someone to call him out was his conversation with Tomomi Minowa. Of course, Tomomi herself wouldn't be the one waiting for him; it would be another person who had an issue with them talking. If Minoru could convince the person who had summoned him that he had no designs on her, he should be able to end this and make it an irregular onetime event.

Once he had cut across a few corridors and passed the side of the gym, the square dojo came into sight ahead.

There were small thickets at the sides of and behind the dojo, and it was fairly dark at this time in winter. It was the first time Minoru had set foot there.

When he turned the corner of the building, walking carefully on the damp and slippery ground, he heard multiple voices coming from his destination.

"Oh, he's here, he's here. You gotta buy me fried chicken now."

"Seriously? He didn't hafta come."

"Hang on, weren't you the one who told me to call him out?"

Looking ahead as he walked, Minoru's eyes fell on a few male students wearing matching Windbreakers. Judging by how they were talking to one another, the two leaning up against the wall were upperclassmen and the one standing a little way away was a sophomore.

Coming to a halt about five meters away from them, Minoru observed the guys wordlessly. This school had never had full-on gangsters or delinquent students, but still, there wasn't even a hint of danger in the appearances of these three.

Although it seemed like they had had a little bet going about whether Minoru would come or not, they really just had the air of exceedingly normal jocks.

Minoru stood there with a mixture of relief and wariness.

One of the upperclassmen broke away from the wall and, with a friendly smile, said, "Uh, you're Utsugi? Sorry for calling you out so suddenly."

"...It's fine."

Minoru observed the three of them further, keeping his words to an absolute minimum.

The long-haired upperclassman who had spoken to him was smiling, but the other one leaning against the wall, who had a bald head like a monk, was sullen despite winning that fried chicken. The sophomore seemed to be the one who'd written the summons and stuck it in Minoru's shoe locker, but he probably just did it on orders.

The long-haired one threw another question—the real question—at Minoru, who had lapsed into silence again.

"It's kind of a personal question, Utsugi, but are you going after our little Minowa?"

Minoru was visited by two thoughts at the same time: *I thought so*, the confirmation, and *No way*, the surprise.

He had thought the summons was related to Tomomi Minowa, but he couldn't believe that just talking to her for the two or three minutes it took to get from the entrance to the classroom would be considered "going after her."

Minoru faced the three—who must be track team members, since they called her theirs—and answered with the words he had prepared.

"We were classmates in middle school, so we were just talking a little." He thought for a moment, then added, "...I'm not really going after her or anything."

But the long-haired one, a thin smile still on his face, tilted his head as if to say, "But still."

"But Utsugi, seems like you don't normally talk to girls at all, do you? What's with you only talking to Minowa?"

"It's not that I...never talk to them. If somebody talks to me, I'll at least answer them..."

"But according to my information, I guess you talked for a pretty long time? Ogucchi, how many seconds was it?"

"W-well, I didn't exactly time it. Um...I think it was roughly fifteen minutes or so..."

Minoru wanted to ask if they really thought it took that long to get from the lockers to the classroom as a retort, but he held back. Even if fifteen minutes became three minutes, that didn't change the fact that it had been a conversation.

So what if I am going after her?

It wasn't like he didn't have any desire to give a cool retort like that. But if he did, the other guys probably wouldn't be able to back down anymore, and Minoru would surely go home and sit with his head in his hands, groaning in regret for an hour or more. Whenever there was trouble, he kept his head down and let it pass. That's how he'd lived for these eight years.

"...Um, I have absolutely no desire to get involved with Minowa, really," Minoru stated clearly, his gaze fixed somewhere around the long-haired one's chest.

But his enemy was more persistent than expected.

"Hmm. But still, what are you going to do if Minowa talks to you again?"

"I d..."

He started to say, "I don't know," but corrected himself just in time.

"I'd say hi, since she's an acquaintance, but—"

"Enough, I'm tired of this."

The guy who suddenly broke in was the bald one resting his back against the wall behind them. With both hands still stuck in the pockets of his Windbreaker, he sprang upright using just the strength of his body, passing the long-haired one and walking toward Minoru briskly.

Coming to a stop right before Minoru, his nose at the same height as Minoru's eyes, he snorted and murmured in a deep voice, "You're a math and science guy, right? If so, you should just keep your nose in those books. There's seriously no way you can mess with our girls."

He was given no opportunity to say that he wasn't messing with them. The bald one pulled his left fist from his pocket and casually drove it into Minoru's stomach—more precisely, he tried to drive it into Minoru's stomach.

Minoru reflexively bent forward and backed away. But there was no way he could have dodged the punch with those movements. The fist, muscled like an adult's, plunged into his solar plexus. Minoru stopped breathing, getting a clear premonition of the hopeless pain that accompanies being hit in the abdomen.

But that pain never became a reality.

That phenomenon was triggered once again. His field of vision changed hues. All sound disappeared and both his feet left the wet ground. *Exactly as if he were detached from the world.*

The bald one's punch dug into his abdomen. Yet there was no pain, no impact, and not even the sensation of touching something. It was exactly the same as yesterday morning when he had made contact with the handles of the racing bike...

No. They weren't touching. With both his eyes wide open, Minoru had seen it clearly. Between the suspended fist of the bald one and the uniform Minoru was wearing, there was a gap, if only just a few millimeters.

Was he pretending to punch me...? Did he stop right before the impact...?

When Minoru looked up as he thought these things in the silence, what he saw was the bald one's violently contorted face. It wasn't rage—pain probably.

He took another breath, and at about the same time, the mysterious phenomenon faded away. The color, the sound, and the feeling of touching the ground returned.

The punch hadn't connected, but Minoru backed away, his body still in the position of escape he had moved himself into. His feet slipped on the damp fallen leaves, and he landed on his backside.

From behind them, the long-haired one gave a compassionate smile, while the sophomore had an odd, tense one. Neither had noticed the strange force that had come over the bald one.

Holding his left fist in his right hand and gritting his teeth, the bald one seemed as if he was desperately suppressing a scream that threatened to burst forth from him. It was the expression of a person who had hit not a soft human body but something like a concrete wall with all their might.

Once the pain seemed to lessen after a few seconds and the bald one exhaled slowly, he looked down at Minoru seated on the ground with an odd look in his eyes.

"...You...," he whispered in a hoarse voice.

He was probably wondering what in the world the sensation he had just experienced was.

Luckily, he didn't seem up to taking deep breaths, so he spit out in a low voice, "Don't get cocky. Next time, it won't end so easily."

When the bald one headed off at a quick pace, the sophomore followed him at a half run.

As the long-haired one passed by after the other two, he called out, "Sorry, Utsugi, but we're just teaching you the ways of the world."

Minoru was barely listening. Inside his head, the words *what if* were playing over and over.

What if...what if, what if in that moment, he hadn't backed away as fast as he could of his own accord? What if he hadn't been able to respond to the punch and just stood there bolt upright?

Was the bald one's fist smashed up all the way down to the bone? He wasn't basing this on anything; it was just a gut feeling. But if that had truly happened, Minoru would believe it without a doubt in his mind.

What was that just now? Just what did that bald guy hit?

Still sitting on the ground in a state of shock, Minoru lifted his right hand and touched his sternum over his uniform.

Nothing was there. But there was something. Something...living.

"...Did you do it?"

The question came out like a gasp, and no voice rose to answer it.

How did I get home from school—?

When Minoru came back to reality, he was on the porch of his house locking up his bike. Looking at his watch, the time was 6:30 p.m. The sky had already gone completely dark, and warm light poured from the living room window as he looked into it from the small garden. His sister Norie had probably come home already.

Hit by a sudden realization, he peered into his bag. The library books he'd meant to return on his way home were gone, replaced by different books. Somehow, he'd apparently managed to get to the city library, return the books, and check out new ones while on autopilot. He walked toward the door to the entryway, thinking absentmindedly that he was lucky he didn't cause an accident.

He had never told Norie this, but on the days when she came home before him, he got just a little bit nervous when he was opening the door. Even though he knew in his mind there was no way it would happen, he ended up picturing it no matter what he did. He wondered if, when he entered the house, he would find Norie on the floor covered in blood.

Minoru traded his bike key, which was still clutched in his left hand, for a large dimple key.

They had a house rule that they always had to lock both the front door and the back door, even when they were home. When he slid the key into the keyhole and turned it to the left, Minoru heard the reliable clunk of the door unlocking and exhaled a bit.

Before he could take his shoes off, he heard the pitter-patter of slippers running toward him. Next, he heard a voice that was gentle in tone but full of energy.

"Welcome home, Mii!"

"Hi."

It had taken him a whole year before he could naturally return her greeting. As he thought this, he changed from his sneakers into the slippers that were there just for him and stepped into the hallway.

Standing before him was a young woman wearing an apron and clutching a ladle in her right hand. She was about the same height as Tomomi Minowa, but even though Minoru had long ago surpassed her in height, she didn't feel petite. Was this because she was related to him as his adoptive sister?

Eight years ago when Minoru had lost his family, Norie Yoshimizu had taken him in and raised him.

"Um, Miss Norie, I've said this a lot, but you don't need to meet me at the door when you're in the middle of cooking...," Minoru said, looking at the ladle.

Norie's smiling face transformed into an unhappy one.

"And I've told you a lot that you don't have to call me Miss Norie, Mii!"

"Even so, I've gotten so used to it by now... Uh, something's rattling around in the kitchen."

At Minoru's words, Norie fell silent for a moment.

"Aaah, the pot's going to boil over!" she yelled, bounding back down the hallway.

Minoru exhaled a puff of air and started up the stairs. As he went, he heard another shout.

"We're having gyoza today! Now hiring one person to fold the dumplings!"

"...I'll be there right away after I change clothes!" Minoru yelled back, dashing up the stairs.

Minoru's large room had tatami mat flooring and was on the second floor of a four-bedroom house built fifteen years ago. Following his policy of having as few possessions as possible, he didn't have much furniture. There was a low bed along the eastern wall, a bookshelf built into the western wall, and a simple desk and chair next to a floor-to-ceiling window on the south side.

There was a notebook computer on top of the desk that was a hand-me-down from Norie, but he didn't have anything like a TV, video recorder, or gaming system. There were only about thirty novels and academic books lined up on his bookshelf, and supposing someone came over to hang out, he would have trouble figuring out how to pass the time. But for better or worse, he didn't have any friends he was that close to.

Minoru put the top and bottom of his school uniform on a hanger and took off his collared shirt and T-shirt. Opening the closet in just his boxer briefs to take out a change of clothes, Minoru's hand stopped suddenly.

There was a large mirror mounted on the inside of the closet door. His half-naked reflection in it drew his gaze.

Minoru had often heard indirectly that people considered him a gloomy guy, and he thought that was exactly right. His eyes had a skeptical look about them, and his mouth was so tight that it seemed he had forgotten how to smile. His bangs, which had grown down past his eyebrows, got in the way when he ran, but he didn't feel like cutting them any shorter. His build was more feeble that it was thin, and the weakness of his neck and shoulders in particular was just like a girl's.

Moreover, the somehow diluted feeling of his hair color confirmed his dreary image. It wasn't that his hair was white, but depending on how the light hit, it could look gray. This wasn't the color he had been born with; it became like this after that night eight years ago. It would be easy to dye it black, but his teachers and classmates had never said anything about it, so he left it alone.

Minoru, checking that nothing about his body had outwardly changed, fixed his gaze last on his bare chest—the exact center of his visible ribs. His white skin showed no injuries, no hollows, and no protrusions.

Still, there was no denying it any longer. What had happened three months ago was not a daydream. Something was lurking there. The thing had brought about a mysterious phenomenon, preventing the handles of the bike and the fist of Minoru's classmate from touching him.

The result was that it protected him from harm, but instead of gratitude, he had a creepy feeling. He thought about all the abnormal things going on, which couldn't be explained by the common sense of the world Minoru had been living in. As he contemplated this, goose bumps popped up all over his exposed skin.

But.

As he whispered, "...Common sense...," in a low voice, his shivering left him.

Common sense. Common sense.

Under the "Common sense" section in Minoru's dictionary, a piece of writing by the nineteenth-century novelist Ogai Mori was quoted.

"Common sense is the capacity to comprehend normal occurrences and take appropriate measures."

If common sense was the ability to understand ordinary things and act accordingly, Minoru had lost sight of that. He wasn't clear on where the line between normal and abnormal was.

Was running ten kilometers every morning normal? Abnormal? Was not having any friends to hang out with on days off normal? Abnormal? How about having someone come into one's house and murder their whole family? And is it normal for the person responsible to not get caught, even after eight years? Is it abnormal?

If all of those things are normal—then one wouldn't be shaking in their boots when their running time improved or when they didn't get injured when they should have because of something that fell from the sky and slipped into their body. Despite the fact that there had been a big fuss when signals broadcasted by an extraterrestrial civilization were captured by a telescope on the moon, things had gone completely silent in less than six months.

Anything that can happen will happen. Or in this world, anything can happen.

Minoru tore his eyes from his reflection in the mirror, put on an old sweatshirt and cotton pants, and left his room. When he went into the living room after carefully washing his hands in the first-floor bathroom and gargling, Norie padded over to him quickly from the kitchen at the back of the house holding a big bowl.

"Nice timing, Mii! I just finished getting the ingredients ready."

"Oh, then I'll..."

As he started to say, "Then I'll help you right now," he looked down at the bowl and was speechless for a second.

"...Hang on, won't this be too much?"

The dense mixture of gyoza ingredients—cabbage, bok choy, green onion, garlic chives, minced meat, and roughly chopped Shiba shrimp—rose to the top of the bowl. Norie and Minoru were the only ones living in the house and neither of them were big eaters, so no matter how he looked at the situation, it seemed like they'd have a lot left over.

But as Norie placed the bowl on the dining room table, she said with a self-satisfied air, "Even if we make too many, they last for a pretty long time when you freeze them. Apparently, the trick is to flash-freeze them after adding a little flour."

Minoru sat down in a chair, thinking that what Norie had said meant gyoza day would be coming again before too long. Lined up on the table, there were dumpling wrappers (premade as usual), a big stainless steel tray to put the finished dumplings on, and a bowl full of water that they would use to seal the dumplings.

Norie sat across from Minoru and gave him a fearless smirk.

"We're going to compete to see who can make more, Mii," she said, suddenly declaring war.

"L-let's not compete over speed… I can't see anything but a depressing future for us if we don't seal the wrappers well enough."

"I'm going to grill the gyoza, so even if there's a little bit of an opening, it's totally fine! On your mark, get set, go!"

…*No wonder she's the deputy chief examiner at the prefectural office.*

Minoru rushed to grab a spoon as he whispered this inwardly. He performed his work quickly, scooping up the right amount of ingredients, putting them in a wrapper, creating a fold, and crimping it together. He had intended to concentrate on what he was doing, but his thoughts wandered little by little to the past.

Eight years ago, when Minoru had been brought into this home after being orphaned, Norie never ran out of smiles, always working to fulfill the roles of both sister and mother.

However, at the time, Norie had just graduated from college and begun working at the prefectural office. He had always thought of her as an adult, but at the time she was a mere seven years older than Minoru was now. Seven years from now, when Minoru was twenty-three, he really couldn't imagine himself looking after a child about whom the only thing he knew was their name.

Come live with me.

That's what Norie had said to a downcast Minoru back then. In a voice without an ounce of indecisiveness or hesitation, smiling gently.

Most of Minoru's relatives had shown an unwillingness to take him in after he lost his family one night in that gruesome incident. Norie's father, who was still living at the time, had also apparently thought it would be difficult; he had already lost his wife (Norie's mother) and was living with just his daughter.

But it seemed that Norie had fervently tried to persuade him.

To Norie, Minoru was the child of a cousin on her mother's side, meaning he was her cousin once removed. Why did Norie, fresh

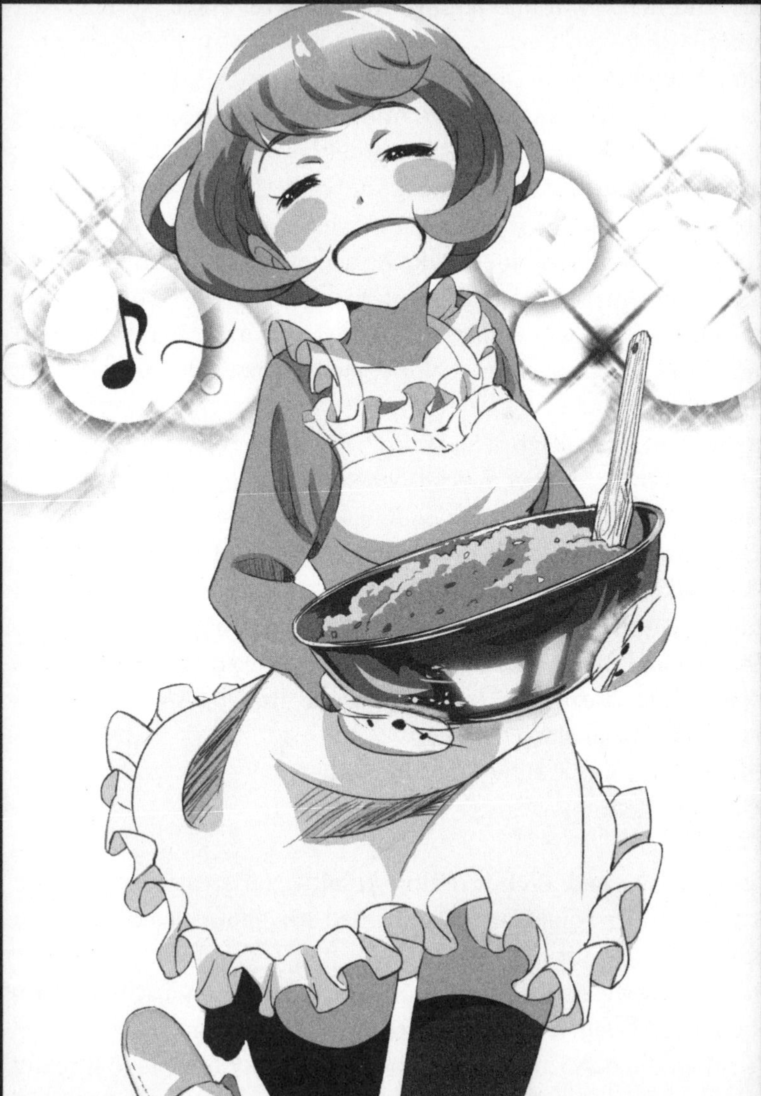

out of college, take a child who she had met few enough times to count on one hand, a child who was separated by five degrees of relatives, and make him into family? He had never asked Norie herself directly.

But about one year after Minoru came to this house, Norie's father, Kouhei Yoshimizu, told him. Norie had lost her mother in a car accident when she was eight, the same age Minoru was. From that time until middle school, she was a child that almost never smiled.

Although for his daughter's sake he had at first opposed arranging an adoption, Mr. Yoshimizu was stern but kind with Minoru after adopting him. He had collapsed four years ago because of a brain hemorrhage and passed away. Norie, too, lost both of her parents at a young age.

In the eight years Minoru had lived with her, the only time the smile had disappeared from her face was when Mr. Yoshimizu died.

"Okay, finished!" said Norie, bringing Minoru out of his reverie.

They had cleaned the bowl out, and the rows of milky-white gyoza inside the stainless steel tray were divided into two groups: one close to Minoru and one on the other side. Norie started tallying the ones she had made, counting, "Two, four, six, eight, ten," so Minoru had no choice but to go along with her.

"Thirty-one for me! How about you, Mii?"

"Um...thirty-three..."

"Ooh!"

Even after he had announced the results, Norie gave him a smile that took up her whole face. She pressed her hands together, which were white with flour.

"Just as I expected, Mii! I'll nominate you for the high school men's event in the All-Japan Dumpling Folding Competition!"

"Th-thank you. So...we ended up making sixty-four. Is that really okay...?"

"Oh, isn't that a nice number? If we make eight each of grilled gyoza, fried gyoza, steamed gyoza, and boiled gyoza, it'll work out perfectly."

"I don't think that's going to work. And you said it was fine for there to be openings in the wrappers, since we were making grilled gyoza…"

"Well, guess it can't be helped. Should I freeze half?"

When Norie started to take the tray to the kitchen, Minoru hurriedly called out to her, "Freeze two-thirds!"

4

He was still in the city of Saitama.

Even if he lived here he could never grow to like it, but it was curious that in the two short days he had stayed here he had developed a certain affinity for a city name that he had at first found laughable. He also might have felt that way because he had been able to find top-quality prey here.

Takaesu finished showering and returned to his room in a bathrobe, pulling the curtains wide when he approached the front window. From the deluxe twin room of the high-rise hotel he had checked in to last night, he got a panoramic view of Saitama's new city center at night. The footbridge that stretched out west from the train station was decorated with lights this time of year, and the quiet twinkling of the innumerable blue LEDs had its own sort of charm.

The large, gently sloping flat surface that spread out directly from the north side of the footbridge might have been the roof of Saitama Super Arena. It looked just like a flat-topped seamount rising from the depths of the ocean. If he could have that whole space to himself to set up a dining table there, it would probably feel wonderful.

As he looked down at the nighttime scenery, Takaesu moved his right hand to pull out a round thing of about two centimeters from a paper bag on the nearby table. He tossed it into his mouth.

The glossy brown color resembled a chocolate truffle, but it wasn't. It was a macadamia nut in its shell, said to be the hardest of the edible tree nuts.

He rolled the macadamia nut—which people usually used a special nutcracker to open—around his mouth for a while, then held it lightly between his first and second premolars.

He slowly, slowly applied pressure. The feeling in his mouth was just like that of biting a steel ball. His upper and lower jawbones creaked, and the masseter muscle that connected them shook. If the average person bit down this hard, they would surely break a tooth.

Of course, Takaesu was not the average person, however. No. He was not a person at all. He was a shark. A shark that swam through the city, devouring people.

There is a shark called the tiger shark. It's a large variety that can grow to a maximum length of seven meters, and it has another name: the man-eater shark.

The tiger shark's teeth are a special shape. They have a double-layered structure with sharp, knifelike points and thick, sawlike bases. This shark, which can break even a sea turtle's shell with these teeth, was Takaesu's third favorite shark.

Imagining himself in the form of a tiger shark, he bit down with all his might. The nut burst open in his mouth with a pleasurable popping impact. The thick shell broke vertically and the one-size-smaller embryo—the part commonly referred to as a macadamia nut—rolled out.

Holding the shell in his mouth, Takaesu spit out only the embryo into the wastebasket.

The shell had broken in two, and he chewed one half on the right side and one on the left. This second battle also ended with his teeth victorious. The shell broke apart, and he crushed it into even smaller pieces. *Crunch. Crunch. Crunch.*

Three months ago, this would have been impossible for him. No, at that point, Takaesu would've had concerns about the hard-baked rice crackers and beef jerky that even children could eat without trouble. At the restaurant he had come to critique, he would've had terrible trouble fooling them if they had sent out stiff *cantuccio* biscuits.

But it was different now. *Crunch, crunch, crunch, crunch.*

On the day that *it* had taken refuge in his lower jaw, Takaesu gained new teeth. Teeth that could crush any food, no matter how hard. Glorious teeth that kept growing stronger the more hard things he ate.

"Chew, chew, chew, chew," Takaesu murmured in a singsong voice as he persistently went on chewing the fragments of the shell, which had become as fine as grains of sand. "Chew, chew, chew, chew."

Suddenly, an indescribable fishiness spread through his mouth. It wasn't the taste of a nutshell. It was the taste of dried-up anchovies… dried sardines.

Chew it up well, Hii. Chew. Chew. Chew more. If you spit it out, you'll get a pinch. There now, chew. Chew. Chew. Chew.

"…!"

He was struck with an intense nausea and gagged a little, but he held it together somehow. The dried sardine flavor went away after a few seconds, so he swallowed the macadamia shell, which was now a paste. Takaesu didn't know if it had any nutritional value in general, but with that his teeth became a little bit stronger.

Shaking off memories of a distant past, he imagined the near future. Was that girl here today as well, running along the road that passed through the new city center below him? Did she go home and eat a full dinner, and was she now deep asleep in her bed, growing a little more?

He painted a picture in his mind of the calcium absorbed by the young girl's body, circulating in her veins and permeating her snow-white bones. That alone brought a gush of saliva to his mouth. There was an itchy, stinging throbbing in the center of his lower jaw. Tossing a new macadamia nut into his mouth, Takaesu rolled it around, pretending to bite it, soothing the thing. He trembled slightly.

Not yet. It was still too early.

He was checked in to the hotel under a fake name, but it was impossible to avoid all of the security cameras in the lobby and the hallways, and the employees of the Italian restaurant he had visited the night before would likely remember Takaesu. He would need to wait at least one more day…no, two more days before taking action.

Luckily, he had his laptop with him, so he could write his draft at the hotel. He would just think of this delay as a spice to increase his pleasure when he bit down on bone.

"Sleep well and grow, Signorina," Takaesu whispered to the young girl who was probably sleeping somewhere in the urban landscape he saw below his window. Then Takaesu bit through the second shell forcefully.

5

Minoru finished flipping through to the end of a running magazine that he wasn't even that interested in and returned it to the magazine rack.

He looked down at the digital watch on his left wrist: 4:25 p.m. Not even thirty minutes had passed since he came to this convenience store, but an employee who had been shooting glances at Minoru— or at least had seemed to be shooting glances at Minoru—for a while was probably thinking, *It's been half an hour already.*

He'd planned on killing some time at the nearby library before his plans at five o'clock, but it was unexpectedly shut down for the day. But the employee wasn't aware of Minoru's circumstances, and he would probably soon reach the limit for how much idle in-store reading he would tolerate.

Akigase Park, where they were meeting, took less than five minutes to get to by bike. There was nothing for him to do for the remaining thirty minutes other than to read a book or something on a park bench while braving the cold wind. Luckily, he was wearing a wool Chesterfield coat over his uniform today, and there was a hardcover book in his bag that he had planned on returning to the library. Rereading a book was nice sometimes.

Having decided on his next course of action, Minoru left the magazine section and headed toward the shelves of snacks.

Minoru didn't have enough willpower to leave the store without buying anything after having stood there reading for half an hour, but it wasn't like he had much financial leeway, either.

While he was thankful to his adoptive sister, who worried every month about whether his allowance was enough, he made sure he got only the lowest possible amount he needed to get by.

After looking around the shelves for a bit, he took one package of mints that came with a small case and headed to the register. Out of the two payment counters, one was closed and the other had two customers already waiting. The customer checking out was a man who was nearly elderly. His basket was jammed full of items, which the female employee was holding up to the bar-code scanner sullenly. In line behind the man was a boy in about third grade, swaying his body around as if unable to wait any longer.

A few minutes after Minoru stood behind the elementary schoolboy in line, the first customer finally finished checking out. As the man made his way to the exit with plastic bags hanging from both hands, the boy moved forward enthusiastically to take the man's place, putting his item on the counter. It was a ten-card package of a fighting-style trading card game that was very popular among elementary and middle school students; even Minoru knew the name.

The boy seemed to want to open it as soon as possible. Without waiting for the employee to hold the package up to the bar-code reader, the boy dropped a few coins he had been clutching in his left hand onto the counter. Immediately after, the employee looked at the register display and said, "That'll be 313 yen."

Hearing that, the boy's shoulders began to tremble.

At first, he looked up at the employee's face, then down at the coins he had just put on the counter. He stopped moving. Minoru leaned over a bit to see what was going on and looked at the counter.

On the glass were three hundred-yen coins and one ten-yen coin. That was three yen short to buy the cards, but the boy was frozen in place and showed no signs of trying to add more coins.

Suddenly, Minoru understood the situation. The sales tax had risen to 8 percent in 2014. It had become 10 percent in 2015, the year after, and this easy-to-calculate number had been used for a while. But this year, it had been raised to 12 percent. Moreover, the sudden talk of a tax increase had thrown the Diet into confusion, and the implementation of the new tax rate had been pushed back to the end of the year, December 1—in other words, five days ago.

The price of the cards in question had probably been less than three hundred yen including tax through November. But because of the 2 percent tax increase, the price had gone up a little bit.

Even though it was only just a few yen apart, it was a world of difference to an elementary school student. The boy finally seemed to understand that the price had changed, and his ears instantly reddened. He dug around in the front pocket of his pants many times but didn't produce any coins to make up the difference. He had probably just run to the store from his house clutching only the allowance that he needed to buy one pack of cards.

Discovering that one didn't have enough money after bringing an item to the register would be incredibly embarrassing even for the teenage Minoru. The boy was completely dumbfounded, as if this was the first time this had ever happened in his life, and he continued to fervently search his pockets with his eyes all the way down.

Minoru felt as if he could see the memory being engraved in the young boy's mind with his own eyes. The boy would definitely recall this moment over and over in the future.

Or the woman working at the register could tell the boy that she would hold on to his cards while he got three more yen from home, pulling him out of his panic and making it possible for him to forget this incident. But she didn't seem to have any intention of doing so. She kept her silence with a scowl on her face, drumming her fingers on the glass surface of the counter.

After the oppressive silence had gone on for about ten seconds, the boy finally seemed to have an idea of what to do next. Plucking his four coins up from the counter, he said, "I don't need it," in a barely audible voice. He turned right around and started to run toward the automatic door.

Minoru had gotten a five-yen coin out of his wallet a little earlier, and it was now clutched in his right hand. At this moment, he dropped it on the floor. The boy turned around hesitantly, and Minoru bent down in front of him, picking up the brassy coin as it spun on the floor. Still crouched down, he held the coin out to the boy with it pinched between his fingers.

"This fell out of your pocket," he called out.

The boy's eyes grew wide with wonder, and he opened his clenched right hand.

Minoru set the five yen on the other four coins atop the boy's sweaty palm and stood up.

"Now that you have this, I think you can buy the cards you wanted earlier."

At Minoru's words, the boy counted his coins one by one with the index finger of his left hand. When he had confirmed that there was 315 yen, he looked up and smiled bashfully. He went back to the register right away and dropped his coins on the counter again.

Once the employee rang up the card pack again and the boy had two yen clutched in his hand, he dashed out without giving Minoru a second glance.

Minoru watched as the little figure disappeared on the other side of the automatic doors. When he remembered that he was in the middle of doing his own shopping, he rushed to put the mints down on the counter. When he glanced up, he locked eyes with the employee, who was giving him a creepy look. As he quickly averted his eyes, Minoru murmured in his head that he would have to stay away from the store for a while.

When Minoru left the convenience store and got on his bike, he peddled against the cold wind that blew in his face. He rode through a residential neighborhood for a bit and crossed a bridge over the Kamogawa River, which was a branch of the Arakawa River. He stood on the pedals to power himself up the narrow path on top of the embankment, and the riverbed of the Arakawa at dusk spread out to fill his field of vision.

Around here, the width of the riverbed was up to 1.5 kilometers, and the embankment on the other side was just like a hazy horizon. He couldn't see the surface of the river because another embankment blocked the view, but the broad swath of green that lay nearby was Minoru's destination, Akigase Park.

The park, one of the largest within the city of Saitama, was on a three-kilometer plot of land that ran alongside the embankment. Inside it there were wooded areas, wild bird parks, and barbecue areas in addition to sports facilities like baseball fields and tennis courts.

There had been a large park similar to this one near the town where

Minoru had lived until eight years ago. On sunny days off, the four of them would go on picnics as a family, bringing a basket packed with lunch boxes.

Shaking his head vigorously to interrupt the thoughts, Minoru came down from the embankment and entered the park. He stopped his bike in front of the directory for a moment, confirmed the route to his destination, and got moving again.

Riding slowly down the path that cut through the center of the park, Minoru saw a wide-open lawn planted with orderly trees come into view. That was where he was headed; it was called the Western Garden. It was probably bustling with groups of families in the spring and summer, but now, in December, there wasn't a soul around.

Minoru got off his bike at the side of the lawn. Stepping onto the withered brown grass, he took his messenger bag off his shoulder and took a seat on one of the several benches there. His watch read 4:40. Another twenty minutes until the person he was meeting would arrive.

He had a book in his bag, but, not in the mood to start reading, he leaned on the hard backrest and closed his eyes. Then the scene at the convenience store played automatically inside his brain.

The reason he had put on such a show to give the boy the five-yen coin was definitely because Minoru felt sorry for him, not because he was trying to help him.

It was because he was sure he would be in an unpleasant mood afterward if he had watched that scene all the way to the end. In other words, at the end of the day he had done it for himself. But that was the action he had taken, and now Minoru was getting a taste of the intolerable feeling of his self-important meddling.

Ultimately, interacting with other people always increased his negative memories. Three days ago, when he'd fled in the middle of his early-morning conversation with Tomomi Minowa on the embankment. Two days ago, when he'd clumsily fallen on his backside in front of the track team guys. And now today with his hypocritical actions.

The marsh where the black water of his memories continued to accumulate tried to capture Minoru and drag him down into it whenever it could. Lurking in the depths of this marsh was that incident eight years ago. The memories of that gruesome tragedy that he could remember clearly second by second, decorated in fear and despair, regret and self-recrimination.

Every time he reexperienced that night, he felt like he was losing something inside himself. It was probably something like the strength to live.

Was there any reason in this world to go on living when it brought such painful feelings? Wouldn't he be happier if he could end his life right away and go to the place where his parents and sister were waiting? Every time he sunk into that marsh of memories, that urge came over him.

The reason he had resisted thus far was because if he committed suicide or something, he couldn't imagine how sad it would make Norie, who had protected and raised Minoru for eight years…or how sad it would make his sister Wakaba, who had sacrificed her life that night to save Minoru.

But if those black memories grew any more than this… If the marsh overflowed inside him…wouldn't there come a day when he could no longer recover from it? He would rather go off to a world without anyone in it. In a place where there were no other humans, his negative memories shouldn't increase at all.

If one reads science fiction or horror novels, they often come across plot developments where the main character is thrown into an uninhabited town and overcome with fear. If he were to be put in those kind of circumstances, Minoru thought he would definitely feel a deep relief before fear.

What if—

Had that *thing* descended from the sky to take Minoru to that kind of world of solitude…?

Yesterday and today, after Minoru had finished his daily running in the early morning, he had tried to reproduce that mysterious phenomenon on the embankment when no one was around. Unfortunately, he hadn't succeeded even once, but that didn't mean the phenomenon had disappeared. He just didn't know how to flip the switch. He had a feeling that if he kept on with his trial and error, he would someday be able to will the phenomenon to occur himself.

Even if he was able to manipulate the power at will, Minoru's true desire couldn't be fulfilled through a physical phenomenon.

Even so, that was fine right now. Because if he kept chasing after it hard, he might really be able to go someday. To a world of absolute solitude, all alone.

As he thought this with his eyelids still closed, the faint sound of footsteps reached his ears. He had heard that light rhythm before. Picking himself up, he looked to the left. In the twilight, most of the afterglow having already vanished, he could see a small silhouette dashing toward him. Checking his watch, it was three minutes until five o'clock. A little surprised he had been worrying for a whole seventeen minutes, he stood up from the bench.

The person Minoru had been waiting for, now standing before him, marched in place for a bit while catching her breath. Even when her breathing had returned to normal, for some reason she made no attempt to speak. Minoru himself actually felt it was hard to breathe, so he pointed to the bench first and said, "Um… Should we sit…?"

At this, the girl in her workout clothes, Tomomi Minowa, nodded firmly and sat down at the end of the bench still wearing her day pack. Minoru sat down as well, leaving a little space between them.

As Minoru was wondering whether he should start talking about something himself, it apparently hit five o'clock on the dot and the solar-powered light nearby flicked on. Tomomi took that opportunity to open her mouth.

"…Sorry for dragging you out this late to somewhere so far."

"…I just go home after school ends, so…"

"You aren't in any clubs, are you, Utsugi?"

"No. I guess I'm in the going-home club. Apparently there are less than ten of us in our grade."

The conversation broke off there again. A few hours ago, when another scrap of paper had fluttered down as he opened his shoe locker, Minoru had thought it might be better to just not look at it. But the precise handwriting he saw when he reluctantly picked it up spelled out a message reading, "Please come to the Western Garden in Akigase Park at five in the evening." It was signed by Tomomi Minowa.

He of course wondered if he should ignore it this time as well. The reason he didn't was that he could feel the powerful intentions behind her signing her full name. The day before yesterday, he came to the conclusion that he would ignore the track team guys' orders. He had no reason to timidly obey those guys, who wouldn't even sign their names on his summons. Or at least he shouldn't have a reason to. As he told himself this, Tomomi once again apologized in a small voice.

"…I'm sorry, Utsugi."

"It's fine… My house isn't even that far from here…"

"Not about that."

Tomomi's expression, which had for an instant held a faint smile, suddenly distorted completely. Transparent droplets welled up rapidly in the corners of her eyes, and Minoru felt like he might stop breathing.

"I heard the older girls on our track team gossiping. They said that the members of the boys' team called you out and…beat you up."

"Huh?"

Minoru's eyes grew round as he listened to the words Tomomi said in a shaking voice. It was true that they had called him out, but everything after that was kind of an overstatement. Although he had been punched once in the stomach, that mysterious phenomenon had kept him from taking any damage at all. Besides, it wasn't something that Tomomi, who had not been directly involved, needed to cry and apologize for.

"Th-that's sort of an exaggeration. I didn't get hurt at all, and all they did was say a few things to me…," Minoru explained hastily, thinking that he was in a real mess.

Anyway, he should have denied being called out at all. Tomomi had probably chosen to meet in a park so far from school because she suspected that his conversation with her was why the guys' team had set their sights on Minoru. Minoru's response had only confirmed Tomomi's fears.

"…I'm sorry…," Tomomi apologized again in a barely audible voice, then covered her face with both hands.

Her weak sobs shook the dry December air.

While Minoru knew he should say something, he didn't know what more he could say. There was no reason he would know. Up until now, he'd always avoided facing girls—no, facing anyone one-on-one like this.

Minoru kept his mouth shut, and Tomomi kept on crying. Ultimately, the one who ended this moment was not Minoru but Tomomi herself.

Suppressing her crying with her mouth pulled incredibly tight, Tomomi rubbed at her eyes with the sleeve of her workout shirt to wipe them. She kept her eyes all the way down as she said in a hoarse voice, "It's probably better if I don't talk to you anymore, right, Utsugi?"

"…"

She likely took Minoru's silence as agreement.

Shrinking her small body down even further, she finished by once again whispering, "…I really am sorry."

With that, Tomomi stood up. Turning her back to him, she started walking slowly not toward the path she had come from, but toward the woods in the center of the park. She gradually picked up her pace, eventually breaking into a jog.

Even after the somehow heavy sound of her footsteps had grown distant in the twilight, Minoru couldn't move. He just sat and stared as a single droplet that shone from where Tomomi had been sitting soaked into the wooden seat of the bench little by little.

* * *

Hmm.

Looking down on the vast park from the path atop the embankment, Takaesu tilted his head slightly.

His prey's behavior pattern was different than it had been before. Although she had passed beside Saitama Super Arena after six o'clock in the evening and gone straight home from there both yesterday and the day before, today she had changed course along the way. Instead of heading for home, she had continued running on the narrow path along the river, went over the high embankment, and entered the park about five minutes ago.

He had kept a distance of more than fifty meters between them, so he found it hard to believe that she had realized she was being followed. Still, just in case, he came to a stop just this side of the park and decided to carefully take stock of the situation.

It was only the third day since he had started tailing her, so he didn't know whether this was irregular behavior. Maybe she headed all the way out to this park two kilometers from her house every Friday, but he had a feeling that today there was something heavy about his prey's footsteps.

He didn't actually believe it, but had the police caught on to him without him noticing? Was this a trap to lure Takaesu out? If he set foot here to hunt his prey, would he become the one being hunted?

In these last three months, Takaesu had already chewed on the bones of four people. There was little chance of the leftovers being discovered, as he had disposed of them discreetly, but twice his prey had been reported as missing persons. Naturally, the police would be moving forward with investigations, and Takaesu couldn't say that it was absolutely impossible for them to be led to him by some unforeseen clue.

That *thing* had given him physical abilities that far surpassed that of the average person and teeth that could easily break a human humerus or femur. However, it was indeed impossible for him to avoid or stop bullets. If he was surrounded by police officers who opened fire with their pistols, Takaesu's biting ability would likely end there.

He wasn't afraid of death. However, what he flatly refused to accept was an unseemly, ugly end. He would rather suffocate to death by getting an overboiled fettuccine noodle stuck in his throat than die because he was trapped by a police plot.

The majority of the park that the girl had gone into was enveloped in darkness, most of the only light being from the roadways in the center and southern parts of the park. Were those pigs lurking out there in the dark? Was this a moment of opportunity given to him by the devil? Or was it a trap set by an angel? Just then—

The northerly wind that had been blowing from behind him into the park this whole time stopped. After a bit, lukewarm air blew toward him from the south.

Takaesu's body, which was layered in newly bought black sportswear, shrank into itself as he let out all the air in his lungs and immediately drew in a long breath through his nose.

He had never tested it, but if there were dozens of police officers lying in wait in the park, he should certainly be able to pick up on a smell like that. What came in on the southerly wind was the smell of fallen leaves piled up on the ground, the smell of marshes thick with green, the smell of lawns withered to brown…and the sweet smell of that girl.

The thing gave a sharp throb in his lower jaw.

It's all right, there's no danger, it whispered to him.

Bite her, bite her, it tempted him.

"…Good idea, *compagno*," he whispered.

Takaesu gracefully dashed down the stairs that led from the embankment down to the park.

* * *

What am I doing?

Racked with self-recrimination, Minoru sighed for the umpteenth time. It had already been close to five minutes since Tomomi Minowa had run off, but he still wasn't able to get up from the bench in the Western Garden.

The reason he had come all the way to this park was supposedly because he couldn't be heartless in the face of her show of determination.

If that was the case, then shouldn't he have been able to respond to Tomomi's repeated apologies with the best words he could muster instead of trying to smooth things over with superficialities? But he hadn't actually smoothed things over at all, because Minoru had just stayed intently silent.

He didn't want to interact with other people. He didn't want to increase his memories. If those were his true wishes, it would be better to just confine himself to his room and not go to school, yet he didn't have the courage. Although he said he wanted to be alone, deep down he was afraid to go off the track that led to getting educated and finding a job. More accurately, he was afraid of the people he knew looking at him with pity and contempt because he got off track. Ultimately, absolute solitude was just a fantasy.

Even if Minoru shut himself away, it wasn't as if he would immediately vanish from the memories of the people around him. In that sense, true solitude couldn't possibly exist.

But the people around me probably aren't as concerned about me as I think. No, I'm sure she's like that, too. She'll probably forget in no time that she talked to me and that she cried earlier. Starting tomorrow, I'm going to go back to a life of not being involved with anyone.

As he was telling himself this, he stood up slowly from the bench—that's when it happened.

"…?"

Minoru got the feeling that he was smelling something strange and furrowed his brow. It was so faint that it wasn't even clear if it was a bad smell. The smell of something burning, of iron, of beasts… If he had to say, it was the smell of violence.

After emptying his lungs briefly, he inhaled slowly through his nose. He wasn't imagining it. In the cold air was something he had never smelled before, a foul smell that, strangely, made his heart stir. On top of that, the smell was wafting out from the wooded area that covered the center of the park. From the same direction that Tomomi Minowa had run off in.

＊ ＊ ＊

Takaesu's right canine teeth made a light grating sound as they rubbed together. The eye sheltered in his lower jaw swelled as if unable to wait for the feast that would soon come to it. That excitement traveled to all thirty-two of his teeth, and they ground together on their own, separate from Takaesu's will.

Hold on, compagno. *It would be such a waste if we were to make a mistake now,* he whispered in his mind, resuming his advance.

He moved through the vast forest at the center of the park with quick steps. Because he was off the path, it would be easy to slip on the wet fallen leaves, and the light from the streetlamps didn't reach where he was. But now, the far-off city lights alone were enough for Takaesu's eyes. Like a man-eating shark cornering its prey, he walked on gracefully.

His nasal cavity had a strong hold on her scent. She was close, probably no more than a hundred meters away. If he strained his ears to listen, he could hear the sound of her running shoes hitting the pavement.

Her gait seemed a bit heavier than it had been yesterday, as if she were tired. Of course, it was optimal for his prey to be in its best physical condition, but her being fatigued would make the hunt easier.

From the right side in front of him, the sound of her footsteps was coming reliably closer, as were the regular sounds of her breathing and the rustle of her workout clothes. On occasion, it seemed like she was sniffling. Had she caught a cold, or was she crying? If it was the latter, had something happened to her in the park?

But really, none of that mattered. All he wanted was her properly developed flesh and her well-packed bone.

Her footsteps came closer and closer. He could see the narrow recreation trail on the other side of the thicket in front of him. A small figure was swaying in the white glow of the LED streetlamps.

Takaesu pressed his body tightly against the trunk of a large, towering camphor tree alongside the trail and waited. The moment the young girl ran in from the right and approached the other side of the tree, he spun himself around and came out into the road behind his prey.

Possibly having noticed the slight sound of footsteps, the girl turned around as she ran. Her eyes grew huge when she spotted Takaesu. The teardrops gathered in those eyes glittered in the LED light. He would taste the tears first, as an aperitif.

As he thought this, Takaesu reached out his thinly gloved left hand and covered the girl's mouth as she prepared to scream.

The vibration of her vocal cords reached his palm but never turned into sound. He came around behind her and pulled her closer, wrapping his right arm around her slim neck.

With his first prey, he had made a mistake when regulating the pressure at this point and crushed the person's cervical vertebrae. Although the final result was still the same, he really did want to savor the sense of energy that living flesh and bone had when he first bit down.

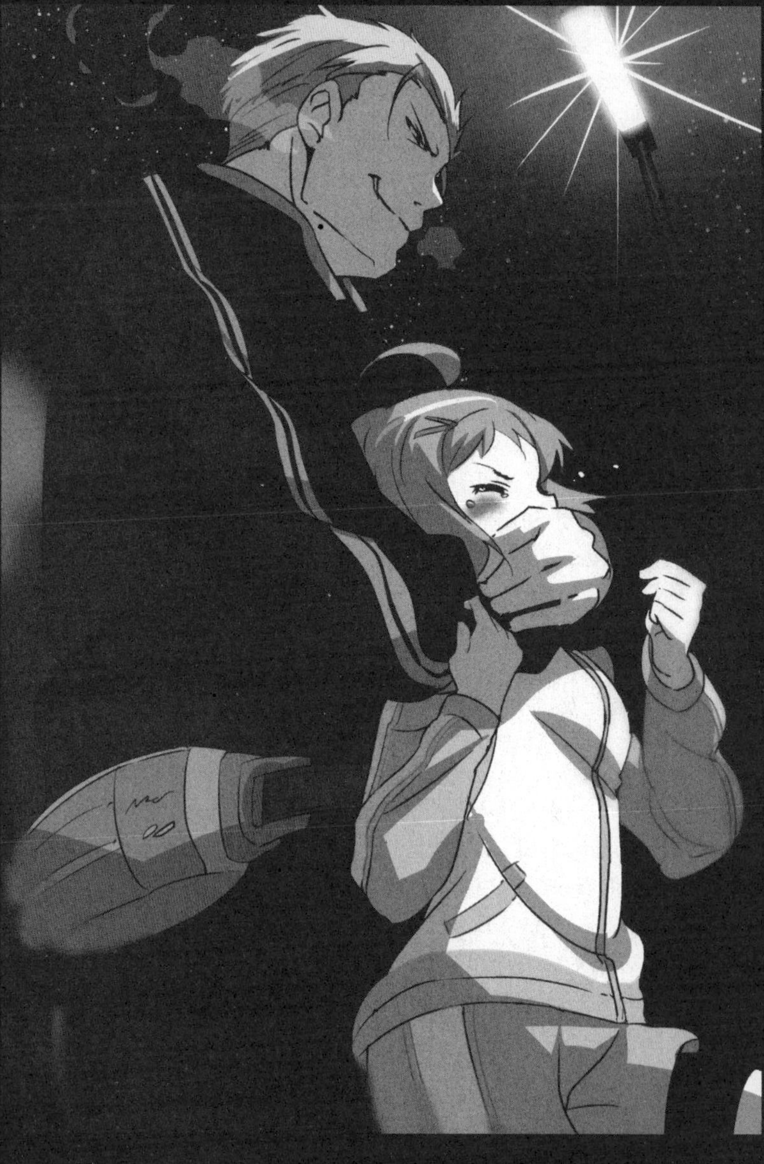

As he pinned down the fiercely struggling girl, he carefully applied pressure with his right arm. People generally think the mechanism in a choke hold that renders someone unconscious is that the artery in the neck is compressed, stopping blood flow to the brain, but that's not exactly correct. To be precise, when a place called the carotid sinus is compressed, the vagus nerve overreacts. This signal reaches the heart, the pulse instantly slows, blood pressure drops, and the supply of oxygen to the brain becomes insufficient, bringing unconsciousness.

That's why, when making someone lose consciousness in a short amount of time, there's no need to completely wring the person's neck. By simply compressing the carotid sinus on the side of the neck under the chin just right—there.

The strength drained from the girl's entire body. Easily lifting up the limp body of his prey, Takaesu left the trail again.

With his canine teeth grating and grating and grating against each other, he began walking in long strides. To the darkness in the depths of the forest where no light or sound could reach.

* * *

In the cold wind, the foul smell disappeared and reappeared. Was there something rotting in the woods, or was someone burning trash? It was a big park, so either seemed possible, but it was mysterious that he hadn't noticed it when he had first come to this place.

The usual Minoru would probably have let it go and walked away, thinking it didn't matter. But an odd foreboding kept him from making his way to his bike.

Was this really even the smell of something rotting or of something burning? Could it be the smell of a living creature? Even if it was, the only things inhabiting Akigase Park were probably raccoons and stray cats.

There shouldn't be any large animals that would do harm to humans. If he shifted his gaze a little, he could see the headlights of cars coming and going over Akigase Bridge just 1.5 kilometers ahead. At this point, Tomomi was surely out of the park and heading onto the embankment path.

Even though he believed this in his mind, the uneasiness that had settled in on his chest didn't disappear.

With all the things going on, my nerves are shot. I'll just go home and bring today to an end. You can't forget things that have happened, but you can put them in the past.

He stepped forward as he said this to himself, approaching his bike parked on the side of the Western Garden. But after just three steps, that smell stimulated his nose again. The more concentrated, more repulsive smell of a beast. It was just as if he had entered the territory of a large, tremendously dangerous carnivore.

"...What is this...?" Minoru whispered as he glanced again at the thicket that was ahead of him diagonally on the right.

Deep in his chest at the center of his sternum, he felt the thing throb. More powerfully than when he had almost been hit by the bike— and more powerfully than when he had almost been punched by the upperclassman.

Sweat had accumulated on his palms at some point, and he wiped them on his pants. Pulling his scarf up to his mouth, Minoru started walking again.

Not to his bike, but toward the jet-black rise of the forest.

$$* * *$$

Still holding the unconscious girl in his arms, a composed Takaesu walked through the woods off the path.

Up until now he'd brought his prey to his car after using similar methods to capture them, but that wasn't an option this time. It would be impossible to move her all the way to the Maserati, which was in the parking lot of his faraway hotel, without being seen by anyone or getting captured on security cameras. He had considered binding her hands and feet and hiding her somewhere in the park while he went to get the car, but with unconsciousness resulting from pressure to the carotid sinus, people recover within a few minutes as long as blood flow returns. There was no way the girl would wait obediently for Takaesu's return if she regained consciousness.

Luckily, this forest was so vast and deep that it was hard to believe it bordered an urban area. It was unfortunate that he was unable to use his favorite dining table, but there was little worry of being disturbed if he used this location for a feast.

Takaesu had walked to the place on the northern side of the park that was farthest removed from the several recreation trails. He put the girl on the ground and noticed an unexpected angular silhouette in front of him.

Muffling the sound of his footsteps, he approached; it was a simple storage shed. The walls were overgrown with ivy, and the paint on the sliding door was cracked. The shed had probably been used to store cleaning supplies and such, but looking at how dilapidated it was, it had likely not been used for several years.

After bringing his face close to the girl in his arms to confirm that she was breathing properly and that there were no signs of her regaining consciousness yet, he laid her down on top of the fallen leaves. Approaching the shed, he grabbed with gloved hands the padlock hanging from the door handle.

It was covered with dust and green rust, but the brass lock didn't budge a bit when he yanked it with all his might. Even with Takaesu's current physical strength, it was impossible for him to break it with his bare hands. He could probably get the door off if he threw his body against it, but the tremendous noise would surely reach outside of the forest.

Still, it would be disappointing to let go of such a lucky find. Although the shed was decayed, it should be effective for keeping down voices—and for heightening the despair of his prey. He removed a wet wipe from the "tool kit" in his pack and wiped the dark gray padlock clean. Suppressing his still-rising revulsion, he opened his mouth wide and put the heavy metal between his front teeth.

He tried adding a little pressure. It was as hard as expected. Macadamia nutshells still had a bit of give, but this didn't bend in the least, obstinately repelling his teeth. He wondered if all of his front teeth would break if he bit as hard as he could. Still, if he wanted to improve any further, he had to raise the level eventually. There were no longer any organic objects that could defeat Takaesu's teeth.

He wanted to bite the lock in half, not crush it. Takaesu took in a lungful of air as he pictured a chisel—and he bit down with all his strength.

A sharp pain ran through the roots of his teeth. A hard clanging sound rang out, and yellow sparks flew from his mouth.

A second later, when Takaesu slowly stood up, he spat out the object rolling around in his mouth into his palm: a lump of brass he had bitten into a semicircle. The little bit of blood sticking to it probably meant that the pressure had ruptured the capillaries in his gums. The thing would probably fix this level of damage for him right away.

When he pulled at the half still hanging from the handle, the U-shaped latch came off. Feeling satisfied as he gazed at the beautiful teeth marks etched into the cut sides of the two metal lumps, he put them into one of his pockets.

When he cautiously pulled open the door, moldy-smelling air flowed out. The interior of the shed was about three and a half square meters. Just as he imagined, there were heaps of cleaning supplies like rakes, bamboo brooms and whisk brooms, and piles of materials like cement blocks and iron piping. However, about half of the floor space was open, and there was a large blue sheet spread out there that was just what he needed.

Lifting up the girl from where she lay on the ground, he went into the shed, then shut the door after putting her on the sheet. There were no windows, so the interior was sunk in near-perfect darkness. After thinking for a moment, he produced a small LED light from his pack and switched it to lantern mode, placing it on top of the piled-up tools. The weak light faintly illuminated the inside of the shed.

Now no one would disturb them. From this point forward, this place was not a grimy shed but a three-star *ristorante*.

After removing the day pack that she was still wearing on her back, he took his nonelastic bandaging tape—an important part of his hunting tools—and wound it around both of the girl's wrists and knees. He stuffed a handkerchief in her mouth and taped over the top of it, wrapping the tape around and around.

When he had finished binding her, Takaesu patted the vaguely conscious girl on the cheek. Finally returned to consciousness, she blinked a few times and focused her eyes on Takaesu's face.

In her large brown eyes, the color of confusion rose first, followed by suspicion and lastly fear. Finally seeming to understand the situation she had landed in, a muffled scream came from the back of her gagged mouth and she backed away from him, her legs moving frantically, shrimplike. However, she immediately bumped into the wall behind her.

"...Don't be afraid, Signorina," Takaesu said in an indistinct voice.

He himself found his pronunciation terrible, but all of his teeth had already begun to swell, and he couldn't seem to enunciate things. In the center of his lower jaw, the thing pulsed as if going mad.

Takaesu grabbed a large iron pipe from the mountain of cleaning supplies and materials thrown on the left side of the shed. The girl's eyes went wider still, and letting out a muffled scream, she pressed her body into the wall behind her.

"Have no fear; I wouldn't use a crude instrument like this," Takaesu whispered in a muffled voice.

Then Takaesu opened his mouth wide. His teeth shone in the light of the LED lantern, and their reflection glittered in the girl's eyes. The center of his lower jaw throbbed with such heat that it was hard to bear. All at once, he released the desire that had been building up in him ever since the night of his last feast.

Crunch. The loud sound came from his lower jawbone. Takaesu's jaw, which had always been robust for a Japanese person, grated and crunched as it grew outward.

It wasn't that the joints had dislocated. The bone itself was expanding through some mechanism that surpassed modern biology.

What's more, the same phenomenon was occurring in his upper jawbone, too. The sharply pointed upper and lower jaws protruded more than ten centimeters more than normal; Takaesu's face was no longer a human one. The girl's eyes were opened as wide as they could go, and her pupils dilated, fear overwhelming her. But the main event was yet to come.

The thirty-two teeth inside Takaesu's quite elongated jaw made high-pitched squeals as they enlarged, becoming double-layered fangs with sharp, knifelike points and sturdy, ax-like bases.

He was a tiger shark. He was becoming a savage man-eating shark that bit open the shells of sea turtles.

The light that he had placed off to the left projected anomalous shadows onto the right wall. If he had been forced to say, his silhouette of vicious teeth—no, fangs—growing from a long jaw could have been that of a new type of human that had the DNA of a shark instead of an ape.

It would probably seem strange and repulsive to obsolete humans, but this was the ideal form that Takaesu had been pursuing for many years: a robust jaw and beautiful, sturdy, healthy teeth that could bite through anything.

Seeing Takaesu's mad transformation, the girl could do nothing but tremble violently. To add to her terror, Takaesu brought the iron pipe in his right hand to his mouth and leisurely bit into the end. The pipe was one of the carbon steel pipes that is often used at construction sites and had a diameter of about six centimeters and a thickness of more than four millimeters. Up until yesterday—no, until ten minutes ago—Takaesu's teeth literally would not have been able to stand up to it even if he had transformed. But the memory of having bitten through the padlock earlier in his normal state gave Takaesu and the thing power.

He sunk his massive canine teeth into the crude iron pipe, an abrasive squeal ringing out. Even a large hydraulic cutter couldn't exhibit this kind of cutting power. He snapped the steel tube apart in only six or seven seconds, just as if it had been a stick of candy.

Takaesu put the bit-off end of the iron pipe inside his mouth and chewed it a few more times. Each time, the shrill scream of metal resounded.

What he finally spat out on the plastic sheet at his feet was a torn piece of scrap metal only a few millimeters long. There wasn't a drop of blood on it.

"*Cattivo*," Takaesu murmured with a sneer, indicating his disgust.

Striding over the piece of metal and taking one step more, he leaned over right before the girl's eyes.

"But your bones seem like they'll taste great."

When he announced this, a muffled scream slipped out from her tape-covered mouth and she jerked her body around like a broken toy. She futilely kicked her legs, which were still bound at the knee, in the air. Takaesu easily caught both of them with his right hand. With no hesitation, he pulled off the running shoes she was wearing.

"...!!"

The girl's screams noticeably intensified. But to Takaesu, it was nothing but background music to increase the enjoyment of the dining experience.

When he had removed her athletic socks, he admired her exposed bare feet intently. They would surely offer the highest quality of firmness.

He wanted to bite into her immediately, but it would spoil the fun if she died so easily; first, he had to prepare to stanch the bleeding. He rummaged around in his pack again and pulled out a zip tie. As he went to wrap it around the girl's calf, Takaesu's hand froze.

He heard a faint snapping noise. Probably the sound of a dry twig breaking.

After a moment, he heard the sound again. There was no doubt about it; someone was approaching the shed.

"If you make noise, I'll kill you right now," he whispered, bringing his strange features near her face and peering into her tear-filled eyes at close proximity.

He put the leg he had seized earlier down onto the floor, went over to the sliding door, and pressed his ear to the rusty iron. He heard a rustling sound at regular intervals. It was the sound of feet treading on piles of fallen leaves. The person was incredibly close to the shed.

He wondered if it was the police, but then realized he could only hear the footsteps of one person. Whether a detective or a member of a SWAT team, no police officer would take action on their own. Then was it a park maintenance person? Had the shed only seemed like it had been abandoned for years because Takaesu's desire to use it clouded his judgment?

He shook his head a bit and glanced at the LED light he had put on top of the cleaning supplies. He wondered for a moment if he should turn it off but decided to leave it as it was.

He turned around and stood at the ready, right beside the door. Whoever it was, he would have to kill them the instant they came in. This time he wouldn't bother with squeezing the person's carotid artery. He would tear through their neck with one bite. It was a shame that he had to put his first-rate prey on hold and bite this inferior bone, but that was what he got for his foolish carelessness.

His jaw, protruding like a shark's, opened wide.

His front teeth, sharp like razors, gleamed in the glow of the LED light.

* * *

After having walked a few dozen meters, Minoru left the recreation trail and stepped into the dark forest.

There was no way the foul smell in the air was something he was imagining now. He could identify it clearly, right down to the direction it was coming from. Before he knew it, the light of the streetlamps no longer reached him, but he had no difficulty walking, probably because his eyesight had become more sensitive than before.

He was aware that he was doing something stupid. Whatever the source of the smell was, it was probably something unpleasant, and he knew he would want to erase the memory of finding it later anyway.

Although it might be better if he turned back, then he would just be struck by the same self-hatred as always. He'd already come this far because he felt uneasy about the fact that the abnormal smell was coming from the direction Tomomi Minowa had run away in, so if he went back without making sure that it was nothing, he would be hit by his own cowardice and coldheartedness.

Is everything I do just for myself, ultimately?

His mouth twisted as he thought this. Right then, his left shoe stepped on a withered branch, making a dry cracking sound. Minoru stopped reflexively and strained to see through the darkness in front of him. He noticed a small shed standing in the clearing a few dozen meters away. It was probably a storeroom or something, but its half-rotted, weather-beaten condition made it seem like it wasn't in use right now.

Even so, Minoru just knew that the smell was coming from there. There was no sign that anything or anyone was around the building. Was it inside the shed? If so, that would mean that the strange stench was not the smell of a wild animal.

It felt like the hair all over his body was standing up. His frozen palms were soaked with sweat. Although he wasn't moving, the stench seemed to grow thicker and thicker. Even when he used his left hand to cover his nose with his scarf, the smell that pierced his olfactory cells didn't let up.

There was something out of the ordinary lurking inside that shed. His right foot unconsciously took a half step backward, and he stepped on another withered branch. His whole body flinched at the sound he had made.

He wanted to turn around right now and run away from the shed. Barely keeping it together, Minoru grabbed the front of his uniform with his sweat-dampened right hand.

When he did this, he felt something itchy and painful in the space between his numb palm and his heart, which was pulsing like an alarm bell.

It was the thing. The small orb that had nestled into his sternum was throbbing with heat. *Don't be afraid. Keep going*, it whispered to him.

Taking a deep breath in and letting it out slowly, Minoru took one step with his right foot, the one that had retreated earlier. Then his left foot. Then his right again. Walking with steps so sure that it surprised even him, he took off his scarf and the bag he wore diagonally across his chest and set them quietly on the ground.

The shed was right in front of him now. When he looked very carefully at the incredibly thin gap between the closed iron door and the wall, it seemed like there was a faint light seeping out.

The beastly smell grew stronger and stronger as he moved forward, but mysteriously, he had no trouble breathing. He definitely wasn't smelling this because the cells in his nose were picking up on some material that had a scent. His brain was taking some sort of information and directly interpreting it as a smell.

As if he were being drawn in by it, Minoru reached out his right hand, clutched the handle of the door, and pulled it right open.

Then he breathed in sharply. A blue plastic sheet was spread out on the floor of the dim shed, and on top of it, Tomomi Minowa was bound at her hands and feet with gray tape and gagged. She still had on her workout top and bottoms, but for some reason only the shoes and socks from both feet had been removed.

"Mi…," Minoru said in a hoarse and throaty voice as he took one step into the shed.

At the same time, Tomomi shook her head violently, her eyes open wide, as if to tell him not to come in. Immediately after, a number of things happened in succession.

The beastly smell, so thick that he could feel even its malice, closed in on Minoru.

Directly to his left, a black shadow flew at him with incredible power.

A long, protruding mouth in an inhuman shape held Minoru by the side of the neck. The vicious and extraordinarily huge sharp teeth touched the skin at the back of his neck.

* * *

Male. Young. High school student. He seemed to know the girl. Same school? Was this *ragazzo* the reason for her tears?

If so, it would've been nice to catch him. What fun it would have been to line them up and take turns biting them. But it was too late. He couldn't stop his jaws, his teeth, or the thing.

It was a thin neck. Slender like a woman's. Takaesu was sure he could cut through to the vertebrae with one bite.

There it was easy to get it between his teeth.

Takaesu thought all of this in the 0.3 seconds after this nuisance had come into view. Tilting his head to the side, he put his mouth on the boy's neck over the stiff collar of his school uniform. The teeth on his right side made contact with the heavy black woven fabric, while the teeth on his left side touched thin white skin. If he bit down like this, he would surely snap right through flesh and bone, revealing a lovely cross section of red and pink and white.

His jaw muscles were ready. He was going to release all of the pent-up power of a shark in one go—

That's when it happened. Something unexpected occurred.

A strange smell hit him right in the face. It was an artificial, chemical, irritating odor that he had never smelled before.

At the same time, the boy's neck swelled up—or it seemed to. Takaesu's teeth, which had cut slightly into the skin, were repelled in an instant by a pressure that surpassed his bite strength. Something unbelievably hard and unimaginably smooth was rejecting his teeth. Pain ran through his masseter muscle on both sides, telling him that the muscle fiber was damaged.

His eyes wide with surprise, Takaesu looked at his own hugely protruding mouth. Then he got an even greater shock.

He definitely felt the sensation in his jaw of biting something. Yet his teeth weren't touching flesh. They were trembling slightly but immobile, separated from the white skin by three centimeters.

But if that was the case, then what was this terrible firmness he felt in the bones of his jaw? Had the boy outfitted the back of his neck with protection made from strengthened glass or something?

No, even if that were the case, Takaesu should be able to easily cut any type of glass or resin in his tiger-shark mode. So was it diamond? Could this completely mediocre high school boy actually have something like that?

Takaesu's thoughts were thrown into confusion—the material was more solid than anything he had ever encountered before, and incomprehensibly, he couldn't see it. Still, he didn't open his jaws. Nothing could exist that Takaesu as a tiger shark couldn't bite through.

Ignoring the grating screams of his masseter muscle, he applied as much force as he could. At some point, the mysterious, irritating odor had disappeared, but Takaesu wasn't aware of it; his attention was focused only on breaking through that transparent something.

As a result, he didn't think of trying to avoid it when the boy, who seemed to have recovered from his shock, swung a clumsy fist at him. Since he had allowed the *thing* to live in his lower jaw, the strength of not only his teeth and jaw but also his physical abilities themselves had skyrocketed. He could take a punch or two from this feeble high school student without feeling any pain. Ignoring the swinging fist, he squeezed with all the strength he could muster—

Impact. His field of vision grew dark, and white sparks flickered. His right temple grew hot as if it were being burned, and soon after he was overtaken with excruciating pain like a nail being driven into him. Even his sense of balance was thrown off as if his brain were being shaken. Takaesu fought to keep his footing, swearing he wouldn't fall over.

He'd been hit. But it hadn't felt like a bare fist. It was a blow from something hard, heavy, smooth… Just like he'd been struck by a polished steel ball at full force. Did that mean that the boy's invisible protection wasn't just around his neck? Was he wearing some kind of glove on his fist that was made of diamond or something else?

No. Could it be…

Pressing his reeling body against the wall on his left, Takaesu tried to thrust the fingers of his left hand into the boy's unprotected stomach. But his fingers didn't make it. Just as he had predicted, they smashed into something right above the gray Chesterfield coat the boy was wearing. It was an invisible wall, smooth, unbelievably hard, and neither hot nor cold.

His whole body. This boy's whole body was protected.

As Takaesu thought this in a daze, the boy raised his right fist again. His movements were that of a complete amateur. But if Takaesu took another blow of the same force as the one before, he would probably pass out this time.

Swallowing an indescribable shame, Takaesu opened his jaw and let go of the boy's neck. He sunk down, the large amount of saliva that had built up in his mouth splashing about.

The boy's fist passed through the space where Takaesu's head had been just a moment ago and crashed into the half-open metal sliding door. There was a thunderous noise as if a large man who took pride in his strength had pummeled the door with an iron hammer. The face of the door was smashed in and pieces of stripped-off paint fluttered through the air. Amid all this, Takaesu struggled to crawl away and rolled toward the outside of the shed.

He rolled over and over like this for about four meters and somehow managed to stand up. A large amount of fallen leaves clung to not just his new sportswear but also his hair. His skin was smudged with dirt. A single line of blood trickled from his temple, and saliva dribbled from his mouth. His brain was so shaken up that he ended up in a squat with his backside stuck out. It was an intolerably ugly position, but Takaesu had no room to get angry.

The boy showed himself in the doorway of the shed, and Takaesu scrutinized him again from top to bottom. He was probably seven or eight centimeters shorter than Takaesu, who was 183 centimeters. He was likely on the tall side for his age, but he had a scrawny build and didn't at all look like he could throw a heavy enough punch to dent an iron door…

No, wait. The shadow created by the LED light that poured out from inside the shed wasn't touching the boy's feet.

He was *floating*. The boy's feet were separated from the concrete of the doorway, albeit by only a few centimeters. Did that mean that invisible shell even went around the bottoms of his feet?

Armor that wrapped around every single part of a person's body without leaving any gaps, was completely transparent and stronger than steel, and even expanded and contracted at will. There was no way something like that could be created with existing science and technology.

As he endured the pain of his swollen, sharply throbbing temple, Takaesu reached a terribly unpleasant conclusion.

It was the *thing*. This high school student standing a mere four or five meters away from Takaesu also had that small orb somewhere in his body. Takaesu wasn't the only human who had been chosen. And the thing gave different powers. Takaesu had gained the power of a shark—and this boy had gained invisible armor.

…Were there still others? Other humans who had orbs dwelling in them? Did they all have strange and dangerous powers, and were they hiding somewhere in Japan?

"…I can't have that," Takaesu murmured in a hoarse voice.

He wouldn't allow something like that. It was unacceptable for anyone other than Hikaru Takaesu to belong to the superior, supernaturally powerful species.

Gnashing his still-enlarged teeth, he made up his mind. He would eliminate them. All of them. The boy in front of him…and all the others who possessed the eye, if there were any. The thing pulsed madly in the center of his lower jaw. It seemed to clamor for him to hunt them, bite them, devour them.

He no longer cared about the pain in his left temple or his warped sense of balance. Still bent forward and spurred on by an overwhelming rage, Takaesu managed to keep himself in check somehow. He would bite the boy next time. He would bite all the bones in the boy's body to pieces through the transparent armor that protected him.

But before that, he should obtain just a little information. The boy could know something about others besides him who possessed the eye.

Sucking in dry air through his slightly open mouth, Takaesu cooled his seething teeth just a bit, then turned to face the boy and started to speak to him.

* * *

The man before him seemed to be saying something, but Minoru couldn't hear it.

Minoru…thought it was male. But he wasn't convinced about the figure's humanity. His height was probably more than 180 centimeters. His limbs were long and his shoulders were broad. He was stylishly dressed in black training wear, and Minoru could sense the thickness of his hardened muscles.

Was he around thirty, give or take? His short hair was styled in a fashionable two-block cut, and everything from his forehead to his eyes gave off an air of intelligence. But the problem was the lower half of his face.

When Minoru had first seen him, he had thought it was a dinosaur. The strangely long upper and lower jaws protruded forward, teeth of inhuman size peeking out. But the form of the jaws, which tapered off at the end, made Minoru think of a fish more than a reptile. What's more, it was a large, carnivorous fish able to attack even humans—a shark.

The enormous triangular teeth were sharp and pointed, and they glistened wetly. Thick bunches of muscle ran down both sides of the face. Those jaws surely hid enormous power, and there was no doubt that one bite from them could easily rip a human body apart.

Just thinking about how those jaws had been around his neck for even an instant sent cold shivers through his whole body.

One minute and a few seconds earlier—

The moment Minoru had opened the door to the shed and found Tomomi Minowa tied up, all his thoughts had stopped. If he had been able to use his head a bit, he probably would have been aware of the possibility that whoever had taken Tomomi was lurking in the blind

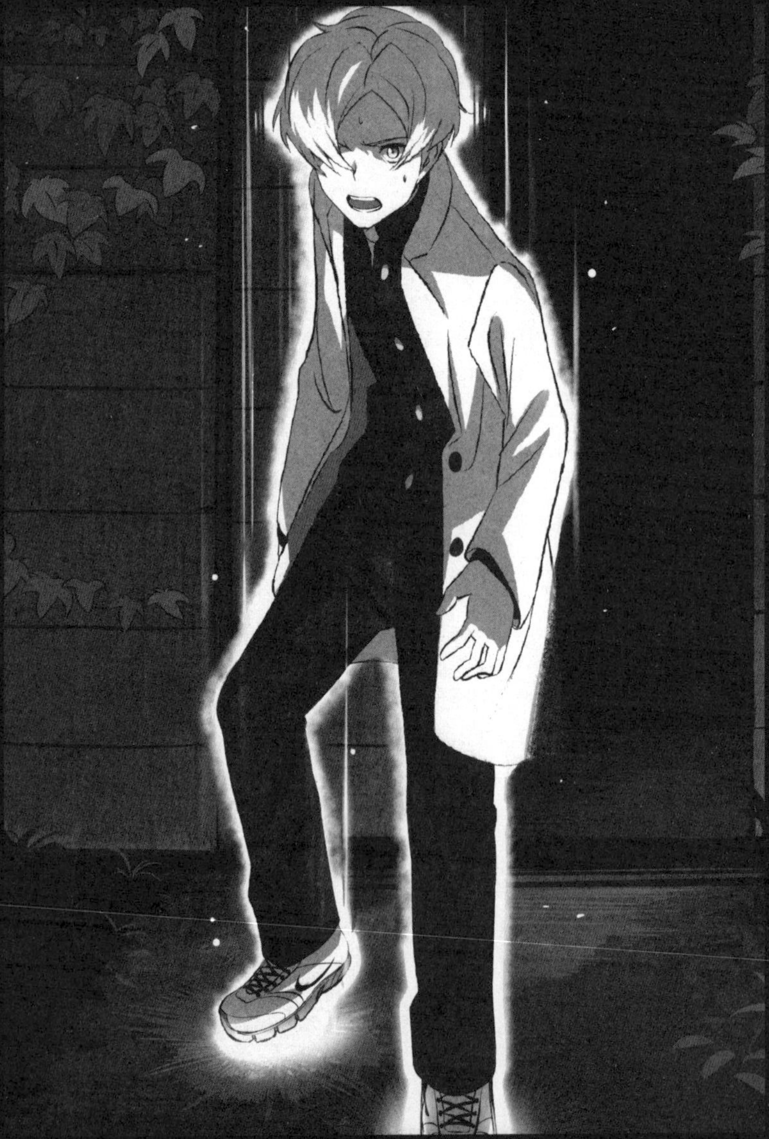

spot behind the door, but he had just jumped single-mindedly into the shed.

Just after, a black shadow had sprung at him from the left—freezing-cold teeth and breath that was hot like a flame touched the back of his neck. At that moment, he felt the thing in the center of his chest shake violently. Then that strange phenomenon occurred once again.

All sound disappeared, his field of vision changed color, and his body floated up just a little. When he felt his attacker's teeth—which had definitely made indentations in the skin of his neck—being pushed back by some unseen force, Minoru finally sensed what was happening to him.

It was a shell. It was a fearsomely hard, invisible shell that could transform at will, and it generated around his body without leaving any gaps. It was about three centimeters thick. It was strange that he couldn't feel the uniform and the Chesterfield coat he was wearing being pressed inside the shell, but he had no room to think about that.

He put all his concentration into making a fist and thrusting it at his attacker. The punch was so clumsy that even he thought it was pathetic, but somehow it connected. Because he felt almost no recoil, he thought he hadn't done any major damage and attacked the same way once more. This time the man dropped down and dodged him, but he stayed on the floor and rolled away out of the shed—this was where he faced Minoru from now.

What in the world was he?

Minoru answered his own question. It was obvious. In the man's chest... No, that wasn't the only possibility. The man was a human, and that orb was dwelling somewhere in his body.

Just as he had imagined so many times, there were others who had encountered it. In other words, the man was one of Minoru's kind.

But there wasn't even a shred of something resembling camaraderie in the eyes of the man with a shark's jaw. His eyes flashed only with cold, murderous intent and seething animosity.

Glowering at Minoru, who stood motionless, the shark man moved his protruding jaws over and over. It seemed like he was saying something, but enveloped in the invisible shell, Minoru couldn't hear the

sound of the wind in the treetops or the sound of traffic on the Akigase Bridge, let alone what the man was saying. But it wasn't actually
silent. He felt as if he could faintly hear a heavy bass sound like the
whump, whump of a machine…or the heartbeat of a massive creature.
He didn't have a clue what the sound was.

There was less than five meters between him and the man. In this
situation, it would be too dangerous to lose the shell. He had never
known how to disarm it in the first place, but still, he felt like he
wanted to hear what the man was saying…

Minoru inhaled the completely tasteless and odorless air. In it, even
the scent of his own body was imperceptible. When he had filled his
lungs, it happened.

The slightly blue hue that covered his field of vision returned to
normal, his body dropped three centimeters, and the bottom of his
shoes touched the wet concrete.

"…!"

The shell disappeared. He almost cried out in surprise but narrowly held it in. If the man realized that Minoru had erased the shell
unintentionally, he would certainly be attacked again. But luckily,
the shark man seemed to think that Minoru had taken off the shell of
his own accord. Moving his mouth again, the man spread his hands
in a sophisticated gesture.

"…Well, well, are you finally in the mood to listen to what I have
to say?"

Originally, the man probably had a beautiful voice that carried
well, but now he sounded just like an alien trying to imitate a human
speaking. His speech sounded strangely warped because the endings
of his words were unclear.

When Minoru stayed silent, the man inclined his head a bit and
went on speaking.

"Young man. I'd just like to confirm something… You have it
somewhere in your body, don't you? The red eye?"

"…Eye…?" Minoru answered reflexively.

The man was clearly referring to the thing buried in Minoru's chest.
But there was just one inconsistency that he couldn't ignore.

The mysterious orb that had descended from the sky three months ago. He had only seen it directly for a few seconds, but Minoru could clearly remember what it looked like even now.

The orb's diameter was a little less than two centimeters. Its surface had a sheen as if it were wet, and a core that was one size smaller was nestled deep under the see-through top layer.

Now that the man had mentioned it, that double-layered sphere really did have some similarity to the eye of a living creature. But—

"Red...?"

That was the only thing that was clearly wrong. The orb that had slipped into Minoru's chest had a light gray permeable layer and a core so black that it seemed to absorb all light. So did that mean the color of each and every orb was different? To start with, how many actually existed in total...?

As if irritated, the shark man stuck his pointed jaw out at Minoru, who was standing stiff as a board.

"So which is it? Do you have one, or don't you?"

"I-I have one... Or there is one inside my body...," Minoru answered in a hoarse voice.

The man nodded, eyes narrowed, and pushed Minoru for more.

"Three months ago?"

Minoru gave a small nod.

"...I see."

When the man closed his massive jaws, both corners of his mouth were tugged up into a vaguely threatening smile that would give a child nightmares.

"Well, your eye seems to have given you quite a pleasant power. Invisible armor that wraps around your entire body... You had me a bit surprised earlier. But what surprised me more was the fact that someone besides me possesses the eye."

The way he spoke felt amiable, but the murderous intent dwelling in the man's eyes hadn't disappeared in the least. No, Minoru couldn't get the wrong idea. Although he and the shark man before him shared the fact that orbs lived within them, the man definitely wasn't someone who he could find mutual understanding with. That's because this man was the one who attacked Tomomi Minowa, brought her to the shed behind them, and bound her hand and foot.

If Minoru hadn't disturbed them…what would this man have done to Tomomi?

Usually, there was probably only one thing that a man would do after abducting and tying up a high school girl, but this man wasn't just a human. He had strangely formed, hugely protruding jaws and enormous teeth with sharp points. Would he have used those teeth to…

The man confirmed Minoru's fearsome imaginings all too easily.

"Well, I'll bite you properly next. No matter how much armor you have, if it only protects your body, I'll find a way. Don't fret; I won't kill you right away. I'll take my time and bite her ever so slowly while you watch, immobilized. No, no, would it be better to reverse the order…?"

"B-bite…? What do you mean, bite…?" Minoru murmured in shock.

The man gave another ghastly smile.

"Hey, hey, when humans bite something, there's only one reason for it, right? To eat, of course. That's what my teeth are there for."

"E-eat… Why would you do something like… Did that eye…get ahold of your brain or something…?"

"It's my own desire, of course. The eye did nothing more than give me the means to do it. I have always wanted to bite people. That's why the eye came to me… By the way, you'll be the fifth person I bite. And the girl behind you will be the sixth."

His strange smile got noticeably bigger, exposing several of his vicious, daggerlike teeth from under his elongated lips.

"Well, then… Shall we have a taste test?"

Licking his lips with a deep red tongue, the man began to close the gap between them little by little. Taking shallow breath after shallow breath, Minoru thought.

This guy is seriously planning to bite Minowa and me to death. I have to hurry and get the shell on again. But I still don't know how to flip the switch.

Three days ago, when I was about to make contact with that bike. Two days ago, when the upperclassman got ready to hit me. And just a few minutes ago, when the man in front of me bit my neck. There has to be some common action that I took each of those three times right before the shell appeared.

The distance between him and the man had shortened to three meters.

...Making a fist... No.

He was two meters away now.

...Clenching my teeth... No.

The man was right before him now, and he opened his vicious jaws as far as they could go. The teeth had a faint metallic luster, and they glinted in the twilight.

...That's it. All those times, and just a little while ago, I breathed like—

Minoru sucked in a sharp breath. But just before the ability given to him by the orb was activated...

Something that Minoru and the fearsome, strangely formed man hadn't even imagined occurred.

A *bam!* rent the air, and directly left of the shark man from Minoru's perspective, a huge amount of leaves that had been piled up on the ground flew into the air.

A figure appeared that had definitely not been there a moment earlier. Her long hair fluttered amid the swirling wind. It was a girl wearing a dark blazer. In her right hand, she had a sort of rod.

"Nn...!"

The shark man swiftly turned back to the right, his eyes wide open as he groaned. At that point, the girl was already thrusting out the black rod she held in her right hand. The moment the tip of it touched the man's right side, intense pale sparks flashed with a crackle.

"Guh!"

At the same time the man's body was swaying back and forth, Minoru let out the breath of air he had just inhaled in shock.

The girl standing just a short distance away in her blazer hadn't leaped down from the treetops or the roof of the shed. Of course, she hadn't been burrowed in the ground, either. She had simply appeared there in an instant.

Her face wasn't visible, hidden by her long hair. Her blazer that appeared pitch-black in the darkness and her gray pleated skirt were probably the uniform for some school. Her legs were covered in similarly black tights, and her shoes were mid-cut sneakers that went up to her ankles.

Her attire was that of a completely normal high school girl. That is, if it weren't for the black thirty-centimeter-long rod clutched in her right hand.

Two electrodes extended from the tip of the rod; it was probably something akin to a so-called stun gun. And although Minoru was completely uninformed about such handheld tools, it was obviously so high-powered that one might think it was illegal.

The shark man had taken a severe electric shock, and he lurched violently backward, his tall figure as stiff as a board. But right before he tumbled to the ground, he stuck his left foot out and managed to stay up. With his whole upper body bent backward, the only thing that was visible was the tip of his long jaw. Suddenly, a ferocious roar burst forth from his jaws, which were opened as far as they would go.

"Gwaaah!!"

If sharks were land animals, that was probably how they would howl. The man's voice was overflowing with enough rage to shake the air, and Minoru's whole body tensed up again.

Under the man's black training wear, his muscles writhed. He had been leaning back, but now his body sprung upright as if propelled there. His arms hung down limply, possibly from the effects of the electric shock, and he stuck out his head and flew at the mysterious girl.

"...!!"

Minoru took in a sharp breath.

Her identity was unclear, but the results were obvious: The girl had saved Minoru. So now Minoru had to save her. Or so he thought—but his body didn't move. His entire body cowered before the shark man's roar.

The jaws with their vicious teeth moved in on the black-haired girl. She tried to pull her body back, pushing off the ground and springing away, but there was no way she could escape. If she was bitten by that jaw, it would take off half her head—

A metallic *shing!* rang out, and sparks flew from the man's closed teeth. He had bitten only air. Just before his jaws closed, the girl had dropped down, dodging the attack by a paper-thin margin.

But the shark man didn't stop moving. He stuck out his jaws once more, persistently trying to bite her. He opened and closed his jaws again with a *shing, shing*, but the girl moved left and right and narrowly evaded him.

The way she moved was amazing—but she couldn't avoid the man forever. Why was she not trying to use that stun baton that was stronger than a normal stun gun? Was it because in exchange for its high power output it couldn't be used continuously?

Minoru once again thought that he needed to help her. He struggled to move his stiff, numb right foot forward. While moving ahead awkwardly, he took a deep breath…

But at that moment, the girl collapsed to the left. Maybe her feet had slipped on the wet fallen leaves.

"Gwah!"

The shark man gave a quick roar and loomed over the girl. Grabbing her with both hands, he opened his jaws at more than a ninety-degree angle, took the girl's delicate neck, and—

"…!"

Minoru had been focusing everything on launching himself at the man's back, but he stopped moving involuntarily.

For the first time, he was able to see the girl's face.

There wasn't an ounce of fear in her clean-cut, coolly beautiful face. Her lips were pulled tight, and her deep black eyes stared directly at the monster who was trying to devour her. The girl thrust the stun baton in her right hand deep into the shark man's mouth, her completely composed expression undisturbed.

Bang!!

There was another explosive sound. The man's massive mouth was filled with pale flashes, and his short hair stood completely on end.

The electricity went on for more than a full three seconds. After this, even the shark man himself probably wouldn't be able to move. As the strength slowly slipped from the man's body, Minoru felt another shiver.

The girl in the black blazer had definitely made narrow escape after narrow escape on purpose. The truth was that although she could have escaped with room to spare, she daringly tried to create an opening for the attack. All that was to ensure that the second shock would incapacitate her enemy—

Just who was she? Both the levelheadedness with which she handled the strangely formed monster and the superpowered stun baton that couldn't be bought on the open market made it difficult to believe that she was the student she looked to be. More important was the fact that she had appeared next to the shark man with no warning. That phenomenon...or that ability.

Did this girl have it, too? That thing?

The moment Minoru thought this was the moment it happened.

The inside of the shark man's mouth was scorched by the electricity, and he completely stopped moving. The thick muscle that bulged from his jaws to his neck convulsed. His long, protruding tongue was charred black, and white smoke escaped from the edges of his mouth. The whites of both his eyes were completely exposed, and he didn't seem to be conscious.

Still, the area around his enormous mouth was trembling like it belonged to a separate creature altogether. His jaws, which had been opened as wide as they could go, closed little by little.

Seeing the sharp front teeth lightly bite the stun baton, which was still stuck in the man's mouth, Minoru groaned in a hoarse voice, "N...no way..."

The high school girl's lovely face tensed as she lay on the ground, as if the current situation went beyond what she had anticipated. Her white hand pressed the switch on the stun baton and there was a third burst of electricity. At exactly the same time...

The shark man's jaws closed with a sharp *shing!* The stun baton split down the middle and the contents of the batteries spilled out, sending white flame into the air.

At that point, the girl's right hand had already let go of the baton. She stood up with agile movements, putting distance between her and the man.

After spitting out the ruins of the flaming baton, the shark man... twisted the charred black edges of his mouth into a sneer.

His eyes, which had been rolled back in his head, trembled and his irises reappeared. The small, dot-like pupils glowered at the girl as his voice rung out indistinctly.

"What a performance that was…"

The man's body weaved as if his wounds were as serious as they seemed, but he faced the black-haired high school girl and stepped forward.

"…I won't let you get away… I don't know who you are, but that doesn't matter now. I'll bite you… I'll bite you down to the bone… I'll bite every last one…"

As he said these hideous words, he slowly and steadily closed the gap between them. The girl, who was standing about five meters away, made no attempt to move. She moved her legs slightly apart and knelt, glaring at the approaching shark man.

What're you doing? Hurry up and escape, Minoru prayed desperately, standing in the doorway of the shed.

From what he could see, the girl didn't have any extra stun batons or any other tools to defend herself with. Assuming she had the same orb inside her as Minoru and the shark man—although he didn't know what color it was—if she could have brought the shark man down with the ability the orb gave her, she probably wouldn't have started off by using a stun baton.

Her mid-cut sneakers were planted firmly on top of the fallen leaves, and the way her gray pleated skirt and long, straight hair fluttered in the wind was natural, so it didn't seem like she had on the same transparent shell as Minoru.

Is she actually…giving up because she thinks she won't be able to counterattack or escape? Is she just planning to get bitten by the shark man and die like this?

The moment he started thinking like this, Minoru clenched both hands hard into fists. He glanced behind him. Tomomi Minowa was on the floor in the back of the storage shed and had seemingly lost consciousness from being so afraid. He felt for her, being bound hand and foot with tape, but she didn't seem to be injured.

He also had the option of picking up Tomomi right now and running out of the park. But the reason Minoru had been able to open the door to this shed was the same reason that he couldn't escape now.

He faced forward again. The shark man and the girl with the blazer were now separated by less than three meters. Minoru filled his chest with air. Consuming a portion of it, he shouted.

"Hurry up and run!"

Then he completely stopped breathing. He sensed the pressure on his lungs gathering in the center of his sternum. He wasn't certain. But the black orb responded to Minoru's will.

The rustling of leaves and the midwinter cold vanished. His body floated up slightly. The invisible shell had been activated. His breathing was the switch after all.

Still holding his breath, Minoru pushed off from the ground through the shell. He drove his head into the shark man's left side as the man tried to turn toward him.

It should have been a tremendous crash, but all Minoru felt was a very slight decrease in his speed. But for the man, it was the same as being hit by a massive lump weighing well over fifty kilograms. He was sent flying without a bit of resistance and toppled to the ground along with Minoru.

Seething with an unnaturally intense rage, the man attempted to shove Minoru aside. As Minoru was desperately holding him down, not breathing started to become painful. Shaking off the fear that the shell might disappear, he let out the carbon gas that had built up in his lungs and inhaled the tasteless and odorless air. He had breathed a bunch of times inside the shell when he was fighting with the man at the entrance of the shed, so this shouldn't get rid of it.

But now he had a new worry. The transparent shell generated at a distance of about three centimeters from Minoru's body. When he had calculated the surface area of his own body in math class, he remembered that it had been about 1.63 square meters. So was the amount of air inside the shell about forty-nine liters? How many more breaths would it take for him to use up the oxygen it included…?

As Minoru considered that, it occurred to him that he should tell the girl to run one more time by just mouthing the words. He turned his face toward her.

But the high school girl in the black blazer wasn't there.

He forget for an instant that he was in the middle of a fight, and his eyes widened. Minoru hadn't taken his eyes off the girl for more than three seconds at most. Wherever she had run to, it should have been impossible for her to cover enough distance to completely disappear from his field of vision. So had she used the same ability as when she appeared?

Whether or not the shark man noticed the girl's disappearance, he was in a mad frenzy, trying to bite into anywhere he could. For the time being, Minoru's shell was warding off the man's teeth, but he had no idea how long it would hold. Would the oxygen inside the shell disappear first, or would it shatter like glass before then?

Suddenly, a huge amount of fallen leaves flew into the air. Right behind where the shark man was grappling with Minoru, the girl stood.

This time, Minoru had clearly seen the moment when she appeared. But still, just as before, he didn't know how she was moving around. As suddenly as if she had teleported, the high school girl had appeared in a place where no one had been 0.1 seconds earlier. What's more, she was clutching a black rod in her right hand—a new stun baton. It was just as if she'd gone to get an extra one from somewhere and just now returned.

Looking at the scuffle between Minoru and the man, the girl scowled and shouted something. Of course, Minoru couldn't hear her inside the shell, but he sensed that she was saying something like, "Get out of the way."

"G-got it!"

She couldn't hear him, either, but after yelling that back to her, Minoru tried to get away from the shark man.

Just then—

Until now the shark man had been raging as if he'd lost all sense, but now the cold light of reason poured from his eyes.

The man took Minoru, who had started to get up, and lifted him and the shell high into the air with both hands. Just like that, he flung Minoru with intense force in what was essentially the pro-wrestling suplex move, aiming for the girl standing directly behind them.

It seemed like this alone was the only thing the mysterious high school girl hadn't been expecting. Her narrowed eyes opened wide and she lowered her body to jump out of the way, but she probably wouldn't make it in time.

They were going to collide—!

Minoru stopped breathing instinctually, focusing his senses on the orb. Just after, Minoru hit the girl face-first as if he were throwing himself over her. He collapsed to the ground with great force, picking up on a refreshing scent and a delicate softness.

He had made it in time to disarm the shell at the last moment, but that had made the impact bigger; he couldn't get up right away. Although the girl was caught under Minoru, she hadn't so much as groaned until she yelled sharply right in his ear, "Move now!!"

It was the first time he had heard the girl's voice. It had a clear note to it that reminded him of the sound of an arrow from a Japanese bow.

He rushed to jump up, but the bottom of his coat and the girl's skirt were stuck together under his right knee, so he had trouble getting away. Giving up on standing, he rolled to the left and put some distance between them.

As expected, she stood up, keeping her body low as she readied the stun baton in her right hand. It was a graceful movement that brought to mind a panther right before it sprang on its prey.

But just after, a look of bitter disappointment came across her face, which was smudged with dirt. What Minoru saw when he rushed to turn around was a black figure cutting its way through the dense bushes at the side of the shed and growing farther away. Occasionally they heard a *snap, snap* sound; it could've been the sound of the shark man biting through branches that were in his way.

If she could move in an instant, she should have been able to catch him with that power. Yet the girl remained in a motionless crouch.

The sounds of the shark man had faded away and disappeared in no time. There were soccer fields and tennis courts in that direction, so he would soon be out in open space. Was the mysterious girl avoiding being seen by people?

A few seconds later, the high school girl picked herself up with a sigh, casually hitched up her skirt, and stowed the stun baton in a holster attached to her right thigh.

Without even a glance at Minoru, who was still sitting on the ground, she turned toward the storage shed and stepped forward. As she walked, she held the small watch on her left wrist to her mouth and whispered into it softly.

"The Biter escaped. One target to protect, one unexpected target to secure. Bring the first and third kits."

...Could a watch that small have communication capabilities? What's a kit...?

As Minoru thought this half in a daze, he finally remembered just who was in the shed that the girl was headed to.

"Oh...Mi...Minowa..."

Calling her name in fragments from his tense mouth, he managed to get some strength in his shaking legs and stand up. When Minoru reached the entrance of the shed, the mysterious girl had already taken the passed-out Tomomi Minowa and sat her up. The girl took Tomomi's pulse with a practiced hand and checked her breathing.

"U-um...Minowa, is she...all right?" Minoru asked as he gripped the edges of the door.

At that, the girl raised her eyes but didn't try to respond. Her stern gaze shot right through Minoru, communicating even her hostility.

A little while later, the girl's lips finally moved.

"Do you know this girl's name?"

Although he was intimidated by her icy tone, he gave a nod.

"Y-yes... We go to the same school..."

"Hmph. On top of being a Ruby, you're a complete idiot, huh? If you target someone from your own school, your identity's going to get discovered right away. Well, that's irrelevant now, though."

Minoru couldn't comprehend what any of her words meant.

"...Ruby? Target...?"

"Knock off that terrible acting. I mean, you and the Biter fought over the girl and had a falling out."

"...Acting...? The Biter...?"

Ninety percent of what she had said was incomprehensible, but he couldn't let those last words go. Taking a deep breath, he replied in a slightly louder voice, "If by 'the Biter,' you mean that monster from earlier, he's no friend of mine..."

Just then—

Minoru noticed a faint sound coming from behind him. The sound of shoes on fallen leaves. He quickly came away from the door and turned around, keeping the wall to his back. When he did so, there was a black figure about five meters away.

He noticed something after he had begun to inhale, wondering if the man had come back. Compared to the shark man—or the Biter, according to the expression the girl had used—the figure was quite a bit smaller in the vertical sense. Even compared to Minoru, the person was probably ten centimeters shorter.

From the figure's height, he thought it might be another girl, but he was wrong. It was a guy of the same age as the black blazer girl or a little older.

He had an olive-colored baseball cap on backward and was wearing a camo-print down vest. On his lower half, he was wearing a loose pair of cargo pants and tough combat boots. Dangling from both his hands were black metal attaché cases.

His clothing made him look pretty domineering, but there wasn't a hint of danger in his face or his expression. His eyes, which gave the impression of being heavily lidded, widened and stared at Minoru steadily—or maybe blankly.

Unsure of how to respond, Minoru just stood there. Then the girl walked out of the shed. She had taken off her blazer and was now in a white blouse, but she showed absolutely no sign of being chilly. Scowling at Minoru with a look in her eyes that was still openly wary, she passed by a little way away from him and stuck her left hand out at the small guy.

"DD, the third case please."

"Ah, r-right."

The young man named DD nodded and held up the attaché case in his left hand. But right before the girl could take it, he swiftly pulled it back.

"...Hey, what're you playing at?"

"Come on, I mean, were you talking about this kid when you mentioned a Ruby to secure? Even though he didn't tie her up or anything?"

"If he tries anything, I'll take him out right away. Just the fact that he fought the Biter without dying is enough proof. Don't let him fool you. The mental interference has already begun. He snatched a girl from his school and tried to kill her."

"Come on, seriously? He's got such a sweet face, though."

"Is that so...? Anyway, who cares. Hurry up and hand it over. I want to take care of this tonight."

"'Kay, got it. You're just as impatient as always, Yumii..."

"Hey, who said you could give me a nickname? It's Yumiko!"

So the girl's name is Yumiko? It seems like that's her real name, but DD can't be his. Or else, with an appearance like that, maybe he's foreign...?

After thinking this, Minoru finally caught on to the fact that they were talking about him. Did "target to secure" mean they were going to capture him? If so, then what in the world did they mean by "take care of this"?

As Minoru went on just standing there, Yumiko took the briefcase, spun around, and announced in a cold voice, "If you don't struggle, we won't get rough with you. I'm going to give you a shot now, but it's only a sedative, so you'll just sleep for a bit. During that time, we'll do a surgical removal and a memory block somewhere in Tokyo, and then we'll let you go home tonight."

As she said this, the case opened with a *click*. Inside were a large syringe and some other instruments side by side, held in place by black cushioning.

Unconsciously taking a step away from the case, Minoru asked her in return, "Wh-what...do you mean, surgical removal...?"

"Isn't it obvious?" Yumiko answered in a slightly stronger voice. "Removal of the Third Eye buried somewhere in your body."

"Third...Eye," Minoru parroted back to her in a mutter.

Third Eye. Although this was the first time he had heard the words, even Minoru could easily guess what they meant. The small foreign body lodged in his sternum. The black orb that the shark man called an eye.

Since they were using a name like Third Eye, these two must be doing research about and analyzing the orbs. And they were probably doing it as part of an organization, too.

Yumiko gave her interpretation of Minoru's silence in a voice that had softened just slightly.

"...The fact that you had a falling out with the Biter means that you haven't been completely taken over yet, right? But if you just leave things as they are, you'll start to attack and kill humans indiscriminately like that damn shark, too. Right now, you can still go back to the life you had. The normal life before the Third Eye took you as its host."

Was it because the hostility in her eyes had lessened, albeit just slightly?

Even in this situation, Minoru couldn't help but sense Yumiko's intense presence again. Her features were solid as if they'd been carved by the inspired knife of a master sculptor. What was particularly striking about her was the color of her eyes, deep like a clear night sky. He ended up staring into their depths like they had just sucked him in.

At this, Yumiko knitted her arched brows together suspiciously and returned Minoru's stare straight on.

"You aren't...actually...?"

Almost simultaneously, DD, who was standing behind them, lifted up the brim of his baseball cap with his right hand as he groaned, "Hold on... Is this guy seriously a Ruby? Couldn't he be a Jet...?"

Here was another term Minoru was hearing for the first time. He tilted his head at this, but Yumiko no longer seemed to have any intention of explaining. She turned around and started exchanging quick words with DD.

"But you're the one who declared that there weren't any more Jets in the Kanto region."

"Technically, I said there were no more awoken Jets. No matter how good my nose is, I can't distinguish the smells of unwoken Third Eyes."

"If it's unwoken, then how did he come out of a fight with the Biter uninjured? If he didn't use his ability, he should've been bitten to death in an instant."

"Th-that's true, but..."

Minoru struggled to understand the content of their conversation, which seemed to be about him.

Could Ruby and Jet be kinds of orbs—Third Eyes? If so, Ruby was probably the red eye that the shark man talked about, but he couldn't tell what color Jet referred to. It was also unclear what awoken and unwoken meant.

The one thing he could be sure of was that Yumiko, DD, and the shark man known as the Biter all had an orb that had descended from the sky living in their bodies. The Biter's enormous mouth and

Yumiko's teleportation were powers given to them by a Third Eye, just like Minoru's shell.

No, powers might not be the only thing the Third Eyes gave them. If he believed what Yumiko said, the Biter had tried to kill and eat Tomomi Minowa and Minoru because of the Third Eye's influence.

So then, will I really start attacking people soon, too...? Minoru thought, halfway in a daze.

That's when Minoru finally remembered something important, an "oh!" slipping out of his mouth.

Yumiko whirled around again, frowning at him with an obvious wariness.

"What is it?"

"Um...before we worry about me, Minowa..."

Tomomi Minowa was still laid out in the storage shed behind them. Although she didn't have any major injuries, being kidnapped by a terrifying monster and nearly killed and eaten must have been a terrible mental shock.

Minoru turned toward the shed and felt slender but powerful fingers grasp his left arm.

"Wait."

Yumiko had closed the gap between them in an instant and was now at close range. In a stern voice that brooked no argument, she said, "Answer my questions honestly. You remember three months ago when you had an encounter with a Third Eye... An orb that came down from the sky, right?"

"...Y-yeah."

"What color was the orb that made you its host?"

The normal Minoru probably would have thought about what answer the other person would like and said that first. But the moment Yumiko's eyes stared into him, Minoru told the truth like they were drawing him in.

"...Black."

"..."

After staring at Minoru for another few seconds, Yumiko gave a small nod.

"...I guess you really are a Jet—you can go."

She took her hand off of him and stepped back. From behind them, DD rushed to chime in, "I-is that okay?"

"You're the one who said this kid isn't a Ruby."

"I-I didn't swear to that."

"Agh, stop going on and on about it already. Go sniff out the Biter or something."

"Can't smell him if he doesn't use his power."

As he listened to this exchange behind him, Minoru returned to the shed at a jog. Tomomi Minowa was laying on top of several piled-up layers of blue sheeting. A black blazer was draped over her body, and although her eyelids were still closed, she didn't look unwell. The tape binding her hands and knees had already been removed, and she was wearing her socks and shoes again.

"...Minowa," he whispered as he knelt down beside her.

Reaching out a hesitant hand, he brought his fingers up to the shoulder of her workout shirt, which peeked out from under the makeshift blanket.

Because too many unbelievable events had happened in succession, his head was still completely jumbled up. But there was one thing he was sure of.

If Minoru had faced Tomomi more earnestly on the bench in the Western Garden. If he hadn't let a crying Tomomi leave without saying a word to her. Then Tomomi definitely wouldn't have been attacked by that fearsome shark man—the Biter.

"...It's...my fault."

It was as if she heard the hoarse voice that he forced from his throat. Tomomi's eyelashes fluttered and her eyelids slowly rose. Under the weak light of the LED lantern, her brown eyes blinking over and over, her gaze focused on Minoru's face. Her lips moved slightly and a nearly soundless voice came out.

"...U-Utsugi...?"

"...Yeah."

Minoru couldn't do anything but nod. Tomomi continued to stare at him for a little while, but she finally said with a faint smile, "...So, it wasn't a dream... Utsugi, you...saved me."

"No...I..."

He was trying to say, "No, I couldn't do anything," but he shut his mouth. His lips felt like they would start trembling, but somehow he forced them into a smile and answered, "Everything's okay now. You can go home right away."

"...Thank...you...," she whispered, smiling faintly. Then Tomomi's eyelids closed once more. Did her heart switch off again, having taken more of a burden than it could bear?

Putting his wrist through the shoulder strap of the yellow day pack that had fallen over next to the wall, Minoru put both his arms under Tomomi's body and picked her up gently along with the blazer.

When he came out of the shed, Yumiko and DD were standing there side by side. Yumiko took a step forward and peered at Tomomi's face.

"She looks okay."

"...Yeah."

He nodded. As he was wondering whether he should thank them, she said something unexpected first.

"Leave her to us."

"Uh... No, I'll take her home..."

"No, she needs to actually be examined at the hospital. And...she's seen the Biter's face. There's a risk of him going after her again. Didn't you even think of that?"

"...!"

The way she said it was harsh, but she was completely right.

Minoru didn't know if the Biter had coincidentally set his sights on Tomomi as she passed through the forest or if he had been targeting her from the start.

If it was the latter, there was definitely a possibility that the monster knew everything from Tomomi's name to where she lived.

But that only solidified Minoru's feeling that it wasn't right for him to do as he was told and leave Tomomi to them, abandoning his responsibility.

"...If so, then shouldn't you have gone after the Biter instead of giving up so quickly? You can teleport with the power of that thing...the Third Eye, right? So you should've been able to catch him easily."

Upon hearing those words, Yumiko's eyes grew stern. This was the part where Minoru would usually shrink back and turn his face away, but just this once, half in desperation, he met another person's gaze.

"...If I could have, I would have," Yumiko murmured as if she were spitting the words out. After taking a deep breath and letting it out, she continued in a restrained voice, "We don't need you to tell us to find the Biter. At that level of damage, he probably won't be able to leave this area for a while... Well, if you're intent on taking her home, I guess we can use her as bait to lure the Biter out."

"...That's not what I...," Minoru shot back at her reflexively.

He bit his lip. Whether or not that's what he was intending, it didn't change the fact that Tomomi's house was dangerous. But still.

"...Then can you really say that the hospital you'd take her to is safe?"

"Definitely more than her house is, at least. And we'll guard her, of course."

"..."

Minoru once again dropped his gaze to Tomomi in his arms. It seemed more like she was sleeping then passed out. There was definitely something capable about her for someone so petite, possibly because her whole body was well muscled. The weight of a human with a life.

But Minoru knew that weight could be easily lost on the slightest whim of fate.

"...What explanation will you give her family?"

"Mm, some deviant started to attack her, but people happened to be passing by, so she's okay...or something."

The one who answered was not Yumiko, but DD. Giving a quick shrug of his shoulders under the down vest, he went on talking.

"This isn't our first case like this. We have the know-how to put her back in her old life after we get her properly protected and treated. That includes psychological care, too."

"But if you say some deviant did it, won't the police come to ask what happened...? And can you keep the police or the media under control? ...Just who are you guys anyway...?"

Minoru had a feeling that Yumiko and DD were backed by some sort of organized entity, and he apprehensively asked them as much. At this, DD gave a wry smile and shook his head.

"Mm, we basically work for the authorities, but we don't have the power to influence the police or the media. We can't tell you details unless there's a formal request for you to work with us and you fill out a bunch of paperwork, though."

"Request to...work with you?"

"Guess that's how it'll probably end up... Here in Japan right now, there's a mountain of Ruby Eyes with homicidal impulses. The Biter from before is one of 'em. It's assumed that the majority of the rapidly increasing missing persons around the country are Ruby victims. By the way, the reason we call them Rubies is that the color of the parasitic orb is red."

After a pause, DD continued to explain.

"On the other hand, there are many fewer of us Jet Eyes with black orbs than the Rubies. You're probably the last identified Jet in the Kanto region. It depends on what kind of ability you have, but I think there's no doubt you'll be asked to work with us. By the way, Jet isn't like the jet from a jet engine. It's from the jet gemstone."

"..."

Minoru stared at DD's face blankly for a moment, then dropped his eyes to Tomomi again.

So there really were two kinds of orbs. The red ones were Ruby Eyes, and the black ones like the one buried in Minoru's chest were Jet Eyes. Humans who had Ruby Eyes as parasites would start to attack other humans like the Biter did. Humans like Yumiko and DD who possessed Jet Eyes were put into an organization by the authorities—in other words, the government—and were fighting the Ruby Eyes...

It was hard to believe. It was more than that; it was absurd.

Minoru raised his head and asked in a hoarse voice, "...Where did the Third Eyes come from?"

At this, the small young man made the most serious expression he had since Minoru met him, pointing the index finger of his right hand straight up. Following it, Minoru looked up. He saw just a few stars twinkling in the gray sky above the treetops.

...*Space?*

...He was saying that...mysterious objects from space took humans as their hosts, gave them supernatural abilities, and made them attack people or protect them?

Give me a break, Minoru groaned inwardly.

If Minoru accepted that, the normal life he'd made the maximum effort to protect would be blown even further away from him. Most importantly, it wasn't like Minoru had the qualifications to join some organization that battled evil.

After all—on that day eight years ago, he'd kept his eyes closed and his ears covered as he hid alone under the floor. And he'd been the lone survivor, sacrificing his beloved parents and sister.

"Hey, you all right, kid? You don't look so good."

At the sound of DD's voice, Minoru widened his eyes with a start.

I'm not here. I'm not anywhere.

He chanted this incantation in his mind, doing his best to sever the pathways of memories that were beginning to connect.

"Oh… It's nothing," he answered, giving his head a quick shake.

He turned his eyes to Yumiko on the right, her mouth still tight.

They couldn't tell him details about their organization and he didn't really want to know, but Minoru was at least certain that they could do things he couldn't. And he was certain that he couldn't be near Tomomi Minowa anymore.

"…I got it. Please take care of Minowa," Minoru said as if he were whispering, holding the sleeping Tomomi out in front of him gently.

Yumiko's arms looked delicate at first glance, but she accepted Tomomi effortlessly. Minoru passed the day pack he had hanging on his right hand over to DD.

"I think Minowa's student planner is in there."

"Understood. We'll use it to contact her guardians."

"…Please do."

Lowering his head a little, Minoru picked up his messenger bag, which he had dropped a little way away. When he just kept walking, a sharp voice called to him.

"Hey, where do you think you're going?"

"Home," he said, standing still but not turning his head as he gave this brief answer.

"Home… You obviously can't. Weren't you listening to all the things DD just said?"

Minoru had expected to hear this to a certain extent, but he shook his head as he continued to face forward obstinately.

"It's not like there's anything else I can do. You said so yourself, didn't you?"

"Even if there's nothing for you to do here, there's a mountain of things we're going to have you do from now on."

A flustered DD interrupted Yumiko's sharp words.

"H-hang on, hang on, let's be a little more peaceful about this, Yumii. I mean, we just found a new friend."

"Calling this guy my friend already is..."

"Whoa, just be quiet for a sec, I'm beggin' you!" he shouted.

DD ran over the fallen leaves with a rustle and came around in front of Minoru. Under his impressively knitted eyebrows, he put on a smile as if trying to smooth things over.

"Um, so, there are a lot of things you want to know, right? If you come with us, we'll tell you as much as we can."

"..."

He definitely did feel like he wanted to know more detail about Third Eyes and the organization the two of them belonged to. But more than that, the resistant feeling that he didn't want to be here anymore was stronger.

Minoru was the one who had created an opportunity for Tomomi Minowa to be attacked by the Biter. Even if she was thankfully unhurt in the physical sense, she probably had deep wounds in her heart. The fact that he had fallen silent and just let Tomomi leave all those minutes ago... No, the fact that he had talked to her for so long on that embankment along the Arakawa River three days ago was something he would never stop regretting no matter how long he regretted it for.

I can't stand for anyone else to get hurt because of me. There's no way, he whispered internally.

"That's okay."

"Huh?"

DD blinked as if he was actually surprised at Minoru's answer.

"You're saying...you don't wanna know? I mean, all of this is completely unbelievable as far as common sense goes."

"...Common sense is nothing but an illusion. Everything happens when it's going to happen."

"Wh-whoa... You're getting pretty philosophical for such a young guy..."

At that moment, he heard a voice from off to the left that sounded like it had lost patience with this exchange.

"Enough already. Just use the stick."

DD's eyes popped out as if startled, and Minoru noticed his right hand twitch. The stick was probably the stun baton that Yumiko had been using. Now that she mentioned it, Minoru had the feeling that the left side of DD's camo-print down vest bulged out just a little more than the right side.

Staring at DD's put-upon face, Minoru prepared himself to stop breathing at any time. Then Yumiko's cold voice rang out again.

"That's how we should treat guys like this, guys who get a look on their face like it's got nothing to do with them even after you've told them about the victims of the Ruby Eyes."

"N-no, no, no, we can't be rough with a Jet like us..."

"Like us? Don't make me laugh," she spat.

The sound of resolute footsteps continued. Yumiko came to a halt on Minoru's left side, very close to him. She ordered in a commanding voice, "Face me."

"..."

After resisting for about two seconds, he turned back to the left.

Still holding Tomomi, Yumiko gave Minoru a piercing gaze, her eyes like crystallized, superheated flames. As he reflexively averted his eyes, Minoru wondered in the corner of his mind whether he'd ever looked straight into another person's eyes like that even once.

"...You lost your right to choose the moment the Jet Eye entered your body," she said, her ringing voice strong in his ears. "Even at this very moment, Rubies are targeting innocent people. You have a duty to go on fighting until all the Rubies are wiped out!"

For Minoru, who always avoided situations where other people would reprimand him, Yumiko's words were like a nail being driven into his chest. But amid that pain, there was also a slight rebellious feeling toward Yumiko's overbearing tone. Minoru clenched both his fists and forced a rare protest from his throat.

"…It's not like I accepted that thing because I wanted to. This is the first I've heard of Jets and Rubies. I didn't know about it, any of it."

"And that's why I'm telling you to be ashamed that you didn't know and to work with us to annihilate the Rubies!"

"It has nothing to do with me. People who want to fight should just fight. Now I'm going home."

Thinking that he would only increase his painful memories if he continued this conversation, Minoru passed by Yumiko on her left and headed out of the forest. But Yumiko blocked him after he had taken a step in that direction, giving DD an order in a voice colder than the December night air.

"Use the stick on this idiot right now. We're bringing him along to headquarters even if we have to do it by force."

"L-like I said, that's kinda risky," he answered.

His tone was as light as always, but there was a hint of anxiety in his voice.

"If we do somethin' like that, there's no way we can persuade him anymore. I mean, the kid's ability is still an unknown. Somehow or other, he came out of a fight with the Biter uninjured. We gotta respect what he wants here, so let's talk things over another day…"

"If he sees the recordings at headquarters, he won't be able to say such naive things anymore. Like how courageously Sanae fights, and she's way smaller than him…!"

There was a name he hadn't heard before in Yumiko's words, which dripped with rage. But Minoru no longer had room to pay attention to it. Driven by an irritation that was unexpected even to him, he spit out in a low voice, "If you want to know, I'll tell you now. If I use my ability, you won't be able to hear my voice, and I won't be able to hear yours. It creates a transparent shell that nothing can pass through. That's why that sort of weapon won't work on me."

"Whoa… Now I get it." His expression turning interested, DD tugged at the brim of his baseball cap and bellowed, "So that's how you kept from getting injured even when that Biter guy chewed on you, huh? Those teeth can bite people down to the bone, though, so that's a pretty major power if it can block them, yeah. This is… Mm… Hey, let's back off here for now. If it's like the kid says, then the stick definitely won't be any help."

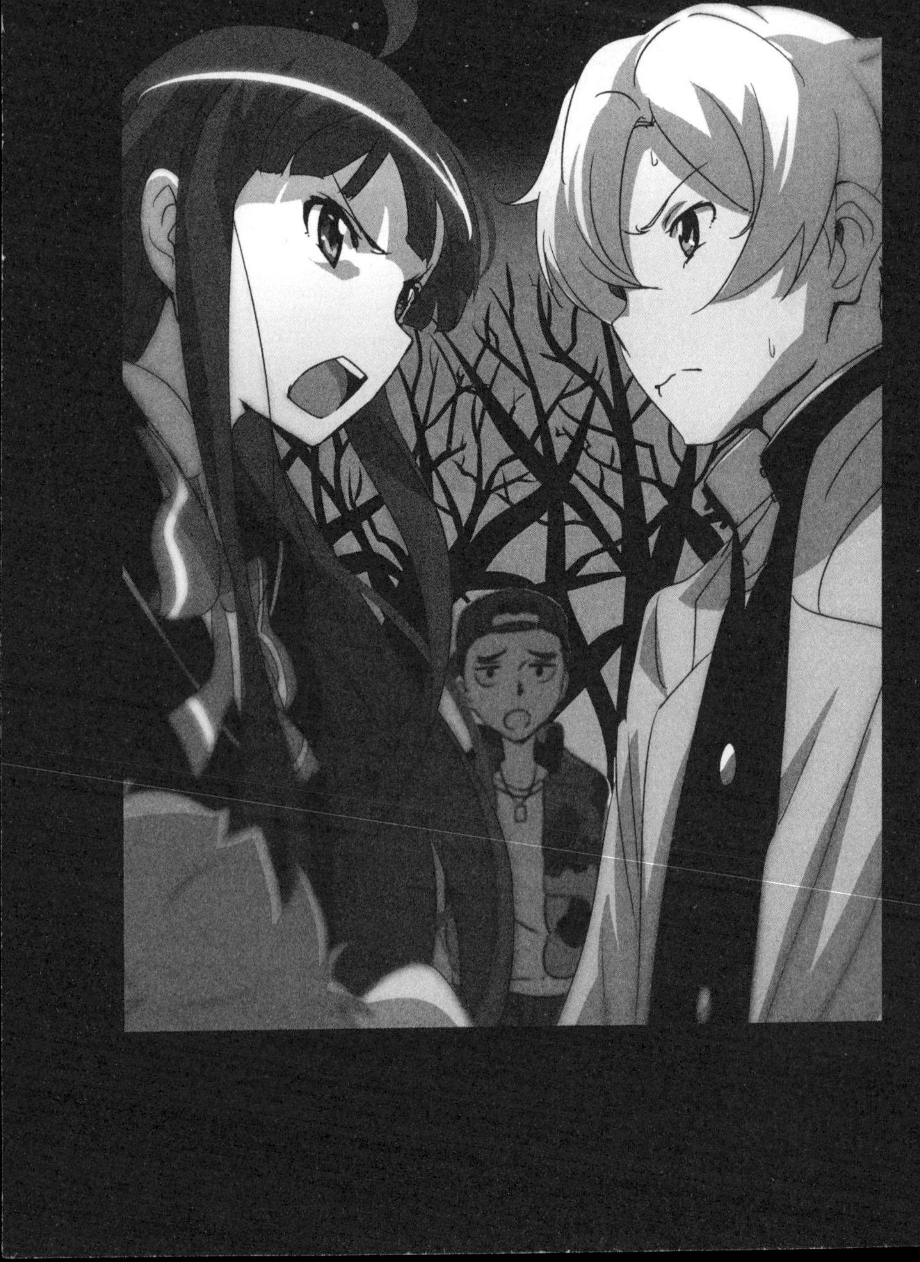

"…"

At this, Yumiko gave Minoru an intense look as if she were trying to knock him out with her gaze in place of the stun baton. Then she let out a short breath.

"…It's kind of suspicious, but it's a little bit interesting if it's true. It really did look like the Biter couldn't bite him even though he tried to…"

"Let's talk things over more peacefully on a new day. Welp, sorry for threatening ya, kid. So we'll talk another day," he said, lifting up his baseball cap slightly.

But Minoru obstinately shook his head.

"I don't feel like talking to you two anymore…so I'll leave Minowa to you."

Glancing at Tomomi, still in Yumiko's arms with her eyes closed, Minoru started walking this time toward the south of the forest.

When he was a few meters off, the two of them called out to him from behind.

"I'm going to give you just one final warning. The Biter's seen your face, too, not just the girl's. The possibility of you being targeted isn't zero."

"It's the smell. Watch out for the smell of the Ruby Eye, kid."

After coming to a halt for a moment, Minoru started walking again as he answered, "I can protect myself."

Even so, as he left Akigase Park and headed for home, Minoru couldn't help checking his surroundings many times. Just wondering if that man was lurking on the dim paths or behind cars parked on the road made Minoru's breathing grow shallow. The feeling of his neck between enormous teeth in that storage shed still clung to his skin.

But if he believed DD's final words, Ruby Eyes including the shark man could be distinguished by smell. Now that he mentioned it, Minoru had originally approached the shed because he was concerned about that strange, foul smell that seemed to belong to a huge beast.

That definitely had to be the smell of a Ruby. It was a smell bad enough that one would have to notice it if it was within ten meters—no, thirty meters.

So at the very least, he wouldn't be attacked by something jumping out of the shadows suddenly. But before that—

He just couldn't believe that everything, including nearly being killed by a strangely formed monster, wasn't some massive piece of fiction.

The Third Eyes were mysterious orbs that came from space. The people they took as hosts started to exhibit abilities that couldn't be explained by known science. Ruby Eyes, who have red orbs living in them, were given not only an ability but also the desire to kill people. Jet Eyes, who have black orbs living within them, were trying to fend off the murderous Rubies.

All of that was hard enough to believe, but what was even more mysterious was why such huge events weren't known to the public at all. If Ruby Eyes attacked people, then shouldn't everything be brought out in the open to draw widespread public attention?

If Minoru hadn't interrupted that twisted man the Biter, there was no doubt that he would've killed Tomomi Minowa. It seemed like Yumiko and DD had been tracking him, but they probably would've been a few minutes too late to rescue Tomomi unharmed.

That's exactly why Minoru couldn't agree with the fact that their organization was trying to deal with this in secret. If there were already so many victims, they should mobilize the police or the military and tackle this on a large scale, not coerce Minoru alone into working with them.

As Minoru thought these things with just a bit of resentment, he bit his lip slightly.

Why was he unable to decide he didn't care like he usually would have? Was it because Yumiko's reproach was sticking with him more than he realized? That wasn't like him at all. The more he got angry and went off like this, the stronger and larger his painful memories would become. That was all.

I'm going to forget. All of it. If the Jet Eyes want to fight the Ruby Eyes in secret, that's fine. It's not something I need to know.

Murmuring this on the inside, he glanced at the watch on his left wrist. The sky was completely dark, but it wasn't even seven o'clock yet. When he got away from the Arakawa River and entered residential streets, he started to see teenagers on their way home from club meetings and salarymen carrying convenience store bags. The memory of having grappled with a fearsome monster with his life on the line just twenty or thirty minutes ago was gradually becoming surreal.

I'm going to forget, Minoru muttered to himself again, pedaling his bike harder.

6

It was so cold that the joints in his extremities creaked. His whole face hurt as if it were scorched. Hunger twisted his insides. But with the energy of his boiling anger, Takaesu was able to silence those sensations.

Nearly six hours had already gone by since he'd slipped into an abandoned building in the process of being demolished about two kilometers away from the park. After midnight passed, the date would change to Saturday, December 7, and there shouldn't be construction either that day or the next. If he let his body rest here for two days, he should recover at least enough to be able to move again.

On the first floor of the large abandoned building, which seemed to have been a warehouse originally, a frigid wind was blowing from all sides and the bare concrete floor was cold as ice. In place of a bed, he wrapped himself in dirty blue sheeting, nursing a bottle of juice that he had bought from a vending machine during his getaway.

Usually he wouldn't drink soft drinks with high fructose corn syrup even if someone asked him to, but he had no choice but to depend on one now. He couldn't even go into a convenience store with his burned-up face, and after discovering that he was being pursued by that strange and dangerous bunch, he needed to lay low in this hiding place until he was able to operate as usual.

He had to sleep and rest his body just a little bit. That's what he thought, but when he made his thoughts a blank, a flame of rage would instantly start to flare up.

"...Quiet now... Calm down...," he whispered without moving his mouth.

That's when he decided to give up on sleep and at least do some quiet thinking.

His long-awaited feast of bones had first been interrupted by the boy with the transparent shell. Then he had been attacked by the girl who could teleport. Although he had somehow managed to bite the girl's stun baton in half, he had been unable to give either of them even a scratch and was forced to flee like some failure.

In that situation, it was the best choice.

Takaesu's reasoning judged that to be true even now, but on an emotional level, it was impossible to accept. He had obtained the power of the strongest hunter, the shark. Wasn't he the chosen one? Wasn't he a proud predator who could bite through anything?

No, it wasn't as if I made some pitiful escape, not in the least.

There were others apart from Takaesu who possessed the eye. The abilities bestowed by the eye varied widely. And there were people hunting those who possessed the eye, probably as an organization. Takaesu had simply given himself some distance for a moment to investigate all of this new information and rethink his plans. Like a man-eating shark slowly circling around its pitiful prey.

Putting aside the boy, who seemed to be an acquaintance of the young girl he had so disappointingly missed out on biting, the teleporting girl had appeared to know from the start that Takaesu possessed the eye when she attacked him. But he didn't understand how she had discovered where he was.

If she had been tailing him the whole time, she should have attacked before he dragged the girl into the storage shed. And if she could use the power of the eye to track him, she likely would have appeared in this building a number of hours ago.

If the tracking abilities of the girl or the girl's companions were limited, they should be far away by now. But with his face like this, it would be difficult for Takaesu to even reach the hotel parking lot where he had his Maserati, let alone return to the hotel room he was renting in the new city center.

If he only had the inflamed burns around his mouth, he probably could have covered them with a face mask or something. But his transformed shark's jaws wouldn't go back to normal, possibly because he'd taken intense electric shocks to the mouth. The fact that he'd been able to make it to this abandoned building without being questioned by passersby was already miraculously good luck.

The reason he'd judged the teleporting girl to be a member of some kind of organization really came down to the effectiveness of that stun baton. The stun guns sold in military magazine advertisements and on the Internet often had taglines that jumped out at one about superhigh voltage products with tens of thousands of volts. They seemed to be extremely powerful, but in truth, what was dangerous for the human body was not voltage, but current—amperes.

In stun guns that used transformers to increase battery voltage, the current strength fell proportionately to below one ampere. Although by appearances they sent bright sparks flying, they almost never caused serious damage to the body.

But the stun baton that girl carried probably used a dedicated high-capacity battery, creating terrible burns in Takaesu's mouth with high-ampere electricity. Naturally, something like that wasn't openly sold in Japan.

The only options were to import it from abroad or to buy something modified through illegal channels. No matter how one looked at it, it wasn't something a simple high school girl could get her hands on just like that.

The girl's teleportation ability that allowed her to appear just when you thought she had disappeared was certainly notable, but it was actually that weapon that required attention. And that was because, put simply, there was some sort of organization backing the girl. In all likelihood, it was an extremely dangerous organization with multiple members who possessed the eye, and their goal was to eliminate others who had it, too.

That's right—dangerous.

Even if Takaesu were surrounded by ten professional fighters it wouldn't be much of a problem, but he couldn't say the same for a group of people who possessed the eye. In reality, that girl had continued to narrowly escape his attacks—which were so fast that an average person wouldn't be able to respond to them—and dealt Takaesu a severe blow. On top of having her physical abilities increased because of the eye, there was no doubt that she had also received some sort of combat training. If there had been just one more opponent like that, he probably would've been completely unable to escape.

What would he do? What should he do?

First, he had to get his wounds healed as quickly as possible and get away from this city.

Then he would gather information. If possible, he would capture that girl or another member of her organization and get them to cough up as much information as they knew. After that, he would hunt them one by one. No matter how much time it took, he would continue to kill them until he alone was the chosen one.

But before that...

Momentarily forgetting the pain of his burns, Takaesu ground his teeth, which were still pointed like a tiger shark's.

Before that, just the boy—

The boy, who had been the first to interrupt his meal, somehow seemed to be unrelated to the girl's organization. The boy had been shocked when he looked at Takaesu's transformed face, and he had come out with these innocent lines like, "Why would you kill someone?"

Surely, Takaesu thought, he would be able to find at least one chance to attack the boy.

He understood that the longer he stayed in the city the greater the danger became, but he just knew he wouldn't be able to let the boy go. That was because that boy with his shell was the only one who could oppose Takaesu's evolution head-on.

The boy's offensive power was far below that of the teleporting girl. Taking one punch had been Takaesu's mistake, but the boy's movements themselves were that of an amateur. He could easily avoid them if he was careful.

But the problem was his defensive power—the terrible hardness of that invisible shell.

"...Grr..."

Just remembering it drew a growl like that of a wild beast from his transformed mouth. The unbelievable hardness that had come across when Takaesu had tried to bite the boy's neck through the shell remained deep in the roots of his teeth even now.

It wasn't at all like the feeling he got in his mouth when he bit something. No matter what the substance, things should at least bend when Takaesu bit them in his tiger-shark mode. But the boy's armor didn't communicate even a micron of sensation to his transformed senses.

Three months ago, when the red eye had descended from the sky to slip into his lower jaw, Takaesu had finally put aside his dentures as real teeth grew in. He had been wild with joy.

He crushed a tankard full of ice. He devoured hard salami. He bit through as many rock-solid biscotti as he wanted.

The more hard things he ate, the stronger his new teeth became. When he became able to eat a T-bone steak, bones and all, Takaesu became aware of the privilege bestowed upon him. And that was to bite. To swim elegantly through the city at night hunting his prey like a superior being, like a predator, and savor delicious bones to his heart's content.

That was why he had to bite the boy. It made no difference that he possessed the eye. There couldn't be any humans who Takaesu wasn't able to bite. Next time, he would bite through that infuriating shell. To do that, he had to heal as soon as possible.

He was a shark. He would be a shark.

For fish, sharks boasted an extraordinary ability to survive. They had a strong resistance to disease, and they could recover even from deep wounds that would kill other fish right off the bat.

Their life spans were long; one male great white shark was identified as being more than seventy years old.

Burns like these would be nothing to a shark.

Picturing himself lurking in the shadows of stones on the seafloor, Takaesu continued to concentrate on enduring the cold and the pain.

＊ ＊ ＊

There was no way he would be getting a good night's sleep.

Minoru was a light sleeper in the first place. That was because he had a habit of forcing himself awake if what he was dreaming took on even the slightest nightmarish cast.

He knew his efforts were pointless. Because the easiest state to dream in was when your body was asleep and your brain was awake—so-called REM sleep—he should sleep deeply if he wanted to avoid dreaming. If he continued sleeping lightly, that alone would raise his chances of straying into a nightmare. Even knowing this, dreams were something he couldn't control himself.

With a sigh, Minoru groped around for the alarm clock on his headboard and got ahold of it, bringing it in front of him.

It was one o'clock in the morning. Normally, he'd already be falling asleep at this time.

Tomorrow—no, today—was Saturday, but Minoru's high school had Saturday school every other week. Unfortunately, he would have to go to class today. Four hours later, he would need to wake up and do his morning run. He did feel like it would be okay to take the day off just for today, since he had experienced all those things, but messing up his daily routine was its own sort of annoyance.

Putting the clock back, he burrowed into his warm blankets up to his head. He felt just a bit drowsy when he closed his eyelids, but the moment he was about to fall right to sleep, he got the feeling he had heard the faint howl of a beast. His eyes shot open. He had actually gotten out of bed, walked to the window, and smelled the outside air from the gap in the slightly opened window frame more than once or twice.

He told himself over and over that there was no way the Biter knew where this house was, but doubts clung to him persistently—was that shark man lurking in the darkness on the street in front of Minoru, staring up at the window of his room?

The existence of that man probably isn't the only thing scaring me, he thought as he curled up in a little ball on his side.

The events of last night were a sign that the peaceful life he had so desperately protected since coming to this city was going to crumble and fall. That was why he felt so uneasy.

The collapse had probably been happening since the day that orb... the Third Eye slipped into his body. But Minoru had kept averting his eyes from reality and denying it until today. With a single phrase, "It doesn't matter," he had disregarded the abnormal improvement in his running time and even the mysterious phenomenon that had kept him from getting so much as a scratch when he was hit by the bike.

But that girl Yumiko's words had mercilessly smashed Minoru's world, and it was starting to transform so much that it would never be able to go back to the way it had been.

Is this power a weapon for fighting the Ruby Eyes who attack and kill people…? Are there people being targeted by monsters like that shark man at this very moment, and do I have a duty to protect them…?

In bed, he gave his head a slight shake and tried to gloss over everything with a wry smile, but his tense mouth wouldn't move.

He was genuinely glad that Tomomi Minowa was safe after having been attacked by the Biter, or at least he thought he was. If his power had helped save her, that should make him happy.

But ultimately, that feeling was just a fringe benefit. It came along with selfish relief that he had avoided seeing her ruthlessly murdered right before his eyes and that things ended without him creating unpleasant thoughts. When all was said and done, it was the same as when he had given the five-yen coin to the boy who was in trouble at the convenience store. If Tomomi had been a stranger whose name and face he didn't know, even if she had been attacked and killed by the Biter without Minoru's knowledge, he probably would've just thought that it was scary and felt bad for her.

That's right… I just need to protect the small world around me.

Whoever Yumiko, DD, and the organization they belonged to wanted to fight, wherever they wanted to do it, and whoever they wanted to protect, it had nothing to do with him. They could just hurry up and catch the Biter, then kill him or give him the surgery.

I've had enough.

He'd had enough of people close to him dying, too. And of those gut-wrenching memories repeating and repeating. He'd had enough of everything.

Suddenly, Minoru shot up in bed.

"Not here. I'm not here. I'm not anywhere," he cried in a low voice as if casting a spell.

The muddy waters of his nearly overflowing memories changed course at the last second, plunging back down to the depths of his consciousness.

It was dangerous for him to question himself in the dark any more than he already had. He would relive that night eight years ago, and it would take away his power to go on living. He couldn't make another suicide attempt. For Norie—and for Wakaba.

When he turned around and looked at the hand of the dimly lit clock, it had only advanced fifteen minutes.

School was a half day, and he could probably make it through even if he stayed up all night. As far as his running—he would make it five kilometers. Giving up on sleep for the night, Minoru turned on his bedside reading light and pulled out at random one of the paperbacks he kept piled on his headboard.

***

When he scratched gently around his mouth with his right hand, pieces of discolored skin flaked off.

The pain from his burns had lessened quite a bit, but in its place he was now tormented by an intense itchiness. The desire to dig his nails in and scratch all over his face as hard as he could was unbearable.

But this itchiness was proof that his wounds were healing. The burning pain he had felt in his joints and muscles every time he moved was now just a stinging stiffness. Takaesu could feel the eye buried in his lower jaw pulsing violently, attempting to restore the damaged areas with all its strength. If his recovery continued to progress like this, his burns would probably no longer stand out within a day.

"…I'm counting on you, *compagno*," Takaesu whispered in a hoarse voice, flopping down on the concrete floor.

The price of this drastic metabolic activity was that his body kept expending massive amounts of energy. When he tried touching his stomach through his training wear, his fat, which had never been ample, seemed to have been almost completely stripped away.

He had long ago passed the stage of hunger; he was now periodically struck by the sensation of an iron vise squeezing his gut. He had drunk the whole bottle of juice a while ago. He'd put an energy bar in his tool kit pack… The moment he thought this, he ended up imagining the flavor of chocolate and his gut ached powerfully and noticeably.

When he gazed at the Panerai watch on his left wrist, it was barely two o'clock in the morning. Dawn was far away, and even if the sun did come up, his face still wasn't healed enough for him to buy anything.

Now, he felt like he could eat a mountain of overboiled fettuccine from a platter. Speaking of that, his article profiling that restaurant needed to be sent out by Monday. He'd left his computer in his hotel room, so he obviously wouldn't be able to write the draft. He should probably at least send an e-mail to the editing department, but he had removed the battery from the smartphone in his pack so he wouldn't be tracked using the signal. If he had the chance, he'd use a pay phone to inform them that the draft would be late...

"...How ridiculous," he murmured, giving a throaty laugh.

He could discard his position as a gourmet food critic anytime. After all, even that was one of the curses *that woman* had placed on him.

And still he was hungry.

He'd drunk all of the juice, but there could still be a fraction of a drop left at the bottom of the bottle. Taking just his right hand out of the blue sheeting wrapped around his body, he searched for the bottle that should have been rolling around nearby.

Then his fingertips brushed against something small.

He grabbed it and brought it in front of him. It was a metal hexagonal nut with a diameter of about two centimeters. After he brushed away the dust with his fingers, it gave off a dim glow in the darkness. Had it not rusted because it was stainless steel?

After gazing at it vacantly for a bit, he leisurely put it in his mouth. He rolled the hard, cold, metallic-tasting lump around on top of his tongue.

...Sweet?

There was no reason it should be. But he definitely picked up on a faint sweetness inside his mouth. A somehow nostalgic sweetness, yet one that made him feel guilty.

Roll, roll. Roll, roll. He absorbed himself in licking it, putting it lightly between his teeth on occasion.

That's right... This was the sweetness of hard candy. The flavor of a big, round black sugar candy.

Hidden in the closet, he had licked intently at the piece of black sugar candy that someone had given him. He had to hurry and finish licking it before he was discovered. But it would be such a waste to just bite it.

Experiencing happiness and anxiety, satisfaction and guilt all at the same time, he rolled and rolled the hard candy around his mouth.

Suddenly, the closet door was ripped open.

What are you eating?!

A shrill, hysterical voice. That woman's voice.

She dragged him out of his hiding spot and forced open his mouth. She pulled the black sugar candy, wet with saliva, out of his mouth with fingers that reeked of makeup.

This! This is what you're eating?! It's just a clump of sugar! Eating sugar will melt your teeth!

Eating sugar will melt your teeth. The phrase he'd heard long ago repeated like a curse. Curling up like an infant without realizing it, Takaesu plunged into a pool of memories.

Hikaru Takaesu's mother was a famous food educator and critic. She was the author of many published books about nutritional education, and she had frequent exposure in all types of media.

On television, she seemed just like the ideal mother: pretty and kind. But Hikaru had almost no memories of being praised by his mother. *Do this. Don't do that. Do this. Don't do that.* Those were all the words he got from his mother.

Hikaru had probably been five years old when his parents divorced.

He remembered his father as being kind. He was a salaryman at a trading company, and the only thing he could have called a hobby was playing pachinko on his days off. He would let Hikaru eat the chocolate and snack foods he won, telling him to keep it a secret from his mother.

Even on the day he moved out, Hikaru's father gave him a ton of candy. Hikaru tucked it away with care in a secret box hidden at the back of the closet in his room.

Hikaru, his mother, and the maid were then the only ones living in that big house in Motoazabu. It was around that time that Hikaru's mother started to get hysterical when she reprimanded him.

At the same time that he started elementary school, he was forced to go to cram school to prepare for middle school entrance exams. Before long, swimming school and English conversation school were added to the list. He had absolutely no time for play, and when he said he wanted a gaming system for his seventh birthday, his enraged mother pinched his ear so hard he thought it would tear off. He was a good student but an outsider in class; he didn't have a single friend.

His mother was crazy about more than just education. She forced the maid to create menus based on her own nutritional theories and strictly forbade eating anything else.

His mother's pet theory was that the foundation of child rearing was to get calcium to kids before anything else for healthy teeth and healthy bones; their dining table was jam-packed with small fish and seaweed. Sweet things were completely banned, and he had to be sure to brush his teeth within ten minutes of eating. She even made him take a toothbrush set when he went to school. When she had discovered him secretly sucking on the candy, she had punished him harder than when he had wanted the gaming system.

And why did his mother make him take such good care of his teeth? That was so she could put Hikaru's picture in her books and magazine articles.

Look how properly she was raising her child. Look how wonderful her theories were. She used Hikaru as material to show off like that. Funnily enough, young Hikaru with his shining snow-white teeth became popular with housewives, and he was even brought in to do a toothpaste commercial when he was eight years old.

Soon, his mother had gone so far as to supplement her claims with the theory that chewing strength nurtures the brain, and even more reforms were made to their diet. For rice, they ate brown rice or rice with grains mixed in. They had small fish that could be eaten with the bones still in them. Their vegetables were all hard stalks. Even snacks were limited to salted beans, dried kelp, and dried sardines. Every time he ate something, his mother would tell him to chew it a hundred times.

Chew it up well, Hii. Chew. Chew. Chew more. If you spit it out, you'll get a pinch. There now, chew. Chew. Chew. Chew. Hii...you have to work hard and eat enough for her, too. So chew more, chew. Chew, chew, chew, chew.

Even when he went into the higher grades of elementary school, Hikaru's grades put him at the top of the class, and as usual, he didn't have a single cavity.

Hikaru became aware of a certain habit around the end of summer break in the sixth grade: grinding his teeth. Without noticing, he had gotten into the habit of rubbing his teeth together hard whether he was in class, studying at home, or going to and from school.

Even when he tried to stop, he just couldn't do it. His jaw just tensed up on its own, especially when he was thinking of his mother, and his teeth made a grinding sound.

It was no big deal, or so he thought. But Hikaru didn't know. He didn't know that excessive tooth grinding was a full-fledged disease: attrition.

A disease in which the enamel is abnormally worn away due to continual grinding of the teeth.

He wore down his permanent teeth, which had just grown in then, enough to expose the dentin. Hikaru became unable to properly brush his teeth because it was too painful. He skipped brushing his teeth at school and fooled his mom by only pretending to brush at home.

Then bacteria set in immediately in his weakened teeth. Cavities sprung up all over the place simultaneously and progressed with incredible strength.

But he couldn't even discuss it with his mother, let alone go to the dentist. His body went cold with fear just imagining…how harsh the reprimands and punishments would be if she knew he had several cavities.

He had them stop the photo shoots for magazines and books for a while, saying that he wanted to focus on studying for his middle school entrance exams. But the truth was, studying was already out of the question because of the pain. Even when he sat down at his desk he was only desperately enduring the excruciating pain, and the days passed by with him unable to get enough sleep. Along with his teeth, all the words and formulas jammed into his head were dissolved by the Streptococcus mutans bacteria and disappeared altogether.

The state of his second-semester finals was wretched. There was no way he could show his mother the answer sheets that had been given back to him. Hikaru hid them in a secret box in the closet.

The excuse that the grading was running late didn't hold up for even three days.

His suspicious mother did a thorough search of Hikaru's room right in front of him, discovering an ancient-looking rice cracker tin at the back of the closet. Raging at Hikaru, who was wailing for her not to open it, his mother pulled off the lid and found the bundle of answer sheets marked with grades that were far below average.

His mother's face went pale and her hands trembled. Then her gaze turned to the bottom of the box. There were the lovingly stored packages of chocolate, gum, and black sugar candy Hikaru's dad had given him before moving out.

His mother's features changed. Her eyes quickly narrowed, her canine teeth were bared, and her hair even seemed to stand on end. There was the face of a demon. Pulling Hikaru down to the floor, his mother opened his mouth aggressively.

The moment she saw Hikaru's teeth, decayed with attrition and cavities, a scream burst from his mother's throat that was difficult to believe came from a human being. That deep, rumbling, lingering voice sounded like the roar of a beast.

His mother ran from the room and returned immediately. Hikaru's mouth was frozen open from fear. His mother clamped down on his front tooth with the pair of pliers she held in her right hand and screamed, *Eating sugar will melt your teeth! I told yooooou!!*

Takaesu leaped up, a muffled sound slipping out of him.

For a moment, he didn't know where he was. After hurriedly looking around in the total darkness in all directions, he remembered the circumstances that had led him to sneak into the abandoned building.

Letting out a long, thin breath, he pulled the blue sheeting covering his body up to his mouth.

It had been quite a few years since he dreamed of that woman. He wiped away the greasy sweat that was flowing down his forehead like a waterfall with the sleeve of his training wear. Sticking a finger into his mouth, he checked to make sure his teeth were where they should be.

Everything was fine. That woman couldn't do anything anymore.

That was because, six years ago on the day he had graduated from college, he had taught her a lesson. Taught her how much she was hated by her own son.

Taking over all of his mother's name recognition and status, Takaesu made his debut as a gourmet food critic, keeping the fact that the majority of his teeth were fake a secret.

There was lingering damage in his alveolar ridge because a layperson had roughly pulled out his teeth while he was still growing, so rather than get implants, he had no choice but to use partial dentures. He had always been afraid it would be discovered someday that he was a food critic with dentures who couldn't chew hard things, but that life ended three months ago. The day that eye given to him by the heavens had settled in his flesh, he put aside his dentures for the new real teeth that were growing in.

…That's right. He couldn't bite his mother anymore, but there was still a person he should bite: the dentist who treated a child that had obviously been abused and accepted a pile of money to keep it quiet.

When he got back to Tokyo, he would pay a visit to that dentist, who was now the only person who knew that Takaesu had dentures.

He would have her examine the teeth that had grown in and fully enjoy the shock on her face before he captured her. He would tie her up on the exam table, pull her teeth out one by one, and chew them up with a crunch as if they were *ramune* candy. There was no need for him to pay an extra fee to have maintenance done on his mouth in an exam room during the middle of the night anymore.

But before that, there was the boy with the shell.

During his brief slumber, the healing of the burns had progressed quite a bit. He didn't feel much hunger, either. Just as if nutrients had seeped out of the stainless steel nut in his mouth.

Roll, roll.

After rolling the nut around inside his mouth a bit—

Grind, grind. Crunch, crunch.

Takaesu bit through the lump of metal and swallowed it.

7

The weekend passed by anticlimactically without a thing happening.

Whether Minoru was doing his run early on Saturday morning, going to and from school, or going shopping with Norie on Sunday, the Biter didn't show himself and Yumiko and DD didn't make contact with him again. In just two days, the events at Akigase Park had rapidly lost their sense of reality.

On Monday morning when he and Norie left the house together, it was starting to feel like everything had been a dream. The presence of the orb settled deep in his chest—the black Third Eye—was the only thing that didn't disappear, but now even that seemed like a part of everyday life.

At an intersection along the way he said good-bye to Norie, who worked at the Saitama prefectural office near Urawa Station, then sped up on his bike a bit. Even when he pulled his face out from under his scarf a little and inhaled the cold air through his nose, he couldn't pick up on that unique beastly smell at all.

But there was still just one thing—no, there were just two things that he couldn't say weren't bothering him, like little thorns in his side.

The first was what DD had called out to him three days ago when Minoru had started to leave the park.

Watch out for the smell of the Ruby Eye, kid.

Even without being told, he went on checking for the smell in the air in that way. But he couldn't get past the feeling that Yumiko and DD had said something important within the conversation about the smell of the Ruby Eye. He just couldn't remember it. Maybe it was a result of Minoru's conscious effort to keep the memories of those events at a distance.

And the second thing was Tomomi Minowa, who they'd taken away to the hospital.

He hadn't seen her at school on Saturday. She shouldn't have any major injuries, so if she was still being treated, was it for a mental issue? That wasn't unreasonable, either; she had seen the terrifying face of the shark man up close. It would be good if she could somehow recover and come to school today, though.

He stopped his bike at the signal to cross the Shin-Omiya bypass and let out a sigh.

At least the incident itself was over. Knowing that he owed the terrible burns he had taken to that mysterious organization, the Biter had no reason to hang around this area for days. He had probably fled somewhere far away a long time ago and was being followed by Yumiko and all them.

The signal turned green, and as he pumped the pedals of his bike hard, he whispered those words deep inside himself for the umpteenth time.

It's over, all of it.

When morning classes ended and the bell chimed for lunch break, the classroom was immediately filled with clamor and the smells of boxed lunches.

Minoru cut across it all smoothly and went out into the hall. Usually he would go straight and head for the cafeteria, but today he came to a halt and looked down the hallway on the right. Minoru's class, sophomore Class One, was on the eastern end of the school building on the third floor. At the far-off western end was Class Eight—Tomomi Minowa's class.

Minoru had no idea what had happened to her after DD and Yumiko had taken her off to the hospital. If he knew her phone number, he could have at least worried about whether to send her a text, but they had never exchanged phone numbers or anything.

He should be able to find out if she had come to school if he went directly to her classroom, but no excuse materialized for why he would be peeking into Class Eight at the end of the hall as he passed by. It also seemed like there would be trouble if the track team guys saw him or something.

Disappointed with himself for thinking these things even for a moment, Minoru started walking not down the stairs, but toward the hall. Even if they saw him, he could be finished with all this if they called him out again. Next time, though, he'd have to be sure not to activate the shell the moment he got hit.

With his shoulders drawn in, Minoru went against the tide of students headed for the cafeteria all the way to the other end of the hall. He furtively peeked into Class Eight through the classroom door that had been left open.

He ran his gaze over the room quickly, but Tomomi Minowa wasn't there after all. Was she absent from school today, too, or had she already gone to the cafeteria or the locker room?

As he was turning these thoughts over in his mind near the door, he heard a low voice from behind him.

"Hey."

Reflexively sucking in a breath, he wheeled around. Standing there was the shark man—no, it was one of the three guys who had summoned him to the back of the dojo. The sophomore from the track team who had seen Minoru and Tomomi talking. If he remembered correctly, they had called the guy Ogucchi.

The only impression Minoru had of the guy from five days earlier was him chuckling in front of the upperclassmen, but now his eyes were sharply narrowed beneath his short hair and his mouth was twisted with displeasure.

"What business do you have in our class, Utsugi?" he asked in a deep voice.

The question made Minoru want to murmur, "Nothing," and slip away, but he stood his ground, slowly letting out the air in his lungs. "Could we talk over there?" he suggested, looking toward the corner of the hallway.

Although the track team member's brow furrowed, creating vertical wrinkles between his eyes, he nodded. They moved in front of a window at the western end of the hallway and faced each other again.

Come to think of it, I only know this guy's nickname, Minoru thought.

"Sorry, I don't know your name," he said as he made eye contact with the guy, who was about the same height as him.

"...Oguchi," he murmured.

Giving the guy a slight nod, Minoru got right to the point with no preamble.

"I was wondering if Minowa is at school today."

"...What's it to you?" Oguchi said, his voice going lower still.

Taking in Oguchi's piercing gaze, Minoru had a belated realization. This guy liked Tomomi Minowa. That's why he was wary of Minoru talking to Tomomi.

Then how about me? he wondered momentarily.

Since moving to this town, he had never felt interested in a particular girl or wanted to become close with one. He had gone on avoiding closing the distance between him and other people, not just girls. That was because he was always afraid that he would end up with bitter memories, painful memories, memories he would want to forget.

Oguchi had surely been overtaken by dark emotions the moment he saw Minoru talking to Tomomi. That's why he had told the upperclassmen and encouraged them to call Minoru out. But there was no doubt that he had regretted his actions afterward. After all, when he had seen Minoru laid out on the ground after being hit, Oguchi's face had been completely contorted.

And he was making the same face now as well.

Gathering what little courage he had, Minoru answered, "…Because Minowa's my friend," without turning his eyes away.

The reason he hadn't uttered one of his usual lines—"it's nothing," "it's fine"—was because a faint voice replaying inside his ear had returned.

You have a duty to go on fighting.

It was the voice of Yumiko, who he would probably never see again.

He didn't think that fighting the Ruby Eyes as a Jet Eye was something he could do. But Minoru felt like Yumiko's words called into question his way of living itself—intent on always averting his eyes from everything these past eight years, saying that things didn't matter or that they had nothing to do with him.

Minoru had talked to Tomomi Minowa a bunch of times, saved her from the Biter, and told her that everything was okay now. After all that with Tomomi, it would be wrong to discard her, saying she didn't matter. And the same thing probably applied to Oguchi, who was right in front of him.

Oguchi heard Minoru's response, and his eyes widened for a moment and his mouth went completely tense. Seeing his bony, athletic right shoulder twitch, Minoru wondered if he wanted to hit him.

But Oguchi relaxed his body after a few seconds and murmured, "…Minowa's gone today, too. She got hurt training on her own last week, and I guess she's been in the hospital for a few days."

"…"

After a brief silence, Minoru nodded and said, "Okay."

Yumiko and DD had probably taken Tomomi to the hospital, called her family there, and given them that explanation about the deviant and all that. Consequently, people had been told by the school that she was injured during independent training.

Minoru knew that Tomomi wasn't physically injured, but of course he couldn't go and tell that to Oguchi. Minoru dropped his head and said, "Thanks. Well, I'll go."

When he had turned in the other direction, he heard a tiny voice.

"Utsugi. You…and Minowa…?"

After considering this question with no verb, Minoru answered truthfully, "It's not like that. But we're friends, so I was worried."

"Huh. Well, see you," Oguchi muttered, going into the classroom through the nearby door.

As he set off for the cafeteria, Minoru suddenly wondered if he should go see Tomomi in the hospital. But he immediately realized he didn't have that right.

Since he had come late, the popular food items were sold out across the board. He wolfed down a Chinese-style rice bowl, which was unpopular but not something he personally disliked. The warning bell rang right as he was going back to the classroom.

Since Tomomi Minowa had been on his mind all morning, he hadn't exactly been paying attention to his classes, so he wanted to do his best in the afternoon. But his thoughts from the conversation with Oguchi kept resurfacing in fragments and disturbing his concentration.

The reason he couldn't get his mind off of Tomomi Minowa wasn't because he had some affection for her as a member of the opposite sex. It was because while she was absent from school, he couldn't yet say that his life was completely back to normal. It wasn't as if he wanted to get closer with Minowa than he was now once she was discharged from the hospital. He just wanted her to get better and run as hard as she used to.

She wasn't injured, so she should definitely be back to school tomorrow or the day after tomorrow. He didn't plan on talking to her, but this anxiety he was feeling should disappear if he spotted her in her workout clothes on the way to and from school or on school grounds.

Minoru made it through fifth and sixth periods telling himself this. Quickly changing his shoes—there were no notes stuck in his shoe locker—he left the school building. As he headed toward the bike parking lot, he breathed in slowly through his nose. The only smells he could pick up on were the scent of dust that was unique to school and the odor of exhaust from cars.

The book he had neglected to return to the city library on Friday was still in his bag. After wondering whether he should head straight home at a time like this, he dispelled the thought; there was no longer a reason to call it "a time like this."

When Minoru arrived at the large library near city hall and stepped into the heated building, the first thing he did was smell the air. Of course, there was nothing abnormal about it. He shrugged, and after dropping his book off at the return counter, he had a sudden realization and made his way to the computer lab.

Minoru slid into the booth at the very end and grabbed the mouse. He started up the browser and entered "Third Eye" into the search bar at the top of the page.

He did have a notebook computer in his room, but he felt a bit hesitant about searching at home for the many words he had heard from Yumiko and DD. He never expected it to happen, but he had the feeling that it wasn't completely impossible for their organization to monitor even the Internet and to locate Minoru's house based on search keywords.

Of course, there were surveillance cameras in the library, too, but it was probably better than his house...

He mulled these things over as he looked at the search results. He had expected this, but the hits he got were full of similarly named company websites and sites related to good luck charms and fortune-telling.

He typed in "Ruby" and "Jet" as additional search terms, but the search results didn't change much. Adding words like "eye," "powers," and "murder," he started to check the sites displayed from the top down, but as expected he didn't find even one site that seemed to contain relevant information.

After dozens of searches, the only information he'd gained that could be called beneficial was about the jet gemstone that DD had mentioned. It was not a mineral, but a gemstone made of fossilized plant matter, and it was spelled the same as the *jet* in *jet engine*. If they'd wanted a black gemstone, they could have gone with onyx or morion. As he thought this, he erased the browser's search history, took a wet wipe from his bag, and wiped down the mouse and keyboard. Of course, he was doing this to get rid of fingerprints, not for the benefit of the person who used it after him.

He walked away from the booth feeling embarrassed by his actions and moved to the magazine reading section. Scanning the rack, he pulled out a monthly science magazine that caught his interest with the words on the cover: *SPN Signal Special Edition*.

He took a seat on the nearby couch and opened the magazine, but the content of the articles just wasn't sinking in. Whatever he did, his thoughts kept drifting back to the abnormal things he had experienced in Akigase Park.

The two types of Third Eyes, Rubies and Jets, had come down from space three months ago, invaded the bodies of dozens or maybe hundreds of people, and given those people supernatural powers.

On top of that, the humans who had been taken as hosts by red orbs, the Ruby Eyes, were even given the urge to kill and began to attack people like the Biter had. That's why those who had the power to oppose them, the Jet Eyes, were fighting the Ruby Eyes. That's what Yumiko, the girl in the black blazer, had said.

It was a ridiculous story, but since Minoru himself had received the invisible shell ability, he couldn't doubt it.

Still, there was some part of it that didn't make sense to him. After thinking a bit, he realized what it was.

The Ruby Eyes had been given power and homicidal impulses. The Jet Eyes had only been given power. It was that imbalance.

What if the homicidal impulse that drove the Ruby Eyes was something similar to hypnotism or brainwashing? Then could they really say that Jet Eyes like Minoru and Yumiko weren't experiencing some sort of mental interference?

My attitude today in front of Oguchi from the track team was really unlike me. Instead of speaking evasively and running away, I faced him, looked him in the eye, and said the things I thought I should say. And it didn't even come to mind that I'd be increasing the memories I couldn't get rid of if I did something like that.

What if that was the result of mental interference...? Nothing about the real me has changed, but could I be getting more aggressive because of the Jet Eye...?

He was putting too much pressure on the magazine he held in his hands, making a little crease in the page. The sound of it brought him back to himself and he hurriedly relaxed his hands.

I'm overthinking this. Everything I do is my own choice.

That's what he told himself, but for a while he couldn't bring himself to stand up. He gazed blankly at the feature story on the page he had open.

Six months ago, there had been an uproar about whether the faint signal captured by the telescope on the moon was a message from an extraterrestrial civilization.

That was because the signal repeated the same number of times as the seven prime numbers from two to seventeen. But no one could decipher the content of this important signal, and things quieted down.

Nobody was talking about it at Yoshiki High School anymore, either, but Minoru still thought about the SPN Signal from time to time. Of course, that was because he had encountered the strange thing that had descended from the sky.

Was there some sort of connection between the signal and the orb—the Third Eye? Or was it just a coincidence?

Yumiko and her organization probably had some kind of information about it, but he wasn't in any kind of position to ask. Depending on how things had gone, he probably could've been given a suspicious shot and had the Third Eye in his chest surgically removed.

No.

If he was even becoming afraid of mental interference, would it have actually been better to just let them do it? Should he have jumped at the chance to escape from that abnormal situation—people who possessed suspicious powers fighting each other—and return to his previously peaceful life?

Taking his gaze away from the magazine, he shifted his eyes to the area around the second button of his uniform. With his thoughts, he approached the black orb that was probably deep inside his chest.

Hey. Did you really come from space? Do you have some connection to the SPN Signal?

What do you want to make me do…?

Of course, he heard no voice answering him. But Minoru felt an incredibly faint throb deep in his chest.

The sensation felt like he might be getting a question in return. Something like, *Do* you *know what to do with the power you've been given?*

Once he had finished reading several magazines and left the library after visiting the bathroom, it was six o'clock in the evening. If he hurried a bit, he should be able to make it home right around the time Norie was starting dinner preparations. He sped down the dark residential streets on his bike.

When he increased his speed, a piercingly cold headwind bore down on him. Wind was pleasant on his morning runs because his temperature was elevated, but peddling his bike wasn't enough exercise to work up a sweat. Minoru's favorite scarf, hand knitted for him by Norie, was hundreds of times better than something off the rack as far as the emotion it contained, but he couldn't say that it was especially great at keeping out the cold.

The wind penetrated the loose stitching unrelentingly and his ears stung painfully. If he activated the shell, this wind wouldn't stand a chance… Although he considered it, he probably couldn't pedal his bike while using his power.

"…Huh, using my power…," he said, voicing his thoughts quietly with a wry smile.

It was a familiar phrase from all sorts of manga and novels, but he never thought the day would come where he'd say it in real life—

"…Ah!"

Minoru's eyes instantly widened.

That was it. The little thorn in his side that had been bothering him. The conversation between Yumiko and DD that he hadn't been able to remember.

Go sniff out the Biter or something.

Can't smell him if he doesn't use his power.

That's what the two of them had said.

He forcefully gripped the brake lever without thinking, and his bike came to a halt with a shrill screeching noise.

If they weren't using their powers, one couldn't pick up on a Ruby Eye's scent.

When the Biter used his ability, his mouth and teeth were transformed into something like a shark's and he could bite through anything. In other words, while he was transformed into a shark man, he was continually giving off that beastly smell.

But to put it the other way, that meant that when he wasn't transformed… When he appeared to be a normal human, he couldn't be detected through smell even if he was just a stone's throw away.

Minoru quickly turned to look behind him. He looked to the left and the right many times, too. There was no one around the little residential intersection. Still, he couldn't say that the man wasn't lurking on the other side of the concrete block wall or that he wouldn't notice that smell right when his head was already being bitten clean off.

He nearly activated his protective shell in fright but thought better of it. Three days ago, he had lost the Biter's scent the instant he put the shell on. Right now, it was more dangerous to block out the smell. The Biter would have to transform right before he attacked, so Minoru should be able to put the shell on in time after noticing that foul smell.

First, he had to get home as soon as possible. He could think of a plan after that. Minoru was able to calm himself down somehow, and he pumped the pedals again.

Forgetting the cold as he exhaled white puffs of breath, he raced down the road home almost nonstop.

When he turned the final corner and saw warm light filling the living room window of his house, his whole body finally relaxed. Norie was probably beginning dinner preparations right about now.

Tonight's dinner was supposed to be the gyoza they had made and frozen five days earlier.

He opened the gate, stopped his bike in its usual spot, and headed for the entryway at a jog. Switching his bike key for his house key, he came to a stop in front of the door. That was the moment.

Minoru felt his heart constrict.

The keyhole where he should have put his key in—it wasn't there.

Above the door handle in place of the keyhole gaped a large hole with a diameter of around ten centimeters. Minoru stared blankly at the hole; he could see right through it to the other side.

The hole hadn't been created with a tool like a drill. The edges of the hole that had been opened in the metal escutcheon plate were jagged, irregular, and sharp, but the cut edge of the inner cylinder shone smoothly. It was exactly as if a beast with a pointed mouth had chewed through it with sharp, strong teeth.

Minoru gripped the handle with his cold, numb right hand and pulled gently. The door opened, gliding open without a bit of resistance. There were no people or animals anywhere he could see—the hall extending straight from the entryway, the stairs going up on the left, or the glass door at the end of the hall that led to the living room. He couldn't hear a single sound. A slightly orange light poured into the hall from the glass door.

His thoughts at a complete standstill, Minoru took off his shoes and stepped into the hall. After dropping his messenger bag, Chesterfield coat, and scarf in the hallway and taking a few steps forward, it finally hit him.

The sound he always heard at this moment. He couldn't hear the pitter-patter of slippers running toward him.

His brain finally started up again, and two thoughts exploded from the center of his mind.

The Biter's here.

Norie.

The only one who could have conceivably bitten through the sturdy dimple key cylinder was that strangely formed shark man.

In other words, there was a possibility that the Biter was lurking somewhere in the house at this very moment. But Minoru charged single-mindedly down the hallway and flew into the living room with enough force to smash the glass door.

"Norie!!"

As he shouted, he looked around the kitchen on the far left, then around the living and dining room on the right. The ceiling light shone brightly and the heater had been left on, but neither the Biter's bulk nor Norie's petite figure was there. When he wheeled around, wondering if they were on the second floor, he stepped on something mushy and soft with his left foot.

"…!"

Jumping back a step, he looked at his feet.

The thing on the floor was a small, milky-white semicircle. Bending down, he picked it up with trembling fingers.

It was one of the gyoza that he and Norie had made together five days earlier. When he had rushed into the kitchen, he saw that the silver tray was flipped over on the floor and dozens of gyoza were scattered around.

It was immediately clear what had happened. Norie had taken the gyoza tray out of the freezer to prepare dinner when the Biter attacked her.

Minoru's eyes pored over the entire kitchen. He didn't find anything that looked like a bloodstain. Next, he prodded the gyoza still clutched in his right hand with a fingertip. The outside was soft, but the ingredients inside were still half-frozen.

With the temperature in the room, the gyoza probably would have thawed all the way to the center within thirty minutes. That meant that the attack had probably happened a mere twenty minutes ago or less.

Dropping the half-raw gyoza in the sink, Minoru left the kitchen again to head up the stairs. When he did so, he noticed that there was a black rectangle placed ostentatiously in the middle of the dining table that hadn't come into his line of sight earlier.

It was the terminal for the tablet that they always had standing up on the edge of the kitchen counter.

Rushing over to the table, he picked up the tablet and pressed the button. The notepad app was displayed. Minoru's eyes pored over the lines written there.

I guarantee that the woman is unhurt. Stay where you are and wait for the next communication. Surveillance cameras have been set up there. If you leave the room, try to contact someone, or try to disable the cameras, I will kill the woman.

The words were clear and concise, which consequently made them surreal. But it felt like the Biter's malice still remained on the glass surface of the tablet even a few dozen minutes after he had typed those lines. Minoru returned the tablet to the table and dropped into a dining chair.

Norie was still alive.

That was the only thing he should believe. If the Biter's goal was to kill Norie, he could have killed her here rather than take the risk of kidnapping her.

But what about the hidden cameras? The Biter had had twenty minutes at the most to attack Norie before Minoru came home. Would he have had time to set up the cameras and connect them to the Internet in those minutes?

Still seated, he swept his eyes all over the living and dining room. It was clean and neat, but since it was far larger than Minoru's room, there were tons of places where cameras could be hidden. And it wasn't certain that the man was using a purpose-built hidden camera. If he had a smartphone running a surveillance camera app, all he would have to do is set it down somewhere.

It was no good. Since the Biter was using Norie's life as leverage, Minoru couldn't leave this room or report this to the police using the landline next to the wall. He had no choice but to follow instructions under the assumption that he really was being watched.

He at least needed to determine if there was a possibility that the Biter was hiding on the second floor while pretending to have moved to a far-off location. Focusing all his neurons on his sense of smell, he inhaled.

It was faint... It was weak, but he had a feeling he was picking up on that smell. Was it a so-called lingering aroma from when he had kidnapped Norie? If that man was lurking on the other side of the ceiling just a few meters away, Minoru should be getting a clear signal even if the man wasn't using his ability. The Third Eye in his chest was completely silent now as well.

The Biter really was far away already.

The initial shock lessened little by little as he became aware of the situation, and in its place a black, cold despair filled his chest.

It's my fault. I'm the one who drew the Biter to this house.

And Yumiko and DD had warned him, too. He had tried to look tough by saying he could protect himself, but he'd only been paying attention to his own surroundings and hadn't even considered the possibility that Norie might be targeted.

If he'd taken their warning more seriously, he could have thought things all the way through. Then he definitely would've realized that the Biter would have ways of locating Minoru's house.

Where had the shark man set his sights on Tomomi Minowa? The most likely possibility was during her morning training or on her runs to and from school. If he had followed her, he would have easily located her house and her school.

And it was natural to conclude that the high school guy who had barged in right before the man was going to devour Tomomi at Akigase Park—that is to say, Minoru—was an acquaintance of Tomomi's, not someone passing by. In that case, if he watched Yoshiki High School's gate, he could've found Minoru.

Third Eyes not only bestowed unique abilities but also vastly increased the physical and perceptual abilities—meaning hearing and sight—of their hosts. He hadn't precisely measured it, but Minoru thought that if he had an eye exam now, his vision would be better than twenty-ten.

Naturally, the Biter probably also had sharp vision. It shouldn't have been hard for him to pick out Minoru from somewhere a sufficient distance away from the school gate, like the roof of an apartment building, and follow him.

Minoru was sure it had happened when he came home from school on Saturday. He hadn't noticed the Ruby Eye smell, but he hadn't known—no, he had forgotten—the important fact that the scent couldn't be perceived when a Ruby Eye wasn't using their ability. So Minoru had carelessly led the Biter right to his home.

It's...my fault.

Once again, Minoru agonized over that realization. He couldn't make any strange movements because the Biter could be watching him on camera, so he desperately suppressed the impulse to scream at the top of his lungs.

It had happened again. He had put his precious family in danger.

No, there was no guarantee that the Biter was letting Norie live like his message on the tablet had said. Right now, he could already be biting her with those shark teeth as her life slipped away.

Just like eight years ago. Just like his father, his mother, and his sister Wakaba.

Was everything happening all over again? Despite living these eight years thinking only of pushing people away and keeping himself from taking on bad memories, had he made the same mistake again?

A faint wail he had failed to suppress slipped from the back of his throat.

Me...me.

Me. If you're going to kill someone, make it me.

Minoru raised his face. He looked around the living and dining room. He didn't know the locations of the cameras, and he wasn't sure if they even existed in the first place. But...

If he got down on his knees and begged...

If I plead as hard as I can, if I say that I'll end my life myself right here, right now, as long as he returns Norie safely...

Then maybe the Biter will listen to my request, since I should be the one he has a grudge with.

There were plenty of knives in the kitchen right next to him. If he drove the one that seemed the biggest and the toughest—the butcher knife—into his chest, he could just die, no matter how many Third Eyes were inside him.

Minoru once again scanned the living and dining room looking for cameras. Fixing his gaze on the area around the TV stand, which seemed like it would have the most hiding places, he took a deep breath. And he clenched his back teeth hard.

This was the turning point.

Was he going to turn his back on his duties and his responsibilities and walk away like he had always done? Or was he going to make the choice to battle fate himself this time?

It wasn't as if Minoru's life was the only thing the Biter wanted. He wanted to bite people to death with those sharklike teeth.

That's why, if Minoru killed himself here, the Biter might take his rage out on Norie.

If there was even the slightest possibility...

If there was still a possibility that he could fight the Biter wherever the next message summoned him to and take Norie back...

Yumiko's voice was in his ear again.

You have a duty to go on fighting.

I don't think I can fight as a Jet Eye against some indefinite number of Ruby Eyes to protect people. But to protect Norie Yoshimizu... To protect my second sister who's more precious to me than anyone else, I know I can fight the Biter as Minoru Utsugi. I have to fight.

After clenching his hands into fists one last time, Minoru slowly released the tension from his entire body and let himself fall back into the chair.

All he could do and should do now was calm himself and wait for the next communication. He would keep down the consumption of his physical and mental energy to raise his chances of winning the fight, even just a little.

Shutting his eyes, he called out to his two sisters inside his heart.

Norie, hang in there. Because I'm definitely going to save you.

Waka, please. Give me your strength.

The time passed as long and heavy as that night had eight years ago.

There was no way he could have an appetite, but he nibbled at a few of the biscuits in the kitchen cupboard and cleaned up the gyoza that had scattered on the floor. It would be a problem if he had to go to the bathroom later, so he had just a mouthful of water.

He sat on the sofa, closed his eyes, and focused on waiting.

When the phone rang at last, it was a little past one o'clock in the morning.

Minoru sprang to his feet, and he had a realization when he reached his hand out to the landline. What was ringing was Minoru's cell phone, which he had left inside his bag in the hallway.

He had to leave the living and dining room to answer. For a moment he wondered what would happen if it was not the Biter but someone else... But he immediately dispelled this thought. The ringtone was from Norie's cell phone. The one calling was probably the Biter, who had stolen the phone.

Running out into the hallway and grabbing up the bag, Minoru took out the phone as he turned right back to the living and dining room. He slid his finger across the screen and put the phone to his ear.

"...Yes?" he answered briefly.

From the other end of the phone line, that man's voice whispered, "Well, what a long time it's been, boy. I apologize for the wait."

"...Is she safe?"

"Don't be in such a rush, *ragazzo*. I had her take some medicine that put her to sleep, so I can't let you hear her voice, but I haven't left a single bite mark on her. Of course, you know...that only lasts as long as you follow my instructions, boy."

There was no strange distortion or huskiness in his smooth tenor's voice as there had been three days ago, maybe because his mouth wasn't transformed at the moment. But Minoru could sense that it dripped with malice and appetite deep within. The Third Eye gave a sharp throb under his sternum.

"I'll follow your instructions. What should I do?"

"Why, it's easy. I want you to come to a certain location now. But it'll be a bit troublesome if you get in touch with the police or that dangerous *signorina* along the way. You'll come out now without hanging up the phone. If we get cut off because of problems with the signal, I'll call you back immediately and you'll answer right away. Are we clear?"

"I understand. Where should I go?"

Although he did ask, Minoru could predict what the man would say. That storage shed deep in the forest of Akigase Park—

But the words that came from the speaker were unexpected.

"First, you'll head toward Keyaki Plaza near Saitama New City Center Station. You've got fifteen minutes. Hurry, *ragazzo*."

He was surprised by the unexpected instruction but had no choice but to follow it.

"I'm leaving right now," he answered.

Minoru slid the phone into his pocket without hanging up and ran back out of the living and dining room. Coming out into the entryway, he shoved his feet into the running shoes that he wore on his morning jogs instead of the sneakers he wore for school. He slipped on a Windbreaker over his coat, left through the unlocked door, and climbed on his bike, completely oblivious to the deep winter cold.

It was about five kilometers to New City Center Station. To get there within fifteen minutes, he would have to ride at an average speed of twenty kilometers per hour. Those numbers were really pushing it for a non-racing bike, especially when riding through an urban area. But the Biter had specified this barely possible amount of time knowing that Minoru possessed the Third Eye.

…Norie. Just hang on; I'm coming right now.

Since the call was still going, Minoru called out to her inside his head as he pushed down on the pedals as hard as he could.

8

The reason Minoru had put on a Windbreaker over his uniform was more to avoid the police than to keep out the cold. Most police officers doing rounds at one o'clock in the morning would try to stop a high school guy if they saw him flying past them in a school uniform.

In reality, he only passed a police officer on a bike once, but no one called out to him, possibly because of the deep hood he had on. Although naturally, even if someone had tried to stop him, he would have sped up and shaken them off.

Speeding through the hushed residential streets, he crossed the bypass. When he came out onto slightly wider roads, he got up from the seat and started pedaling standing up. Although he was on the highest gear of his three-speed bike, the resistance was too light for Minoru as he was now.

The towering skyscrapers of the new urban center appeared ahead of him, piercing the night sky. As Minoru gazed up at them, pressing his right foot down on the pedal with significantly more force, it happened.

Clang! After this impact, the resistance on the pedals completely disappeared. The bike seemed like it would tip over to the right, but Minoru just barely regained his balance and braked. When he peered down at his feet, the broken chain was drooping down to the surface of the road.

He had neither the time nor the tools to fix it, so his only choice was to leave the bike there. When he glanced at his watch after leaning the bike against the side of the guardrail, there were three minutes and thirty seconds left in the fifteen-minute time limit. He would have to run the last kilometer and a half on foot.

"...Norie...!" Minoru called to his adoptive sister in a hoarse voice, tearing off down the path in the dead of night.

In the heart of Saitama's new city center, there was a large sky deck called Keyaki Plaza. On winter nights it should've been illuminated with blue LED lights, but the time period when they were switched on had ended and only the weak light from a smattering of streetlamps shone.

Minoru dashed up the stairs from the ground to the deck. He breathed heavily as he leaned up against one of the countless keyaki trees that were planted there. He looked down at his watch once again. There were twenty seconds left.

This was the first time he had pushed his running skills to the limit since the Third Eye had come to live in him. Thinking in the corner of his mind that the world record for the 1,500-meter run was somewhere around three minutes and twenty-five seconds...he pulled the phone from his breast pocket and spoke in a small voice to the man still on the other end of the line.

"I'm here."

After a pause, that voice answered.

"Yes, I'm keeping a close eye on you, boy. What happened to your bike?"

"...!"

It wasn't a bluff; the man really was watching. He quickly ran his eyes over the surrounding area, but it was long past the time when the last train of the night departed, so there wasn't a soul in the plaza.

"...It broke along the way, so I ran here."

At this answer, a low chuckle came from the phone.

"That's quite a disaster. But I'm impressed that you made it in time without having to come crying to me. She must be quite important to you."

"What did you expect?!"

He felt like he was close to raising his voice against his better judgment but barely held himself in check. There was no one around, but there were probably police posted on the opposite end of the plaza. Taking his voice back down to a whisper, he continued.

"I followed the instructions, so let my sister go."

"Hey, hey, boy. I told you this was the first thing you had to do, didn't I? Naturally, I have your next instruction prepared. Look to the north side of the plaza."

"…"

Suppressing his irritation, he looked in the direction he was told to. A wide footbridge extended to the north, crossing over a road and connecting to a sky deck of the same height. Right at the end of it, the shadow of a huge structure rose up like a hill. It was Saitama Super Arena, the largest multipurpose hall in Japan.

At the same time as Minoru looked up at the arena's roof, a voice came from the cell phone.

"Head to the side of the Super Arena on your right. Don't let any police or guards see you."

"…The right side…"

The Biter's intentions weren't clear, but all Minoru could do was obey. After looking around the area once more and confirming that no one was around, he ran off, keeping his body low.

When he had crossed the bridge and come onto the sky deck next to the arena, he moved eastward in the darkness alongside the wall. He reached the corner after a few dozen seconds, went around it, and looked to the north. There, wide stairs continued up along the side of the building.

Putting the cell phone to his left ear, he said, "From here…"

Minoru had started to ask what he should do, but the Biter interrupted him with the third instruction.

"Go a little farther and there'll be a door to the emergency stairs on the left. Open it and go up."

When Minoru went forward as he'd been instructed, he did see a metal door. Naturally, the door would have been locked most of the time, but the doorknob had been completely cut out. Just like at Minoru's house, the Biter had eaten through it.

Shuddering at the power it would take to get through that thick steel like it was nothing, he pulled open the door. The emergency stairs were right there in front of him, so he muffled the sound of his footsteps and went up.

He came upon another door with a broken lock after going up seven floors, and when he passed through, it came out onto the top-floor terrace.

He looked quickly to the left and the right, but there was no one here, either. Even when he looked up, there were only huge protruding beams that supported the roof high above him.

"...Where are you?" he said into the cell phone in a subdued voice.

Then, after a few seconds of silence that seemed meant to keep Minoru in suspense, a low voice answered.

"Here's your next instruction. If you come around to the back of the terrace there's a ladder that will take you up to the roof. Climb it and come up."

"To...to the roof?!"

"That's right. It's spacious and it feels great. Hurry up, *ragazzo*."

"..."

Minoru looked up one more time, the cell phone still clutched in his hand. The roof of Saitama Super Arena sloped down from the front of the building toward the back of the building. In areas near the front, it was about twenty meters above even from the terrace where Minoru was, and probably more than sixty meters from the ground.

Was the Biter really in that sort of place? Wasn't this some kind of trap? He considered these things, but his only option was to keep obeying the instructions until he had taken Norie back.

He ran to the southern side of the top-floor terrace. The end of the roof that stuck out above his head sloped down farther and farther. When he reached the back of the building, the roof was about five meters away from him.

And when he turned the corner, there was an aluminum ladder there just as the Biter had said. He grabbed the ice-cold metal and started climbing at once.

At last, he reached the top of Saitama Super Arena. The huge roof looked just like a massive glacier falling from the night sky.

The slope, which rose slightly in the center, stretched upward from

Minoru's location toward the front of the building. The scale of it was overwhelming. The actual incline was probably less than ten degrees, but from Minoru's location, it felt like a steep cliff.

Minoru stood still as the cold moon showed its face from a tiny gap between the clouds in the faraway sky. The moon on December 10, 2019, was a waxing gibbous moon, just a little bit short of a full moon. Even so, Minoru's eyes, strengthened by the Third Eye, were filled with bright moonlight. It made the large slope with a width of 150 meters and a length of 200 meters glitter silver.

Then Minoru saw it.

Near the highest point of the huge roof. A single figure standing upright in the center of the slope.

The figure moved his left arm and held something close to his face. After Minoru did the same, pressing the cell phone to his head, a calm voice flowed out.

"Here's your final instruction: Come here."

Then the figure hurled the phone in his right hand far away. The call was cut off at the sound of the impact.

Minoru flung off his Windbreaker and put his cell phone in the front pocket of his uniform.

Tearing his right foot away from the stainless steel sheeting the roof was made from, he stepped forward. Next came his left foot. Right foot. Left foot. Steadily increasing his speed, Minoru dashed about two hundred meters up the slope in one go.

When he was ten meters in front of the figure, Minoru came to a halt.

That man—the Biter—was standing near the edge of the roof with the hint of a smile on his face.

He gave a completely different impression than he had three days ago. He was wearing not training wear, but a dark-colored suit, and his shoes seemed to be of high quality as well. Most importantly, his face wasn't transformed.

Seeing the Biter's bare face for the first time, Minoru saw he had a stylish and intelligent appearance. The skin around his mouth, which should've been burned black from the stun baton, had healed beautifully in just three days.

Minoru had a feeling he had seen that face somewhere before, but before he could remember, the Biter spoke to him in his unfiltered voice.

"How wonderful to see you. Quite a nice view, don't you think?"

The nighttime view of central Saitama would have been spread out behind Minoru, but he questioned the man in a tense voice without taking his eyes off of him.

"Where's my sister?"

At this, the man shrugged and gestured diagonally behind him with his right arm.

Six massive beam-like structures stuck out far from the southern edge of the huge roof. These protrusions were about three meters wide and stretched out into the open air. Close to the end of the third beam from the left lay a petite figure. In an instant, Minoru's eyes confirmed that it was a woman wearing an apron who was bound with tape. She seemed unconscious.

Norie!! he screamed in his mind.

In that instant he felt as if he might run toward the beam, but he somehow managed to stay put.

The smile on the man's face grew bigger as he watched Minoru like this.

"Don't worry, boy. I've only put her to sleep with a strong sleeping medication. I said this on the phone as well, but I haven't bitten even a single finger."

"…"

Right now, he had no choice but to believe what the man said. But it was clear that Norie had been put in an incredibly dangerous situation. It was close to a seventy-meter drop from the tip of the beam to the ground. To fall from there would be certain death.

No.

Minoru alone might be able to come out alive if he fell. He had never tested it, but there was a possibility that his protective shell, which had staved off the Biter's teeth, could withstand a fall from seventy meters high. But Minoru couldn't cushion Norie's fall. The shell was hard enough to bash in a metal door; if he screwed things up, he could damage Norie more than the asphalt would have.

He understood all over again what a self-centered power this was. Minoru's shell cut him off from the world, creating a physical solitude. He could block out all danger outside of the shell, but he couldn't save anyone but himself. It was the ultimate self-protection, only concerned with his own safety.

That's exactly how I've been living.

As he thought this bitterly, he was forced to make a decision.

There was only one way to get Norie back safely. That was to rescue her from the dangerous tip of that beam and to bring her down the ladder behind him. But there was no way the man standing right there in his way would sit back and watch Minoru do that.

There was nothing to do but fight him and take him down.

Just as if he had taken a peek inside Minoru's head, the Biter lifted the corners of his lips in a sneer.

"Have you set your mind to it, boy?"

Wordlessly, he moved his head up and down in a small motion.

Things were as surreal as ever. He was standing on the roof of the Saitama Super Arena, which he was used to seeing on his way to and from school but had never looked at from the top. He was facing a fearsome monster who had already bitten and killed numerous people, and he was doing it alone. That monster and Minoru himself had received supernatural powers from mysterious orbs that came from space. Everything was like a poorly written joke.

But there was just one thing he was sure of. He had to protect Norie.

The man in front of him would probably kill Norie after Minoru. The man's words and actions themselves were rational, but deep in his eyes, hatred and desire danced red like flickering embers. Minoru didn't know if this was the mental contamination of the Ruby Eye as Yumiko had said or if it was something the man had always had—but at this point, it was the same either way.

If Minoru was killed, Norie would die, too.

The Biter watched Minoru as he focused his consciousness on the Third Eye buried in his chest, preparing to put on the protective shell whenever he needed to. The Biter's smile deepened a bit further.

"That's good, *ragazzo*. Truthfully, when I saw you at the park, you yourself didn't tempt me much… But that expression of yours is giving me more of an appetite."

His body swaying, the man rubbed the underside of his chin with the back of his right index finger.

"Well, then, before we fight, I suppose I'll have you answer a few questions. I'm the sort who likes to learn about my food in detail…"

Why do I have to give that kind of special treatment to a guy who's trying to eat me?

Although his mind resisted the concept, he continued thinking things over, his mouth in a tight line. There was no guarantee that Minoru could bring down the Biter on his own, so it wouldn't cost him anything to use up a little bit of time on this.

That was because when the Biter had used his ability to break into Minoru's house and the door to the emergency stairs at Saitama Super Arena, he should have produced that smell for at least a moment, even if Minoru hadn't been able to pick up on it.

"…Then I'd like you to answer a question for me first."

At Minoru's answer, the man nodded with an air of generosity.

"That should be fine. What would you like to know? I'll answer what I can."

"Why did you choose a place like this?"

It seemed that he hadn't expected that question, and the Biter chuckled after blinking a few times.

"I was convinced you'd ask me a personal question. Although I wouldn't be able to answer those… One reason I chose to meet you here is because it's a suitable place for my dining table. It's spacious and actually quite extravagant, don't you think? It's just like being on the ocean floor."

It was strange to think that the top of a roof more than sixty meters above the ground was comparable to the ocean floor. Still, Minoru also had the sense that he could understand just a little. But he kept his comment to himself and pressed for more.

"And the second reason?"

"Simply because we won't be disturbed here… Now then, it's my turn, boy," the Biter said as he gave a quick wave behind him. "Is that woman your real sister?"

"…"

Minoru was under no obligation to give honest answers to the guy who was trying to kill Norie. But he got the sense that he would be found out if he lied and the discussion would break down, so he couldn't help but shake his head.

"She's not. She adopted me when I was a kid."

"Oh ho…"

"Now it's my turn. You said earlier that I 'didn't tempt you much,' so why are you targeting my sister and me?"

The Biter made another elegant gesture as he responded to the question.

"To be precise, I said, 'You yourself didn't tempt me.' However, your ability is intriguing. What is that transparent shell made of? How hard is it? And why did a power like that spring up…? I'd very much like to know."

He spread his arms a bit, then crossed them over his chest.

"So tell me, *ragazzo*. Why did she adopt you? Did something happen when you were a child perhaps…?"

The Biter leaned his upper body forward, practically licking his lips. The depths of his long slitted eyes were tinged with a pale red light.

Minoru had a sensation as if the memories of eight years ago, shoved deep down into his consciousness, were cracking open slightly.

He clenched his teeth hard. He was under no obligation to tell some guy like this the truth, but he felt like the man would see through a lie, and he had his reasons for needing to drag out the conversation for every second he could.

Taking a few breaths, Minoru answered in a restrained voice.

"Because a sicko like you…murdered my family."

In that instant, the corners of the Biter's mouth twitched upward. His now-exposed teeth seemed to have a metallic luster. He had been leaning forward, but now his body sprang back forcefully like it was attached to a spring. The Ruby Eye let out a gale of laughter.

"Ahah-ha-ha-ha-ha-ha! So that's it, now I see, so that's what it was! Your whole family was killed… And you're the only one who survived. *So that's why you got that shell.* Excellent… This makes me want to bite you more and more! I bet your bones must taste like tears!!"

Crunch.

The peculiar sound came from the jaws of the Biter, who was bent over backward. A foul, beastly smell that was savage and brutal and cruel made a direct assault on Minoru's senses. The smell of the Ruby Eye.

"Ah… It's no use, I can't hold back anymore. Let's bring this Q-and-A session to a close. Well, then, let's enjoy this until we've had our fill…"

Crunch. Crunch, crunch.

"A feast…for just…you and I!!"

The Biter's pointed lower jaw stretched and stretched up toward the sky, the bones making a *crunch, crunch, crunch* sound. When he sprang upright again, he was no longer human. The shark man that Minoru had seen three days ago in Akigase Park was there.

Inside the savage smile playing across his massive mouth, rows of knifelike teeth glinted in the moonlight.

"Well, then, to start, I'm going to test you one more time as a tiger shark!" the Biter announced in a strangely warped voice as he tilted his body forward even more. Thick bundles of muscle heaved under his straining suit.

The shell. I have to get it on, Minoru thought, a heat coming over him like the core of his brain was burning up.

But it wouldn't activate.

His breathing, his lungs, wouldn't listen to him. He just panted in rushed, shallow breaths over and over. He couldn't perform the movement that was the key to activating the protective shell: taking a deep breath, holding it in, and putting pressure on the Third Eye in his sternum.

The Biter's shoes pushed off from the roof's steel sheeting. The tall figure was coming at him full tilt just like a shark. His triangular jaws popped open.

Giving up on activating his ability, Minoru desperately dove to the right.

The shark fangs passed only a few centimeters from Minoru's left shoe. Diving in headfirst, the Biter had ended up biting the steel frame of about fifty centimeters thick that was holding down the stainless steel plates of the roof.

Amid the huge crashing sound of the impact and the flying of bright sparks, the Biter chewed off a part of the steel frame as if he were biting into a pastry.

"...!!"

Minoru narrowly avoided falling and his eyes widened in shock. Since he had seen the bite marks left on his door at home and on the door to the emergency stairs of Saitama Super Arena, he had assumed that the Biter could bite through even metal. But still, he had never thought that the man's teeth could be this sharp.

Even for a large diamond cutter, it would take a few minutes to cut a steel frame of that thickness.

If he were bitten without the shell on, even an arm or leg would be taken off in an instant.

Calm down. Calm down and take a deep breath.

No matter how much he thought this, his lungs wouldn't listen to him at all. The air was forced back as if the very end of his trachea were blocked off.

Having tottered back up to his feet, the Biter spat out a huge lump of metal and charged ferociously. This time he opened both arms wide as if to stop Minoru from escaping by jumping aside.

"Shaaaa!" he cried as he drew near.

Minoru dodged the shark's teeth by dropping down. But if he stayed that way, he would be forced down onto the roof.

Resolutely, he dove headfirst at the Biter's waist, slipping behind him through his long legs. He did a forward roll and stood up just like that.

He still hadn't caught his breath. He needed to just start over again. But how? The Biter had those deadly teeth and those long arms. If he caught Minoru, it would be over in an instant.

At that moment, the running shoes Minoru was so used to wearing rubbed against the stainless steel plate at his feet with a squeak.

That's right. That's what I can do now. Something I might even be better at than the Biter. And that's—running!

Instead of turning to face his opponent, Minoru leaned forward and pushed off from the roof as hard as he could.

He had a feeling that man-eating shark was right on his heels. With a shiver, he felt the sharpness of those pointed fangs on the skin at the nape of his neck. Kicking away the urge to cower, Minoru tore off down the vast roof of the arena in a straight line.

Sprinting wasn't really his strong suit, but he knew how to run. Keep one's shoulders relaxed and really swing the arms with a good rhythm. Push off from directly below the center of gravity, staying aware of one's core.

Sprinting was anaerobic exercise, so he didn't breathe. His diaphragm, which had been about to spasm, stopped moving. The carbon dioxide trapped in his lungs escaped. The sound of the Biter's footsteps grew farther away. His thoughts, which had been overtaken by panic, gradually calmed.

The jet-black Third Eye in the center of his sternum gave a throbbing shiver.

It's working!

Suddenly braking with both his feet, he filled his empty lungs with cold air.

Hold in. Push.

His field of vision took on a blue cast, and all sound and temperature disappeared. His body floated up three centimeters.

When he turned around, he saw the silhouette of the shark man flying toward him with arms outstretched, the skyscrapers that stood on the other side of Saitama Super Arena in the background.

"Whoa… Whoa, whoa, whoa!" he shouted inside the shell.

Turning to face the Biter, Minoru charged at him headfirst.

Even when he collided with the Biter's chest through the man's suit, he felt almost no impact or recoil. It seemed that even the three laws of motion were bent by some kind of mechanism when the shell was on. Minoru was clearly the lighter of the two men, but the Biter was the only one who was sent flying.

The shark man was thrown against the steel plate on his back. This time it was Minoru who came flying at him.

Doing as he had seen on fighting shows, Minoru straddled the Biter and swung his clenched fists in turn.

The first swing connected with the Biter's shoulder. The second caught him in the throat—but the third punch with his right fist, which he had been aiming for the lower jaw, was stopped along the way.

The jaws suddenly opened wide and took hold of the fist through the shell.

This time Minoru felt a sharp, hard impact. On the other end of Minoru's arm, which wouldn't budge whether pushed or pulled, the Biter's eyes gave off a red gleam.

* * *

The right side of his chest where he had taken the head butt hurt like it was burning, and his left shoulder and collarbone twinged where he had been punched. He might even have cracks in the bone.

He may have slightly underestimated the *ragazzo*'s physical abilities. Takaesu hadn't expected the boy to outrun him, since he himself sweated at the gym every day training... And he hadn't expected the boy to whip around and charge at him, either.

Those weren't the only events he hadn't predicted.

He hadn't said this to the boy, but there was one more reason that Takaesu had chosen the roof of Saitama Super Arena for the fight. The entire roof was covered in coated stainless steel sheeting, making it easier to slip on than dirt or asphalt.

The transparent shell the boy cloaked himself in had an unnaturally smooth surface and was fearsomely hard. The boy's feet should slip on the metal plates, supposing it was a glass-like substance with an uncommon strength, leaving him unable to move properly. However, when he had braked suddenly and body-slammed Takaesu, the boy's balance hadn't been thrown off in the least.

It seemed as if the boy had a more solid hold on the roof plates than Takaesu in the rubber-soled walking shoes he'd worn.

He didn't understand exactly how that could be possible. But the powers granted by the eye were out of the ordinary in the first place. Anything could happen.

It was just like how Takaesu had managed to recover perfectly— no, beyond perfectly—in that abandoned building with no food or water.

He had taken light damage from the unforeseen counterattack, but he had gotten ahold of the boy in any case. No, he had gotten him between his teeth. At this point, he wouldn't let the boy go, and he wouldn't let the boy do anything. Like this, he would first tear off the boy's right arm along with the shell. Takaesu would enjoy his screams as he was writhing in agony, and then he would devour the left arm as well. Next would be the right leg. Then the left leg. Since the boy could run so fast, Takaesu would be able to get a taste of great, solid bone.

Once the boy was unable to speak because of heavy blood loss after losing all four limbs, Takaesu would eat the woman in front of him, too. To keep her alive, he had gone so far as to use his stock of barbiturate sleeping pills that had been so hard to come by. She was apparently the boy's adoptive sister, but that actually might give things a stimulating and emotional flavor...

When he thought this, a strange stab of pain shot through a deep place in Takaesu's head.

Ignoring this, he pressed down on the boy's body with his right knee as he simultaneously yanked on the arm in his mouth, dragging the boy down to the left. Of course, he didn't open his jaws. After straddling the boy and blocking a blow from his left fist, Takaesu unleashed the bite strength of tiger-shark mode.

"Gugururu!"

The savage war cry escaped from his throat. The muscles around his jaws creaked. His fangs quivered under the terrible pressure.

However...

Just like three days earlier, the boy's shell neither strained nor bent. With a hardness that went beyond that of matter itself, it resisted the power of the tiger shark and refused to break down. The feeling in his mouth told him that he probably couldn't break it even if he went on biting it like this for dozens of seconds.

But you know, boy...I'm not the same as I was three days ago, either, he whispered to himself with the arm still between his teeth, the right corner of his mouth lifting in a sneer.

In the back of the frozen building, Takaesu had been near death. Although the burns around his mouth were healing, the overconsumption of energy could have killed him. What saved his life were the stainless steel bolts and nuts that had fallen on the floor here and there.

According to common sense, humans couldn't derive even a single calorie from metal whether they sucked on it or chewed it up. But there were living things in the world that consumed iron. These iron-oxidizing bacteria derived energy from converting bivalent iron to trivalent iron, and then they multiplied.

Takaesu didn't know if the same kind of mechanism was at work in his body. But the reality was that every time he ate one nut, his hunger subsided and the healing of his burns progressed.

Crawling around the dusty floor in the dark, Takaesu picked up the metal lumps one after another when his fingers brushed over them. Then he brought them to his mouth and devoured them. Like an infant with no self-awareness or a wild beast.

It was humiliating, yet at the same time it gave him a perverse sort of joy.

This was actually what eating was. Artfully crafted cuisine and decorated tables were nothing more than affectation.

At some point, the metal nuts had started to seem as sweet as candy and the bolts as appetizing as cookies. Takaesu went on devouring the metal like mad and fell into a deep sleep once again, his stomach full. He didn't have any more dreams of the past.

When before long dawn broke and he awoke feeling refreshed, his jaws were no longer transformed; they had returned to their usual shape. His injuries, which had probably been bad enough to call third-degree burns, had completely healed, and even when he moved he felt absolutely no pain. That wasn't all. All of his teeth had taken on a silvery gleam as if the metal had been incorporated into his tissue. When he flicked a tooth with his finger, it made a clear ringing sound.

Disguised as a jogger, Takaesu returned to his hotel and checked out after taking a shower. When he clutched the steering wheel of his Maserati in the underground parking lot, he already knew what to do next.

He was going to find that boy and locate his house. He would follow him and attack in a deserted area, or if that was difficult, he would take a family member as a hostage to lure the boy out. Considering the girl with the stun baton and the organization looming behind her,

Takaesu knew it was dangerous to stay in the city, but he couldn't let this go until he'd settled things with the boy.

He really was going to bite him this time. Because Takaesu had been reborn as a stronger, bigger, more beautiful shark.

"Guh, guhg, guhgugooo!!" Takaesu roared with the boy pinned down and his right arm still held in Takaesu's mouth.

The red eye pulsed furiously in the center of his lower jaw. His teeth and the bones, tendons, and muscles of his jaw all grew as hot as a flame.

With a strange *crunch, crunch, crunch!* sound, his jaws—no, his entire head—transformed. The burning pain and a pleasure many hundreds of times stronger pierced his body.

At long last…in the end…he could finally become that shark. The biggest meat-eating fish in history. The absolute ruler that reigned over the sea. Takaesu's second favorite shark. Scientific name: *Carcharocles megalodon*. English name: Megalodon.

* * *

Minoru looked up in shock at the Biter's face as it went through with its new transformation.

The jaws, which had until now stuck out more than ten centimeters more than a regular person's, grew bigger and longer. The bridge of the Biter's nose merged with the end of his upper jaw, drawing a smooth curve from his forehead to the back of his head. His eyes moved to the sides of his face, growing small and round. His neck also became oddly thick, and his necktie and the buttons of his shirt tore and popped off.

And his teeth, which had been double layered with a knifelike row and a sawlike row, became triangular like the points of huge, fixed swords.

The creature holding Minoru's right arm in his mouth was the perfected version of the shark man. From the neck down he was still a human wearing a suit, but all the skin visible to Minoru was dyed a bluish black.

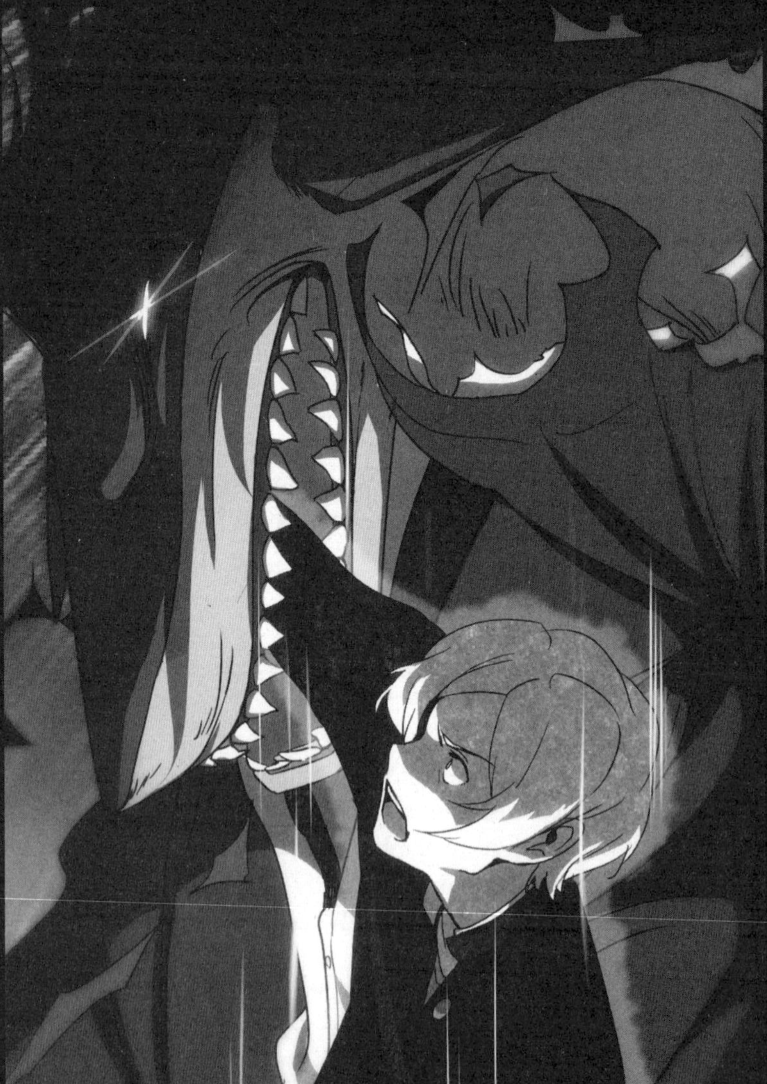

The jaws seemed to have reached a width of twenty centimeters, and thick bundles of muscle rippled on their sides. The teeth had a silver-gray, metallic luster, and they glinted in the moonlight.

It's no good. The shell is going to get crushed.

The moment Minoru sensed that, he shouted, "Whoooooa!!"

Up until now he had allowed his right arm to be bitten, but now he desperately thrust it deep into the man's mouth. His fingers—technically, the protective shell wrapped around his fingers—buried themselves in the soft tissue of the man's throat, and the shark man's head moved backward slightly.

In an instant, Minoru pulled his right arm back with all his might. He could feel the tips of the fangs grind against the invisible shell as he somehow managed to pull his arm out. In that moment, the upper and lower jaws crashed together with violent intensity and orange sparks flew through the soundless world.

This time the massive jaws came at him determined to latch onto his head, but Minoru evaded them by leaning to the left. With the same force, Minoru dealt a blow to the Biter's side with his right knee.

The moment the pressure on him lessened, Minoru rolled out from under the man and freed himself. He stood up, ran like he was going to go around behind the shark man, and put some distance between himself and the other man.

He could still breathe, but it was difficult. Was the oxygen inside the shell actually close to running out? He couldn't lose consciousness now, so he was forced to remove the protective shell.

The same moment the sole of his running shoe touched the steel sheeting, the thick stench of the Ruby Eye that had been growing all this time pressed in on him.

"...!"

It made him want to stop breathing involuntarily, but he endured it and took a deep breath.

Finally, the shark man staggered back to his feet and turned around. His height had grown as much as his head had enlarged, and he was probably at least 190 centimeters now. The muscles of his arms and legs had swollen as well, and the sleeves of his suit and the seams of his slacks were ripped in places. He had long ago lost his tie, and the buttons of his dress shirt had popped off all the way down to his stomach. The exposed muscles of his chest were just like that of a bodybuilder...no, a wild animal.

Even with more than five meters separating the two of them, he was overwhelmed by the man's physical power to destroy. Minoru picked up on it in the air. He inhaled another big breath and tried to activate the protective shell again.

But just a moment before he could, the Biter gave a twisted smile and spoke.

"Hah-hah-hah... It's too bad I can't see myself..."

It was an inhuman voice, a mix of hoarse bass notes and a lot of scraping noises. The form of the lips and teeth and tongue was indeed completely different from that of a human, so the words themselves were irrational. The monster, who seemed to have crawled out of a nightmare, went on speaking as he stared at Minoru with eyes that shone with a strange red luster.

"It almost makes me want to have you take a picture of me with your cell phone. Even if I told you what I ate to become like this, you probably wouldn't believe me, hah-hah."

The shark's mouth sneered. The exposed fangs gleamed viciously.

"By the way, *ragazzo*, I wonder if you know how many kilograms per tooth the occlusion strength...that is to say, the bite strength, of humans is?"

"..."

He gave his head a small shake. At this, the shark held up the index finger of his right hand professorially.

"Well, then, I'll tell you. For an adult male, it's about sixty kilograms, although there are individual differences. For lions, it's four hundred kilograms. For crocodiles and hippos, it reaches one thousand kilograms. Those are about the highest numbers for land animals."

"...Are you trying to say that your bite strength is around that much?" Minoru asked in a hoarse voice.

The Biter sneered again.

"Unfortunately, land creatures and such are irrelevant. The largest of the rulers of the sea, tiger sharks and great white sharks, have an occlusion strength of two thousand kilograms. You could say they are the strongest among modern animals... But as far as extinct species, there are some that surpassed them.

"The well-known dinosaur Tyrannosaurus rex apparently had an occlusion strength of five thousand kilograms. How extraordinary."

"What's your point?!" Minoru shouted.

He couldn't stand listening to the scholarly lines coming out of the shark man's mouth amid this nightmarish spectacle. He did have reasons to want to use up time, but he was also worried about Norie laid out there on the beam in midair. If the sleeping pills wore off and she woke up in a panic, she might fall from the beam.

But the Biter wagged the index finger he was holding up and continued speaking further.

"Don't be in such a hurry, *ragazzo*... Now then, did the strongest occlusion strength in history belong to T. rex? The answer is indeed no. In the oceans 5.5 million years earlier, there was a king that boasted an actual occlusion strength of fifteen thousand kilograms, three times that of T. rex. That's around fifteen tons per fang, probably enough to easily tear through even the thick skin of whales. Even you have probably heard of it. That absolute ruler was the most powerful shark and had a length of a little over ten meters...*Carcharocles megalodon!*"

His voice suddenly growing louder, the Biter shouted, "And now! The extinct Megalodon has risen above eternity and been resurrected! ...In other words, as me—!!"

The man's feet dashed against the steel plating with a *bang*.

The Biter sprang at Minoru with a speed unimaginable for such a massive body. Bounding to the left to avoid him, Minoru activated his ability again.

But this time, he wasn't certain that the protective shell would be able to keep those fearsomely huge teeth at bay. He could no longer use the strategy of attacking with his fists as he let the man bite him as much as he wanted.

If I make it home alive, I should find a way to look into just how many tons of force the shell can withstand.

After considering this somewhere in the corner of his mind, he shook the thoughts away. Right now he needed to focus on ways to defeat the monster that was right in front of him.

If the Biter's weapons were jaws that could bite through even iron, Minoru's weapons were his fists covered by the shell. On top of being able to punch without worrying about damage to his wrists or the bones of his hands, his fists were as hard as steel. Because of this, he could expect them to exert about as much power as a hit with a large hammer—if they connected.

"Wh...whoa!"

Minoru had stuck out a fist as he came around on the Biter's right side, but it flew through only air. The Biter had jumped out of the way in an agile movement. Minoru narrowly avoided the fangs that came at him a moment later. He swung his fist at the man once more, but he dodged it again.

He was aware that the big swings of his punches revealed him to be inexperienced. But Minoru, who really was a complete amateur, didn't have the faintest idea of how to punch. Little by little, the Biter began to evade Minoru's punches with room to spare, while Minoru began getting scraped by the Biter's fangs.

If things went on like this, he'd get caught eventually.

A weapon. Didn't he have any other weapons aside from his fists?

Kicks would probably be more powerful than punches, but they were out of the question. He'd either fall over the moment he kicked or his leg would be bitten.

If things were going to be like this, should he have brought a kitchen knife from home? No, if he put on the shell while holding a knife, it would be flung inward and he might cut himself.

What am I going to do? What can I—

As he barely continued to attack and defend, Minoru had at some point been driven to the eastern edge of the huge roof.

He couldn't go back any farther. Possibly realizing this, the Biter spread his arms wide and closed the gap between him and Minoru little by little.

He wouldn't be able to dodge the next attack. If he jumped back, he would fall to the terrace on the highest floor or to the road surrounding Saitama Super Arena if he really messed things up. From this location, it would be about a sixty-meter fall...

Wait.

Hadn't he already thought this through earlier? And from the other way around?

That was right. He did still have a weapon. A huge one that left no chance for escape.

Squatting down, he glanced to the right.

As if sensing that Minoru would try to escape that way, the Biter shifted his center of gravity as Minoru dove at him in one leap.

Norie, I'm coming right back, so just stay there for a little bit longer!!

As he spoke to his beloved sister inside his heart, Minoru bent his knees and pounced on the Biter. Pushing off from the plating of the roof as hard as he could with both feet, he leaped straight back.

Right on the verge of sinking his teeth into Minoru's face, the Biter's eyes grew huge. He stuck his left hand out behind him, but it was already too late.

Intertwined, the two men who possessed Third Eyes shot off the edge of the roof.

* * *

Absolute faith in his own power.

Takaesu in Megalodon mode had that unshakable faith, but he hadn't thought that the boy did as well. His reason for thinking this was that the boy had made awkward escape after awkward escape, not allowing his shell to be bitten.

That's why Takaesu hadn't imagined this. He hadn't imagined that the boy would actually fling himself off a roof sixty meters high, taking Takaesu with him.

"Graaa!" Takaesu roared in a mixture of rage and horror as he desperately tried to grab hold of the roof's edge.

But his outstretched fingers only grazed the concrete beam.

Directly below the roof, there was a terrace on the top floor that connected to the emergency stairs. But with this amount of force, they would fly past it and fall all the way to the ground dozens of meters farther down.

When he'd chosen the roof of Saitama Super Arena as the location for the battle, he had of course considered the risk of falling. However, be that as it may, the roof was about thirty thousand square meters wide. As long as they fought in the center of it, there would be no way to fall, and the boy wasn't likely to go near the edge, either.

He couldn't believe that, despite his predictions, he'd gotten so absorbed in the hunt that he drove the boy to the edge...or that the boy had sprung on him without Takaesu seeing through his plan to take them both down together.

How foolish. How foolish. Had even his brain actually become that of a shark?

It was too late for regrets. Somehow, he had to minimize the damage from the fall. To do that, he could use the boy as a cushion...

No, no, that wasn't right. The boy was wrapped in a shell harder than iron. If Takaesu fell on top of that it would double the impact. He had to get away from the boy. He had to get away and fall on top of the bushes or the trees lining the street.

After running through all of those thoughts in an instant, Takaesu tried to push off the boy who clung to him. But the boy's arms had a tight hold on him and Takaesu couldn't peel them away.

The ground was coming up fast already. The spot where they were falling was a wide sidewalk bordering the eastern edge of Saitama Super Arena. He wouldn't be able to avoid smashing into the asphalt. The only thing he could do now was believe in the power the eye had given him...no, in the power he had found on his own within himself.

He would endure it. He would survive.

"Grrooooo!!"

As he released a fierce roar at the rapidly approaching ground, Takaesu stiffened all of the muscles in his body.

Impact.

First, everything he could see turned a pure white, then immediately went black.

* * *

Since the Biter had twisted his body right before they hit, Minoru landed on the road on his left shoulder.

There was the feeling of a sudden slowing and the feeling of pressure as if the core of his body was being pushed on. *That was all.*

He'd made a huge crater in the asphalt, yet Minoru hadn't even felt an impact, let alone pain. The invisible protective shell had completely blocked the fatal blow to Minoru's body that a sixty-meter vertical drop would have dealt him.

What in the world is this shell?

This was the first time that Minoru had felt something akin to fear about his ability, but even that was only for an instant. Right now, he was nothing but thankful. Because the Biter, who'd fallen at the same time on his right shoulder, was lying a little way away on the road, unmoving.

An inky black pool of blood was spreading out underneath his massive body. The tips of his hands and feet alone were convulsing with irregular twitches.

He was dead—or was he? Had the "weapon that left no chance for escape" Minoru used—in other words, the asphalt-covered ground— destroyed the Ruby Eye who was so proud of his menacing power and toughness?

That would mean I killed him.

The realization came on him suddenly, and he deactivated his power without thinking. The soles of his shoes stepped on asphalt debris, making a gritty, crunching noise.

There should have been an unbelievably deafening noise when they fell, but a complete silence hung over the world.

On the right was the wall of Saitama Super Arena. On the left was a road hemmed in by train tracks. Geographically, the only ones who would enter this road were cars headed for Saitama Super Arena's underground parking lot, and the parking lot had already closed quite a few hours ago. There was no sign of security guards or police running over, either.

Minoru stood still for a while, hearing only the sound of the northerly wind shaking the leaves on the trees lining the street.

Fight the Biter and take him down… He had intended to harden his resolve to do just that. But now he realized that he hadn't been prepared enough to consider what it meant to take him down.

Unconsciously, he had been avoiding the word *kill*. It had been the same as a message in an RPG to defeat a monster, to punish it.

Ultimately, Minoru hadn't been able to look reality full in the face until the very end…

As he thought this, Minoru cautiously took one step toward the Biter, then another.

The Ruby Eye was lying facedown. His head was still the sharply pointed one of a shark. Even the hair that remained on the back of his head had become blue and needlelike. If he was going to stay like this, not returning to his human form, how could his body be disposed of? And was it even Minoru's responsibility? But how would he do it?

As Minoru considered this, taking another step forward, it happened.

He heard a weak yet strange sound.

Crack, crack, crack. Crunch, crunch, crunch. Like something hard being crushed. No, to be precise—like something hard being crushed by teeth.

"—!!"

His eyes widening in horror, Minoru jumped back a step.

A moment later, the Biter's huge body moved as if it were on a spring. When his sturdy right arm slid out like a serpent and grabbed Minoru's right ankle, Minoru flung it off with all his might. Without even time to put on the shell, he plunged backward into the bushes between the sidewalk and the roadway.

Minoru couldn't get up immediately. Right before his eyes, the Ruby Eye he had just believed to be dead dragged himself up.

He had taken serious damage. There was no doubt about that. His white shirt was dark with blood, and blood still dripped from his lower jaw. But something else was also dropping to the ground. The Biter's mouth kept making tiny movements, and from the corners of it, fine little pieces fell one after another.

Crunch, crunch, crack, crack.

He was eating. The street. Lumps of asphalt.

When Minoru looked, there was a large hole at the Biter's feet. It wasn't one that had been created by the man's fall. He had bitten it open with his massive fangs.

"...*Cattivo*," the Biter spat.

Minoru couldn't even identify what language the word was from. The shark man lifted his face, and the edges of his mouth twisted in a smile.

"...Well, I suppose there are similarities between the main component of asphalt, hydrocarbon, and the main component of rice and bread, carbohydrate. Once you eat them, isn't it all the same?"

"...You can't... No matter how much of a shark you are, there's no way you could digest asphalt...," Minoru muttered blankly, still toppled over.

As he did so, the countless lacerations carved into the Biter's upper body closed up little by little.

His ability to recover was unbelievable.

"Ha-ha... Don't underestimate a shark's power of digestion. Sharks can also recover from wounds that would instantly kill any other fish," the Biter claimed as if he had read Minoru's thoughts. "...But it is true that a fall from that height was a bit much to bear... It would be an annoyance to climb up there again; should I have you reschedule for a new time and place? You can just keep lying there."

Turning to face the other way, the Biter started walking slowly. As far as Minoru could tell from the way he was avoiding using his right shoulder and dragging his right foot, there was definitely still remaining damage.

In the direction the Biter was heading was the slope that continued down to the underground parking lot. Did he have his car parked inside? If he took the car, there was obviously no way Minoru could catch him by running.

Minoru should finish him off while he was hurt. If he lost sight of him here, he would probably go after Tomomi or Norie once his wounds were healed.

Even though he understood that in his mind, Minoru stayed buried in the bushes, unable to move.

He wouldn't be taking him down, he would be killing him. Although he was this strangely formed shark man now, Minoru would be taking the life of someone who had started off human. The weight of that action pressed down on Minoru and drained the power from his limbs.

I can't do it. There's no way I could kill a person. I never once considered something like that. I didn't even imagine it. That's why it's impossible. I can't fight any more than this.

And even the Biter might have been just a normal person before he had encountered the Third Eye. If mental interference affected him and he was forced to kill people in a so-called brainwashed state, then do I have the right to punish him for those sins?

That's right... I can't do it. Whether it's the Biter or anyone else, taking someone's life by my own choice... That's not something I'm...

No. That was wrong.

There was just one person who Minoru could kill without a moment's hesitation if he had the chance. Minoru had within him a murderous intent that would never disappear no matter how much time passed.

The perpetrator who took the lives of his father, mother, and sister. The perpetrator who hadn't been caught even after eight years had passed. Minoru didn't know what they looked like or what their name was or even their gender, but whatever the person was like and whatever the circumstances were, that was the only person he could kill.

He wanted to kill them. He wanted to kill them in the most brutal way possible.

The Biter had done the same thing. He himself said that he had already killed four people before he attacked Tomomi Minowa. Whether he was or was not being manipulated by the Third Eye, that didn't change those facts.

The victims probably had families, too. Families pushed down into the same abyss of grief, anguish, and despair as Minoru.

It did have something to do with him. It did matter.

Even if he didn't have the right, Minoru had the duty. The duty to take down—no, *kill*—the Biter here and prevent him from taking the next victim.

The Biter had already finished descending the gentle slope and was now making his way into the parking lot. The lot's business hours were over, so the interior was pitch-black. His huge back sunk down slowly into the darkness—

Balling up his fists and clenching his back teeth, Minoru tore himself away from the bushes.

He stood up. He put his left foot forward. He pushed off from the pavement with determination.

He ran. He dashed down the long slope, came out through the

pedestrian walkway next to the bar gate, and ran into the underground parking lot.

There were almost no cars in the large space dimly lit by green emergency lights. But at the Biter's destination was parked a large sports car with a flashy exterior.

Pouring every last ounce of determination into his voice, Minoru yelled out to the large figure that swayed irregularly.

"Wait!!"

The strange silhouette came to a sudden stop.

"Are you going to run away with your tail between your legs because of a little fall from a roof?!"

The figure was briefly still, then slowly turned around.

"...Run away...?"

Deep in the darkness, his eyes gave off a red light.

"Ha-ha-ha... What daring things you say, especially when you yourself fled in panic on the roof like a little sardine."

"Yeah. But I won't run anymore! Right here, I'm going to...kill you!!"

Minoru's declaration reverberated through the large parking garage.

The red eyes gave one slow blink. Minoru was struck by the feeling of the temperature plummeting but gathered his mental strength and continued to stand his ground.

"...Kill me...? You, the prey...are going to kill me, the predator...?"

The Biter took a step forward with his right foot, the sound of it solemn.

"Are you saying that you, with only that single thin layer of that measly shell, are going to kill me, the truly superior species...?"

Next came his left foot. The black figure was becoming larger at a speed beyond what could be accounted for by perspective.

"I can't allow that... I'll have to teach you just how foolish and sinful those words are..."

The Biter's muscles bulged as his bones squealed. His countless fangs glinted viciously in the hazy light.

"I'll bite you... I'll bite you...bite you, bite you, bite you, bite you, bite yoooou—!!"

With this strange war cry, his massive body leaped into the air.

At the same time, Minoru pushed off from the concrete floor, too.

He activated the shell. He clenched his right fist as hard as he possibly could.

"Waaaaaaah—!!" Minoru screamed as he drove his fist toward the shark that was descending on him from directly above.

The fist wrapped in the shell smashed into the tip of the Biter's pointed nose. The bluish-black skin split, tears radiating outward, and huge amounts of blood sprayed into the air. But after the shark turned his head to the left and deflected the fist, he opened his jaws as far as they could go and took Minoru's entire head into his mouth.

   ✳ ✳ ✳

Rage.

A rage like something he had never felt before—a fierce rage that surpassed even what he had felt when his mouth was being scorched by the girl's stun baton raced through Takaesu's entire body.

Was it because he'd gotten caught up in the boy's plan and taken an unsightly fall?

Was it because he'd been in such a mess that he'd eaten asphalt to heal his wounds?

Was it because the boy had rained those disgraceful words down on him, saying that he'd fled with his tail between his legs?

It was, and it wasn't. This rage had existed deep in Takaesu many hours before…since the time he'd raided the boy's house and abducted that woman, the boy's adoptive sister.

Truthfully, he'd intended to kill her right away.

Compressing her carotid sinus would do nothing more than knock her out for a few minutes. This time he would be passing through the center of an urban area, so it would be a nuisance if she came to in the trunk of the car. He would be killing the boy right away anyway, so as long as she seemed to be alive when looked at from a distance—no, even if the boy spotted that she was dead, it wouldn't be much of a problem.

But once he had silently chewed through the key cylinder, opened the door to slip inside, and stood behind the woman as she made dinner preparations in the kitchen, Takaesu was overcome by a certain indescribable sensation. He hadn't even been able to recall what he came there to do.

As she checked the heat of the gas stove where she'd placed a frying pan, she spoke to Takaesu in a bright voice as he stood there behind her. "Welcome back, Mii. You came in so quietly today. Wait just a minute; I'll get dinner ready right away."

In reality, Takaesu probably stood frozen behind her for only about a second. But in that second, he felt waves of confusion and turmoil like he'd never experienced before. It might have had something to do with the atmosphere that filled that space.

The smell of freshly cooked rice billowing out from the rice cooker. The light sound of oil popping in the frying pan. The apron strings swaying along the woman's small back.

The atmosphere that these things came together to create should have been something unreachable for Takaesu. Still, he was enveloped by the sensation that he had returned home from a place that was cold and dark.

Someone was speaking to him with a smile on her face as she sat in a chair on the other side of the table, which would soon be set with rows of dishes.

As a reward for getting 100 percent, I made your favorite spaghetti and meatballs today, Hika. Eat a lot and chew it well...

Once he had become aware of things again, Takaesu had his right arm wrapped around the woman's neck and was carefully pressing on her carotid sinus. When the strength soon drained from her petite body, he laid her gently on the floor.

This wasn't what he had planned. Knowing this, he tried to make himself break her cervical vertebrae, but his right hand around her thin neck could only tremble and didn't have an ounce of strength in it.

Since the red eye had come to dwell in his body, Takaesu had already taken the lives of four people. And when he'd tied up his prey on the big dining table in the basement of the villa and chewed on their bones from the feet up, he hadn't felt a bit of hesitation.

But no matter how many times he tried to put some force into his right hand, the muscles of his arm would only quiver, not obeying Takaesu's will. The eye pounded in his lower jaw and called for him to kill her, kill her. But this voice that had always been pleasant now brought only a dull pain in the center of his head.

Unable to avoid changing his plan, he'd had the vaguely conscious woman take some of his valuable barbiturate sleeping pills.

Then he shoved her in the large suitcase that he had originally prepared to carry her corpse in. He went so far as to leave the zipper open a bit to keep her from suffocating.

He left a message for the boy on the tablet he had found in the dining room and left the house. He piled the suitcase into the back of the minivan that he had parked nearby. The car was something that he'd stolen yesterday up north. His beloved Maserati would attract too much attention, and the trunk was small. He'd also had another motive for the trip.

By the time he was gripping the steering wheel and starting to drive toward the new city center, he had stopped thinking about the reason his right hand hadn't worked.

But deep in his subconscious, he already knew. It was a fact he never wanted to admit to. The fact that he hadn't been able to kill the woman even though he'd planned to was because he sensed in her the aura of a mother.

Takaesu had killed his real mother the day he graduated from college. For twenty-two years, she had been his ruler, constantly giving him countless commands and refusals, pains and humiliations. Now he had removed her from existence.

He took the plan he had perfected over time and put it in action. The moment he did, the only things that existed inside his heart were hatred and bitterness at having had his teeth pulled out with pliers. In the six years since then, he had never once regretted it.

That's why this was unacceptable. It was unacceptable for him to feel something maternal in the woman, who was nothing more than bait to lure the boy out.

Because he, Hikaru Takaesu, was the superior species that had discarded all worthless emotions. Because he was a predator who swam elegantly through the city hunting humans as prey.

He would prove it.

After he broke open both the shell and the boy's head, he would return to the roof of the arena and bite the woman to death as well. If he did that, Takaesu would wipe out the weakness left within him.

"Garraaaa!!"

Channeling an energy that was probably rage into a roar and dispersing it, Takaesu bit. And bit and bit.

Every time the boy's swinging fists hit his chest and shoulders, his muscles were crushed and his bones creaked, but he ignored the pain and continued to bite.

"Grrrooooooo!!"

Another hoarse howl shot from his throat. The eye in his lower jaw was pulsing stronger than it ever had before, and something hot permeated his entire mouth. The tendons and muscle connecting his upper and lower jawbones made a stretching noise as they enlarged.

Takaesu's mouth already took up more than 70 percent of his head. The fangs grew bigger and bigger. They grew thicker. The roots of his teeth penetrated deeper and deeper into the alveolar ridge so that they could endure the intense pressure. A pain shot through his nerves, worse than what he had felt when the stun baton burned him.

Despite this...

The boy's shell continued blocking Takaesu's teeth without even a sound of protest.

Even if this was a supernatural phenomenon created by the eye, the shell was made of some sort of matter. So, then, was it really possible for it to take this much pressure without deforming even a little?

No. It shouldn't be. If he mustered just a little more strength...just a little more, it would certainly break.

He heard a strange clicking sound coming from inside his body. Unable to take the extraordinary pressure, the bones of his jaw were cracking and being restored immediately. Tendons and muscles were being created by the same process, and every time his skin split and then closed, drops of blood went flying.

And yet—the shell didn't break.

It was so hard it was unreasonable. This was certainly the final test that Takaesu would be put through. The moment he bit through the boy's shell, the weakness in his spirit that couldn't shake off the phantom of his mother even now would fade away. Then Takaesu could become a true predator...a real shark.

That's right, I...I am a shark.

Takaesu's favorite shark. The shark he identified with more strongly than the mako shark, which swam the fastest; the tiger shark, which could break open even sea turtle shells; and the emperor Megalodon, which was the most powerful.

That was the gray nurse shark.

It belonged to the order Lamniformes and the family Odontaspididae. It was a maximum of about three meters, almost never attacked humans, and had an incredibly ordinary form.

But among the approximately five hundred species of sharks, there was only one characteristic that no shark but the gray nurse shark had: oophagy, cannibalism.

Gray nurse shark fetuses eat not only unfertilized eggs, but also other shark embryos in their mother's womb.

Takaesu was the same.

From the earliest time he could remember, his mother had told him over and over that he should have been twins, a boy and a girl. Hikaru and Akari. Apparently they'd even picked a name for her.

But the only one born was Takaesu. He didn't know what specifically had happened, but as a result of some little mishap in early pregnancy, one twin was absorbed into the other—namely, Takaesu. It was a rare phenomenon called "vanishing twin," and it seemed to be an underlying cause of his parents' divorce as well.

Whenever she could, his mother would tell him, *You have to work hard and eat enough for little Akari, too.* When she was enraged, sometimes she would go as far as to say, *After all, you ate her.*

He was in third grade when he learned about the ecology of the gray nurse shark from a field guide in the library.

He had thought, *It's the same as me.*

I'm not human. I've always been a shark. That's why I ate my sister inside Mama's belly.

If I'm a shark, it's okay if I don't have friends. It's okay if I have to have sardines as a snack.

I'm a shark. I'm a shark.

After his mother had pulled out nearly all of his teeth with pliers, those magic words were the only thing that gave him emotional support. Sharks lost and replaced teeth endlessly throughout their lives. So someday, he'd get new teeth, too.

Three months ago, the magic words had come true.

And now the time to prove that truth had come.

He could admit it; the boy's shell was essentially the hardest of any material in existence. But Takaesu's teeth were the strongest of anything ever created.

When he bit the shell open, Takaesu would go over the final wall. He would shed all human weakness and human foolishness and become a real shark.

"Garaaaaaaa—!!" Takaesu howled from his throat, which was starting to close up from the continuing enlargement of his muscle fibers.

As his mouth continued the cycle of destruction and regeneration, a spurt of blood like a flame burst forth from it.

Suddenly, all sound disappeared. It was as if even his inner ear had been converted to muscle.

What do I care? Just make everything into jaws.

The moment after he thought this, he felt a sensation like both eyes bursting as his vision was enveloped in darkness.

The taste of blood disappeared. The metallic smell disappeared as well. The pain that made his face feel like it was burning disappeared.

I'll give it to you! I'll give it all to you!

Takaesu screamed inside himself in silence.

I'll give you everything, so take that hopelessly hard...hard...

What? What am I biting? Why can't I remember...?

My brain... Even my brain is turning to muscle...

The only thing that was left was the sensation of something warm pulsing in the core of his body. The pulsing intruded all the way into his brain and changed to muscle, taking away his memories and sensations.

Inside Takaesu, the memory of becoming a predator three months ago disappeared. The memories of his six years of success as a gourmet food critic disappeared. The memories of going through his student days desperately hiding the fact that he had dentures disappeared.

The memories of his mother pulling his teeth out with pliers, his mother making him memorize his multiplication tables, his mother making him chew on sardines, his mother praising him for getting a hundred on a test disappeared.

The memories of his father giving him candy on the day they said good-bye and the memories of taking a walk with his father on the riverside as they held hands disappeared.

Takaesu's head was now nothing but an enormous mouth and a clump of muscle fibers to move it. There was a thunderous howl not belonging to a human.

A huge volume of blood spurted from him. All of his muscles contracted, pushing past their limits—

In the next instant, his jaw made a stuttering motion. Countless silver lights scattered, twinkling beautifully as they flew through the air.

What had broken was not the boy's shell, but the teeth that gave Takaesu his identity.

Immediately after...

The lump of flesh that had been the face and head and brain of the human Hikaru Takaesu burst open with violent force. Dark blood and chunks of flesh were blown outward like a waterfall. One of the teeth that was mixed in there shot into the ceiling of the parking lot and carved a deep hole in it.

The body had lost the entire head, and only part of the lower jaw remained. It slid wetly down that transparent shell, which had held out to the end without so much as a sound of protest, and fell to the asphalt.

＊ ＊ ＊

He heard an irregular chattering sound.

That's strange. I should only be able to hear that bizarre heavy bass sound inside the shell, Minoru thought vaguely until he finally realized the source of the noise was his own teeth.

He was completely unable to stop the shaking of any of the muscles in his body, not just those in his jaw. It was like ice water ran in his veins instead of blood. He was numb and tingly from head to toe, so much so that it was a mystery how he was still standing.

This was the second time—no, maybe the third time—he'd been this close to death in his short sixteen years of life.

On that night eight years ago, Minoru had been hiding in the storage compartment under the pantry floor and didn't see the murderer's face. Minoru had always regretted that, but after being this close to the literal "jaws of death," he could do nothing but stand frozen in fear.

The Biter's rows of teeth that had so solidly held on to Minoru's head were instruments of destruction. Their dull gleam concealed over-whelming power. Each of the massive teeth was like a blade honed with many layers of malice and murderous desire.

He had thought it was over. That there was no way the shell could hold off that kind of power.

In that short time, he even imagined how things would go the moment the shell was disabled. Would it shatter into countless frag-ments like glass? Would it be stretched out like rubber? Or would it pop and disappear in an instant like a bubble? And when would that time come?

He would kill the Biter. Minoru had already resolved to do that much. But he hadn't known that battling to kill or be killed would be so terrifying or so grotesque. It was a clash of naked hostility with-out even a shred of heroism.

Of course, there was hatred inside Minoru, too. Hatred for the per-son who'd killed his family. Hatred for the Biter who'd tried to kill Tomomi and Norie. He didn't think that the energy of those hatreds was weaker than the hatred the Biter aimed at him.

But whether he could channel it into power was another question altogether. The Biter used hatred and murderous desire as energy to fight. This made Minoru realize that he wasn't equipped with the cir-cuits for that. Or maybe that was exactly the difference between Jet Eyes and Ruby Eyes.

That's why Minoru hadn't even been able to heave a sigh of relief, let alone raise a cry of victory, when the Biter's head caved in as if his inability to control his own excessive murderous desires imploded it, or even when the man's massive body had collapsed to the floor as it scattered huge amounts of blood and flesh.

"...This...," Minoru whispered as he watched blood like black rain pour down on the shell that had protected him to the end. "...This..."

...*Isn't a fight*. That's what he wanted to say, but the words wouldn't come out.

The Ruby Eye Biter was dead.

His ruthless, headless corpse lay on the ground. All of the memories he had built up scattered meaninglessly and left the world. And this was indeed something Minoru had done. Even if he had only stood there, Minoru had killed the Biter using his own power.

Was this the inescapable conclusion? Or did another option exist?

No voice answered these questions. Minoru averted his gaze from the corpse on the floor before him and staggered up. This action sent every last drop of the blood that had pooled in a hollow of his shell dripping down to the parking lot pavement.

When he deactivated the protective shell after retreating a few steps, the sick smell of blood pressed in on him and Minoru screwed up his face. He had hesitations about leaving the Biter's body on the floor like it was, but nothing could be done about it now. He had to hurry back up to the roof of the arena and rescue Norie from atop the beam—

The violently expanding air beat against Minoru's back. Then the sound of the synthetic rubber soles of someone's shoes scraping against the asphalt echoed. He nearly put the shell on again reflexively, but stopped himself and turned around.

Standing at the nearest end of the slope that led to the exit of the parking lot was the high school girl wearing a black blazer. It was Yumiko. The only thing he knew about the Jet Eye was her name. Just like three days ago, she had a large stun baton in her right hand.

Running her gaze over the Biter's body on the ground and Minoru standing far back, she brought the watch with communication capabilities to her mouth and whispered a brief message.

"DD, I found him. The underground parking lot."

She dropped her left arm and jogged over with a stern expression. Her small lips moved to speak.

But the one who spoke first was Minoru. He hurled words at her in a volume that surprised even him; he was almost shouting.

"How can you show up when everything's over?!"

The reason Minoru had tried to use up time before beginning the fight with the Biter was that he had anticipated—no, expected—that Yumiko and DD would notice the smell of the Ruby Eye.

It was selfish of Minoru to expect a rescue when he had refused to work with the two of them. He had that much self-awareness, but he just couldn't keep himself from yelling.

"Didn't you tell me?! Didn't you say you'd find the Biter?! So why... are you so late...!"

"..."

After biting her slightly parted lips harshly, Yumiko asked in a low, restrained voice, "So you fought the Biter alone? Are you all right? You're not hurt?"

The unexpected question knocked the wind out of his sails and he nodded.

"...I'm not in any pain at the moment..."

"I see. Just in case, I'll make arrangements to have you taken to the hospital."

After returning the stun baton to the holster on her right leg, Yumiko started to raise the wristwatch to her mouth again.

"Oh, w-wait!" he broke in hurriedly. He was hesitant to rely on her after his yelling, but he couldn't say so. He turned his gaze to Yumiko and explained quickly.

"My sister was left behind on the roof. The Biter attacked her and made her take some medicine... I have to hurry and save her, then take her to the hospital—"

But Yumiko held up her left hand to interrupt the rambling Minoru, then nodded.

"It's okay, DD brought your sister down from the roof. She doesn't have any wounds, and her vitals are strong."

"...I-I see..."

He breathed a sigh of relief.

Holding up her watch, Yumiko contacted someone as she walked toward Minoru.

"We're done here. The Biter is no longer active. The kid's all right, but we're going to have him seen to just in case. Bring the car around to the underground parking lot once you've recovered the rescue target."

After ending the call, she turned her gaze to the strange figure of the body on the ground a little way off. Next, she looked up at the roof, making an expression as if she had been convinced of something.

"The car will come right away... I'd like to confirm something, just in case... The Biter... You were the one who...?"

"...Yes. I'm the one who...killed him."

"Huh," she answered briefly.

Yumiko looked straight at Minoru. He did his best to look back into her eyes, so deep and dark they seemed to see straight down to the bottom of his soul.

He thought she would probably reprimand him like she had three days ago. That was because, although he had let his emotions get the better of him when he shouted at Yumiko earlier, he was aware that 70 percent of what had brought on Norie's abduction by the Biter was his own negligence and thoughtlessness.

But Yumiko defied his expectations, her long hair swinging as she bowed low.

"I'm sorry. We're in the wrong this time. Yesterday, the Biter broke into a construction company in Kumagaya. There was no one there since it was Sunday, but one car was stolen. DD and I interpreted this as him escaping to the north, so we took Route 17 up there... But today we finally realized it was a feint and came back. Judging him to be an impulsive-type Ruby Eye because of the tendencies associated with his MO and ability was our mistake..."

"..."

This was a drastic change compared to three days ago. Minoru was confused by Yumiko's attitude, which could even be considered admirable.

His rage from a few minutes ago seemed to have completely dissipated as he listened to her explain. In its place, a doubt rose up in his mind.

"But...you have a so-called teleportation ability, don't you? If you used that, couldn't you have transported yourself in an instant...?" he asked.

At this, Yumiko gave a faint, wry smile and shook her head.

"My power is different than what you'd call teleportation. How can I put it...? It amplifies my ability to accelerate and just moves me straight ahead. I can't go through obstacles or anything, so there's no way I could use it to travel long distances. If I collided with a building or a car while accelerating, I'd probably die."

Minoru nodded, thinking that was probably why she hadn't been able to chase the Biter as he ran through the bushes three days earlier.

"So... That's what it is, huh? The Third Eye abilities are kind of... useful and inconvenient at the same time...," Minoru muttered, thinking of how he couldn't hear any sound from outside the protective shell when he activated it.

"Just what standards are used to determine the powers..."

"Oh, that... It's based on the memories of the Third Eye's host...," Yumiko began to say, looking down.

The sound of an engine coming down the slope interrupted the conversation.

What appeared was an ordinary black minivan. After the van entered the underground parking lot, the engine stopped and the driver's side door opened. DD jumped down wearing a camo-print vest just like the one he had on three days ago, although this one seemed to be a black-and-gray one for night missions.

He slightly lifted the brim of a baseball cap in the same color and beckoned to Minoru once he had seen him. Yumiko nodded, too, so Minoru jogged over to the car.

When DD opened the left rear sliding door, Minoru's eyes flew to the petite figure laying on top of the fully folded-down rear seats.

"...Norie!" he shouted in a strangled voice, bending his upper body into the car.

After clutching her in his arms frantically and bringing her out of the car, he knelt down on the floor and spoke to her again.

"Norie... Are you okay? Norie!"

The body of his adoptive sister, wrapped in a light Windbreaker to maintain her body temperature, was shockingly light. Her eyelids were still closed and her face looked white as a sheet under the emergency lights. He had a feeling that her lips moved ever so slightly at Minoru's voice, but she didn't regain consciousness.

"She's still under the influence of the sleeping meds right now, but there's no danger to her life, kid," DD said.

Clapping Minoru on the shoulder as if to reassure him, DD walked over to the Biter's body on the ground a little way away.

He peered into the huge open wound and then looked up to the ceiling. As if he understood what had happened from this alone, he bowed his head with the same serious attitude as Yumiko.

"Sorry, kid... And thank you. We'll make our apologies and

acknowledgments again another time. First, we gotta get you and your sister to the hospital. You okay with letting us pick the location like we usually do?"

"Y...yes."

When Minoru nodded, DD turned his gaze to Yumiko.

"I asked the chief to collect the Biter's body. He was just on his way to the hospital, so I'm having him drop by here first. I think he'll be here in like twenty minutes, so can ya stand by here till then, Yumii?"

For a moment, Yumiko made a disgusted face at the thought of being left in a dark underground parking lot with a corpse, but she nodded in compliance.

"All right. For now, just hurry up and take these two to the hospital."

"Got it, got it. —Oh yeah, just a quick check first to be sure. Kid, the Biter's Third Eye disengaged, right?"

"D-disengaged?"

Unaware of what the word meant, Minoru tilted his head.

"Disengaging is a phenomenon where, after a host dies, the Third Eye leaves the body and floats into the sky as it glows," Yumiko explained. "It nearly always happens the moment the heart stops."

"Uh...into the sky...?" Minoru muttered as he looked up.

Yumiko and DD looked up just the same. The ceiling, covered in concrete and exposed piping, had a dark hole with a diameter of about five centimeters bored into it. But it wasn't the Third Eye that had made it.

Bringing his face back down, Minoru spoke as he recalled his memories of a few minutes earlier.

"Um...the Biter's head was blown off in front of me... His body collapsed just like that... But I don't think there were any glowing things flying around..."

Hearing this, Yumiko's eyes grew wide.

"Oh, but there's a hole there."

"One of the Biter's teeth that was blown off embedded itself in there and left the mark. See, if you look closely, you can see something silvery deep in—"

Before Minoru could finish his sentence, Yumiko yelled, "This is bad, DD, it didn't disengage! We have to extract the Third Eye fast or…!"

Simultaneously, the three of them looked at the headless corpse of the Biter laying a little way off.

The head was still missing. But at some point, it had stopped being a corpse.

The right arm, bent at a strange angle, was trembling as its fingers dug into the pavement. It was trying to lift up the torso.

Unable to believe what was happening right before his eyes, Minoru just blinked over and over as he clutched Norie's body to him tightly. But the thing that used to be the Biter's corpse didn't stop moving. It tried to distance its torso from the ground with awkward movements, the joints of its arm making disgusting crunching noises.

The bleeding from the neck had mostly stopped already. A large amount of viscous liquid oozed from the massive lower jaw, half of which remained, covering the exposed cross section. Foamy pink bubbles continued to rise up and then burst; was it because air was going in and out of the trachea?

"…But… It doesn't even have a head…," Minoru whispered in a hoarse voice.

The Biter had compared himself to a shark. But there was no way any shark could live after losing its brain.

Despite this, the thing that had been a corpse just a few dozen seconds earlier was moving more and more intensely. Finally, even its legs were shaking, and once the soles of its shoes touched the ground, it tried to stagger to its feet.

Thick new flesh was rising from the place where the head had come off, fusing with what remained of the lower jaw as it widened into a shape that resembled a trumpet. Minoru thought it looked exactly like the mouth of a lamprey—but immediately after this crossed his mind, countless sharp teeth grew in, bursting through the writhing flesh.

With a *whoosh*, air mixed with a mist of blood erupted from the dark hole that had been the Biter's esophagus.

Every time the broad chest moved like a bellows, blood that had flowed into the trachea was expelled.

After these motions continued for a few seconds, the thing that had been the Biter suddenly stopped moving.

Underneath the round "mouth," some of the flesh moved around, wet with mucus—

Deep within the flesh that had divided into left and right like a vertically opening eyelid, it was just as if a red, glowing orb was showing its face. Even Minoru immediately understood that it was the Third Eye that had latched on to the Biter.

That was definitely an eye. Its color and structure were completely different from a human eye, but he clearly felt the magnetic gaze it gave off.

Next to Minoru, DD gave a low groan.

"Is this...a physical transformation–type Ruby Eye doing a runaway? It's like...a completely different creature..."

"A...runaway...?" Minoru asked in return.

Not looking at him, DD explained in a hoarse voice, "That's what we call it. When a host takes a fatal wound and their heart stops, Third Eyes normally disengage right away. But in some cases when the brain takes serious damage but the body's still fine, the Third Eye itself starts to control the body."

"What happens...after that...?"

"In all the earlier cases without exception, the Ruby Eyes started to attack living things around them indiscriminately. But their hearts stopped right away because of massive blood loss and they disengaged."

"B...but his bleeding's already stopped..."

"This is the first time we've seen a runaway with a Ruby Eye that transformed its own body like the Biter did. The fact that it can heal wounds this bad... Seems like even if we wait..."

"It seems pointless to wait," Yumiko whispered in a resolute tone, finishing DD's thought.

"I can't imagine it surviving for long, but this doesn't seem like a situation where we can expect an immediate disengagement, either. We have to do something about it before that thing gets out into the city or something."

"Something...like what?"

"Kill it again."

Yumiko looked at Minoru with completely calm eyes.

"It's okay, DD and I will take care of it. Get out of the parking garage with your sister."

"B...but will you be okay against that guy with only the stun baton...?"

As they were talking, the monster was trying to complete even more transformations.

Its arms grew thick like a bodybuilder's, the sleeves of its suit ripped all the way to the shoulders, and the expensive-looking watch on its left wrist popped off into the air like it was nothing. The centers of its enlarged hands split horizontally, and it looked like sharp fangs were growing from there, too. It seemed like the hands alone, not to mention the round mouth on the head, could break Yumiko's favorite stun baton with no problem.

But Yumiko nodded with an expression of determination, and a faint smile played at the corners of her lips.

"I'll show you how my ability is really used," she said, hiking her skirt far up with her right hand. A holster of a different shape from the one on her right leg was attached to the upper part of her slender left leg. From it she pulled out a large combat knife with a *shing* sound.

The blade, imposingly thick and easily twenty centimeters long, glinted in the glow of the emergency lights.

Slowly leaning forward, Yumiko whispered in a low voice, "DD, cover me."

"I'm supposed to be behind-the-scenes support, but sure...," he grumbled.

DD stuck his right hand into the bottom of his camo-print vest and, surprisingly, pulled out a small handgun. It was automatic and equipped at the end with a tube that seemed like a silencer. That's all Minoru knew, but if DD was bringing it out in this situation, it had to be real. He took the safety off with an experienced hand and pulled back the slide with a slight *shick* sound.

When DD whispered, "Okay," Yumiko turned to Minoru behind her and said, "Once we start attacking, back away slowly so you don't attract the thing's attention. When you've got enough distance, go up the slope and outside."

"O-okay."

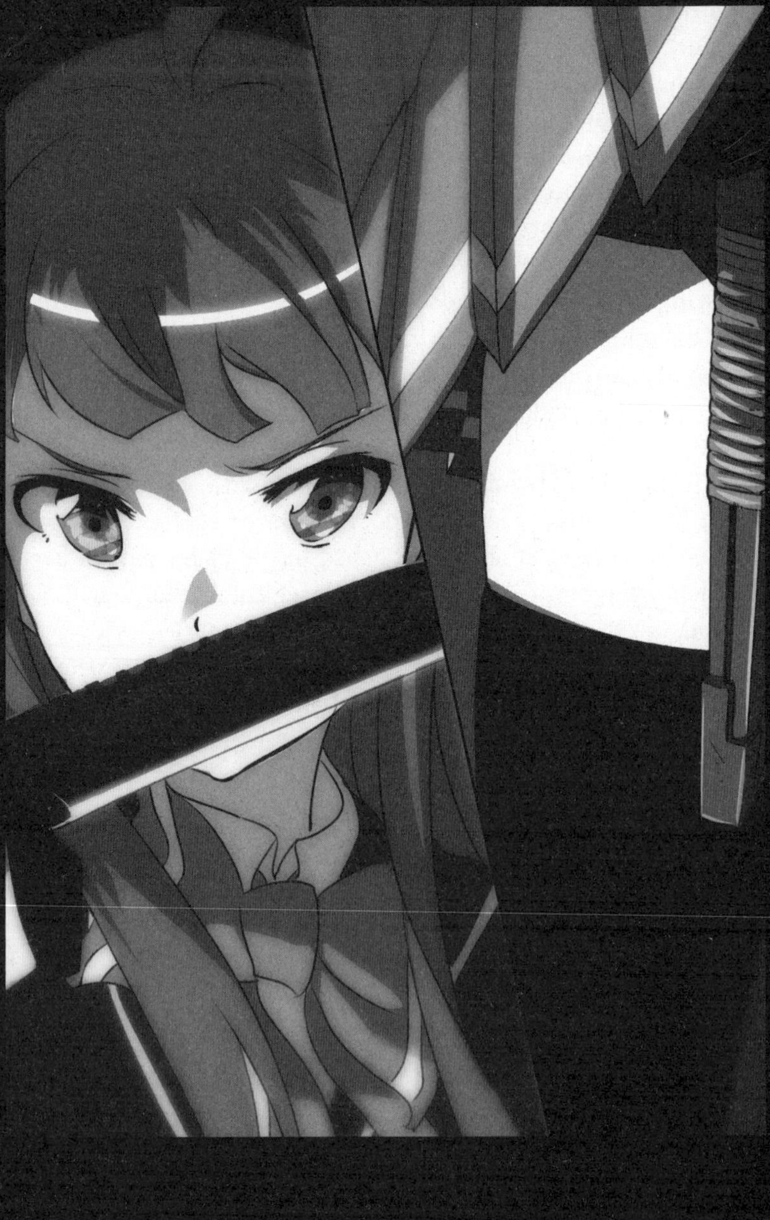

He wondered what he was supposed to do if Yumiko and DD didn't come out, but he didn't have time to ask.

Yumiko and DD caught each other's eyes and—

"Go!"

On this brief signal, DD pushed off from the asphalt first.

The underground parking lot was big, but it was laid out in a grid pattern with thick pillars standing in rows. He started running in a straight line, heading for the pillar to the left of the runaway Biter.

The monster's red eye swiveled around and followed DD's small form.

"Gruf," it groaned, rounding its back like a beast about to set upon its prey.

Aiming for its upper body, DD took one shot after another with the handgun in his right hand. With a *scritch, scritch* sound like something being clawed at, the fabric barely covering the Biter's body burst here and there.

"Groh," the Biter groaned again.

His countless teeth growing in concentric circles moved furiously, but he didn't collapse. Scratching at the ground with both hands, he took a stance similar to a crouching start facing DD, who was running toward him from the right side.

The moment the monster's left side was exposed, that's when it happened. Yumiko took a big step forward with her right foot, stepped on the asphalt floor, and pushed off.

Although it was a casual step without a bit of force, Yumiko's body vanished into thin air in an instant.

It made a *pop* like the sound of an impact, and a large amount of air came rushing toward the space where Yumiko had been a moment earlier.

"Gogwaaaaa!"

The monster gave a rage-filled, thunderous roar, and Minoru hurriedly shifted his gaze in front of him.

By then, Yumiko's attack against the monster had already succeeded. The combat knife was stabbed deep into the left side of the monster, which had been chasing DD and trying to rush at him. Yumiko's hair and skirt flew about furiously in the wind as she clutched the knife, telling of the fearsome power of her charge.

Retreating cautiously while carrying Norie as he'd been instructed, Minoru thought inwardly, *I see now.*

To borrow Yumiko's words, the acceleration—that is, the kinetic energy—created by pushing off from the ground with her left foot was amplified dozens of times, sending her charging straight ahead at a furious speed. That was Yumiko's ability.

In that case, the knife was certainly many times more compatible than the stun baton. The speed of her charge simply added to the strength of the weapon. On top of that, after seeing that furious charge that could only be described as teleportation, it was probably impossible to escape even with the reaction time of someone who possessed the Third Eye.

The monster seemed to have taken a deep wound in its lung, and another huge amount of blood spurted from its mouth.

"Gagrooooo!!" it screamed in agony and rage.

Still, without falling, it tried to cut Yumiko down with the fangs growing on its right hand.

But right before the attack hit her, Yumiko tilted her body back and pushed off from the floor with a *thump*—then disappeared. A spray of blood that flew from the wound in the monster's side was caught in the swirl of air that rose up, shooting around the room as a mist.

Yumiko appeared about ten meters back, the soles of her sneakers making a scraping noise as she braked. Then she pushed off from the ground in front of her again. With a *pop* in the air, she vanished.

She reappeared this time plunging the knife deep into the Biter's back, retreating again in an instant. By the time her opponent responded and swung its arm around, she had already traveled far away.

With deep wounds in two places, the monster reeled and fell to one knee.

Even the runaway Biter, with its extreme healing ability, seemed unable to replenish the blood it had lost. It had bled a huge amount from Yumiko's two knife attacks and from when its original head was blown off. For an ordinary person, that amount was probably enough to make them lose consciousness or die.

The red light emitted by the Ruby Eye blinked irregularly like a badly connected electric light.

Red mucus sprayed from its mouth every time it took another heaving, rushed breath.

Finally, the monster fell to both knees as if it couldn't endure the weight of its huge body. The mouths that had appeared on its palms raked the asphalt with crunching sounds, but it no longer seemed to have the strength to stand. The interval between the flickers of the Ruby Eye's light grew longer and longer.

What in the world are you? Minoru murmured in his mind, holding his breath as he watched over this scene.

The Third Eyes came down from space, latched on to humans, and gave them strange powers. Even after the host lost its life because the power became too great, the Third Eye manipulated the unconscious body and tried to attack other living things.

Just what meaning was there in that? What could be necessary about this kind of ugly and miserable conclusion?

It seemed like Yumiko and DD were thinking the same sort of things. They both came to a stop, watching the monster with pained expressions.

Finally, Yumiko clutched the knife in both hands and readied it on her right side. She put out her right foot and squatted down.

The monster raised its upper body up high, seeming to sense something.

Yumiko pushed off from the ground.

The air crackled. A dust cloud swirled up. Charging through a distance of about ten meters in an instant, Yumiko drove the knife into the heart at the center of the monster's chest, which was wrapped in thick muscle—

There was a shrill metallic *clang*. Orange sparks rent the air.

Minoru's eyes widened. Inside the torn shirt where the heart should've been, a fourth mouth had appeared.

The inside of the vertically torn skin was flesh colored like a pomegranate, and there was a row of sharp fangs around the edges. The mouth wriggled furiously, determined to bite through the blade of the knife it had firmly in its grasp.

For just a moment, Yumiko wavered between letting go of the knife and retreating or plunging it in as it was. And the monster didn't overlook this paralysis.

It flung its left arm out furiously, smashing right down the side of Yumiko's body. Without an ounce of resistance, her delicate body was sent flying and slammed into a concrete pillar a few meters away.

"Ah…"

At the same time, Minoru sucked in a breath…

"Yumii!"

DD readied his gun and charged. Yellow flashes burst one after another from the end of the silencer. But by covering its body with both its thick arms, the monster kept the bullets from hitting its trunk.

A dry metallic sound rang out, and Yumiko's knife held in the monster's chest splintered from the middle. Just like that, the mouth ground up the thick blade like it was biting through a cracker.

"Graaaaa!!"

Possibly having regained energy from eating the metal, the Biter leaned back its massive frame and howled loudly. The one eye set in the main mouth glittered a deep red like the color of blood.

DD pulled the trigger twice more. One shot missed and the other hit the monster's right leg. But he wasn't able to fire the next shot. The monster's right arm stretched out more than five meters like a snake, bit into the barrel of the gun, and took it out of DD's hand.

The gun was instantly smashed, snapping sounds accompanying its destruction, and the mouth on the monster's right hand swallowed it. DD instantly tried to jump back, but the monster dealt a heavy blow directly to his side with its left hand.

"Guh…"

DD went flying with terrifying force, slammed against a far-off pillar, and toppled to the floor.

Without even glancing at the seemingly unconscious DD anymore, the Biter's one red eye turned to Yumiko once again. She was still conscious but wasn't yet able to stand. The massive body took a huge leap and landed right in front of her. It leaned far forward and stretched its round mouth more than five centimeters, mucus dripping on Yumiko's gray skirt and getting it dirty.

At this point, Minoru probably could have escaped the threat of the monster if he had run at full speed up the slope and gotten away from the arena as instructed.

But that option didn't even occur to him. Before he knew it, Minoru was already shouting loudly.

"Stop—!!"

When the Biter, who had been trying to eat Yumiko, twitched at the sound of his voice, it turned its strangely formed head 180 degrees around to face backward, the red eye inside the mouth looking at Minoru.

The monster's response was quick. After leaving Yumiko, it charged straight at Minoru with movements like that of a large primate, the fangs on both hands digging into the asphalt. The thick smell it gave off, the most brutal Ruby Eye smell he had ever encountered, was a direct hit to Minoru's five senses.

"Grrrrr…"

The wet groan escaped from the hole in its trachea. Despite having lost its head, the body was now even larger than when it had been human. It was closing in on him right before his eyes. The fangs, which were growing in layers on the head, squirmed noisily. The mouths on its chest and hands clicked open and closed, over and over.

Taking a determined breath and getting ready to activate the protective shell—Minoru shuddered violently.

He couldn't do it.

If he used his power now, Norie would be flung from his arms and out of the shell.

The four jaws moved in on Minoru, who was frozen in a half-standing position, and Norie, who was still slumbering.

What amounted to many hundreds of fangs were glinting in turn.

While time flowed slowly as if it were being compressed, Minoru suddenly recalled a certain scene three months ago.

It was mid-September.

A typhoon had passed through in the middle of the night, and there was still a strong wind when Minoru went out for his daily early-morning run. Minoru had run the wet streets from his house to the Arakawa River. As he looked up at the clouds that flew past in the sky with tremendous speed, he suddenly had an idea and headed for a bridge he never crossed.

The state of the Arakawa River was completely different than in the daytime. True to its name, which meant "wild river," the riverbed was filled with swirling muddy-brown water. He could almost feel in the soles of his shoes the pressure of the water that thundered as it struck the girders of the bridge.

While he was staring down at the swirling surface of the water, a voice played inside his ear.

You can't do that, Mii. You can't ever go near the river after a typhoon.

It was a kind voice that had spoken to a young Minoru a long time ago, the voice of his older sister Wakaba.

Why had he forgotten it? If he had remembered, he wouldn't have come to see the river.

He lost more memories of his sister every day. The only memories piled up in that place were bitter and painful and sad.

If…

If he jumped into that river now…then would the raging current wash everything away for him? Would it carry him to the place where his sister and father and mother were waiting?

Minoru gripped the railing strongly with both hands.

That's when he had the feeling someone was calling him. Taking his eyes off the muddy-brown water, he looked up at the gray sky.

At first he thought it was a bubble. The small grayish thing that looked like a bit of foam gently floated down.

Finally, he realized that there was no way it could be a bubble. That was because there was a powerful southerly wind blowing from in front of Minoru. Whatever it was, it should have been blown apart in an instant if it were something light enough to float in the air.

But the round object descended from above Minoru's head, completely ignoring the wind. His eyes widening in amazement, Minoru lifted up both hands and cupped the object gently in his palms.

When he brought it to his face, it was something he had never seen before. Shut inside the transparent gray orb was a pitch-black orb one size smaller. It looked similar to a marble, but it drifted lightly on his palms as if it had no weight at all.

Finally, the orb rose up soundlessly, floated quickly through the air, and touched Minoru's chest.

The moment it slipped through the fabric of his running clothes and touched his skin, he felt a faint warmth. It was just as if someone had touched him gently with their fingertips.

After standing there blankly for a bit, Minoru rushed to pull down the zipper and look at his chest.

The orb wasn't anywhere there, but the skin above his sternum was a little red. However, this discoloration also disappeared within a few seconds.

What was that just now? Or was I dreaming standing up?

Inclining his head, Minoru started to walk back along the path across the bridge. He had already forgotten the urge that had begun to swallow him earlier.

Those were all the memories he had surrounding his encounter with the Third Eye. Minoru hadn't seen the Third Eye itself for more than a few dozen seconds directly.

Minoru felt something as he stared close-up at the runaway Biter's "eye"—in other words, the first Third Eye he had seen in three months. He felt some sort of purpose concealed deep within the orb.

It was something completely different from the malice, murderous desire, rage, and hatred that had dwelt in the Biter when he was human. An absolute logic of a different sort, far out of the reach of Minoru's comprehension. Not the pitch-black eyes of the great white shark or the compound eyes of an insect with a metallic glitter, but eyes that concealed a much deeper, darker remoteness.

Minoru just went on staring into the eye of the monster that was now truly trying to kill him.

It came closer as mucus dripped from those teeth, which had been able to crush even a thick knife. The hole in the center of its mouth writhed and writhed as if it were starving.

Although he knew he had to escape, had to just save Norie, his body didn't move. The bottomless pool concealed in the red eye sucked in even fear and uneasiness.

That was when—

The monster's gaze dropped a tiny bit. Minoru just knew that it had seen Norie in his arms. The inhuman light of the Third Eye flickered ever so slightly.

It was just for an instant, but Minoru had felt something humanlike in the monster's eye. It was the wavering a person felt simply because they were human during times when they were confused, distressed, or in pain.

The monster stopped moving. A low groan that sounded like "grph" slipped from the depths of its grotesque mouth. It pulled its face back. It put down its hands, the teeth clicking away. The monster backed away little by little.

When it was a few meters away from Minoru, whose eyes were wide with shock, the monster swung around. Then, changing directions completely, it released a savage war cry as it started to run.

It was running toward Yumiko, who had just now finally stood up. She was pressing on her right shoulder with her left hand as if it was still damaged. She no longer had the knife in her right hand and was now unable to pull out the stun baton.

She was powerless in the face of the huge beast that was about to attack her.

And yet the power of the determination that dwelt in her black eyes still hadn't disappeared. She quickly dropped down, putting one leg behind her and one in front.

"Groff!!"

The monster leaped at Yumiko as its starved howl thundered out.

Right before its arms touched her with their exposed fangs, Yumiko pushed off from the ground with her right foot and accelerated.

But the place where she appeared was a mere three meters away. On top of that, she failed to brake and sunk to one knee.

The monster's response was quick. Digging into the asphalt with the fangs on its left hand, it used the hand as a fulcrum to change directions, maintaining the power of its charge as it leaped.

Yumiko barely managed to stand up and accelerate again, but she made it an even shorter distance than last time.

Did Yumiko's ability of amplifying her acceleration require a sufficient initial movement to travel a distance of dozens of meters? Yumiko charged by powerfully pushing off from the ground with the leg strength of someone who possessed the Third Eye, then creating intense acceleration. Was she limited to going only two or three meters if she launched herself with a stagger?

The monster followed Yumiko and charged again. She narrowly

slipped past its right arm, which shot out like a snake, but one tooth caught the ribbon on her school uniform, and torn fabric flew through the air like blood.

That was when Minoru made up his mind and began to run. But he wasn't headed toward the slope. Laying Norie in the shadow of a concrete pillar, he ran all out toward the runaway Biter.

Even though he understood mentally that Norie's safety was his top priority, he just couldn't abandon Yumiko and DD to escape. He was never again going to sacrifice someone to survive. No way.

Noticing Minoru's footsteps, Yumiko spun around. Minoru couldn't hear what she was trying to shout; she was probably calling him an idiot.

Activating the protective shell, he ran right past Yumiko.

When the monster's eye caught Minoru's approach, it didn't waver in the least.

The Ruby Eye glinted, containing only an inhuman determination to eliminate. It came at him from the left and right with palms that had sprouted fangs.

Both hands bit into him from above the shell, but Minoru shoved down his fear and pushed off fiercely from the floor. He slammed his head into the Biter's chest.

The huge body lifted up. At the same time, Minoru shouted.

"Whoooooooh—!!"

Wrapping both hands tightly around the Biter's torso, he gathered all his remaining strength into his legs and pressed forward.

Run. He was going to run.

Maybe all that running I did was for this moment right here.

As he thought this, Minoru ran. Still lifting the Biter up, he dashed through the vast underground parking lot in a straight line.

Finally, he could see one car in front of him. A large dark blue sports car. The car the Biter had probably prepared for his getaway when he was still human.

"Come…oooon!" Minoru screamed as he slammed himself and the Biter's body into it.

The elegant line of the rear fender crunched in. The rear window shattered everywhere, and the trunk sprang open.

Blood erupted from the Biter's strangely formed mouth and the wounds made by Yumiko's knife, raining down on the protective shell. But the monster didn't stop moving. It tried to bite Minoru to death with the huge jaws on its head as it waved its arms around wildly.

Minoru gritted his teeth and stared at the line of fangs gnashing over and over a mere three centimeters from his face.

Judging by the size of the jaws, he wondered how much pressure was being put on the protective shell. This occlusion strength could be several times that of the human Biter as a Megalodon.

The circles upon circles of innumerable teeth writhed as if they had minds of their own, trying to break the shell. Even if a tooth happened to break under the pressure, another one would immediately come up from inside to fill the hole.

Minoru's whole body was numb with a fear as cold as ice. His heart pounded so hard it was painful, and his breathing grew shallow. But Minoru did his best to endure it. He could endure it because of the heat of the small life in the center of his chest.

The crimson Third Eye glowing right in front of Minoru had chosen the man called the Biter to kill people. In that case, why had the jet-black Third Eye sheltered in Minoru's chest chosen him?

Right now, he still didn't know. That was probably something he would never be able to know.

But just for the moment, he was going to trust it. To trust his own intentions, his wish to save someone besides himself.

Gritting his teeth, Minoru balled up his cold, numb right hand into a fist—and threw a punch with all he had.

The shell-covered fist plunged into the monster's left side. He hadn't really been aiming for it, but that's where Yumiko had stuck her knife in deep.

The runaway Biter leaned its massive body back, flailing both its arms wildly. Its fanged left arm sliced easily down the back of the sports car.

In the next instant—

A huge amount of transparent liquid gushed out from inside the car, soaking Minoru's shell and the Biter's body.

Water? Did that guy have a bunch of mineral water piled up in his trunk or something?

After thinking this, Minoru dispelled the thought right away. He couldn't smell anything, but this wasn't water. It was *gasoline*.

"...!!"

The idea that suddenly sprang to his mind took his breath away.

The fear came first, telling him it was impossible, but then he shook that fear off, knowing he had to do it.

But gasoline alone wasn't enough. There was one more thing he needed.

He raised his face. The Biter had released Minoru's head from his mouth and struggled in anguish, as if maybe the gasoline had gone down its trachea. This was his only chance.

Enduring the fear, he took a big breath and—deactivated the shell.

Taking care not to breathe in any of the fuel that was probably evaporating in the air, he shouted one short, loud phrase.

"Light it up!!"

Having heard his voice, the Biter immediately made a fierce move to sink its teeth into Minoru. If Minoru had been just a tenth of a second later in putting on the shell again, he probably would have lost his head. Shuddering at the sight of the fangs that stopped with a *bang* right in front of him, he waited for that moment.

Finally—

Long hair flew into view on his right side.

He looked over. Yumiko had teleported there and was standing about five meters away. The stun baton was in her right hand. But there was a hint of hesitation in her eyes.

As he pinned down the runaway Biter with the strength of desperation, Minoru yelled, aware that she couldn't hear him.

"I'm fine, so just throw it!!"

As if his words had reached her—

With a nod, Yumiko turned on the stun baton and hurled it at Minoru and the Biter. Trailing an afterimage of sparks through the air, the stun baton slowly approached and—

Minoru's vision was dyed a bright orange.

Rather than saying it caught fire, it was closer to an explosion. Minoru reflexively turned his face away from the flames that spread instantly with a roar.

But the invisible protective shell perfectly blocked that intense heat given off by the blaze—and the radiant heat from the resulting electromagnetic waves. He unconsciously inhaled at the sight of the rampaging crimson brightness a mere three centimeters away.

The runaway Biter's body was also enveloped in bright red as Minoru pinned it down.

The tatters of the Biter's suit fabric burned up instantly. The bluish-black discolored skin was burned to a blackened crisp as he watched, too. Flames swallowed up the sports car, small explosions going off in succession.

Holding down the incoherently raging monster with the power of desperation, Minoru shouted.

"Just…stop already—!!"

The mucous membrane inside of the enormous mouth started to grow inflamed. The hole of the trachea was probably shaking violently because the monster was screaming, but the sound didn't reach Minoru's ears. The Third Eye burrowed into the mucous membrane as if to escape the intense heat, but the blaze relentlessly scorched the flesh and turned it to ash.

Originally, human bodies contained a large amount of water and shouldn't burn easily even when doused in gasoline. However, possibly because of the transformations forced through by the Third Eye, the monster's body burned intensely in a fierce column of flame as if the body itself were flammable material.

Minoru could feel the sturdy flesh rapidly shriveling through the protective shell. The limbs burned up first, the exposed bone separating from the joints and tumbling to the floor.

Suddenly, the almost entirely burned torso shrank drastically, and a tiny amount of mucus was expelled from the small hole in the place where the mouth had been.

That was the final act of the monster's life. All strength suddenly drained from the weakly moving body.

Then Minoru saw it.

No longer bright, the Third Eye broke like a piece of glass art.

From inside it, a red ball of light flew up at tremendous speed.

When the light hit the ceiling of the parking lot, it made a large hole with a diameter of about two centimeters and passed through it. It pierced through the floor above, and the floor above that—through

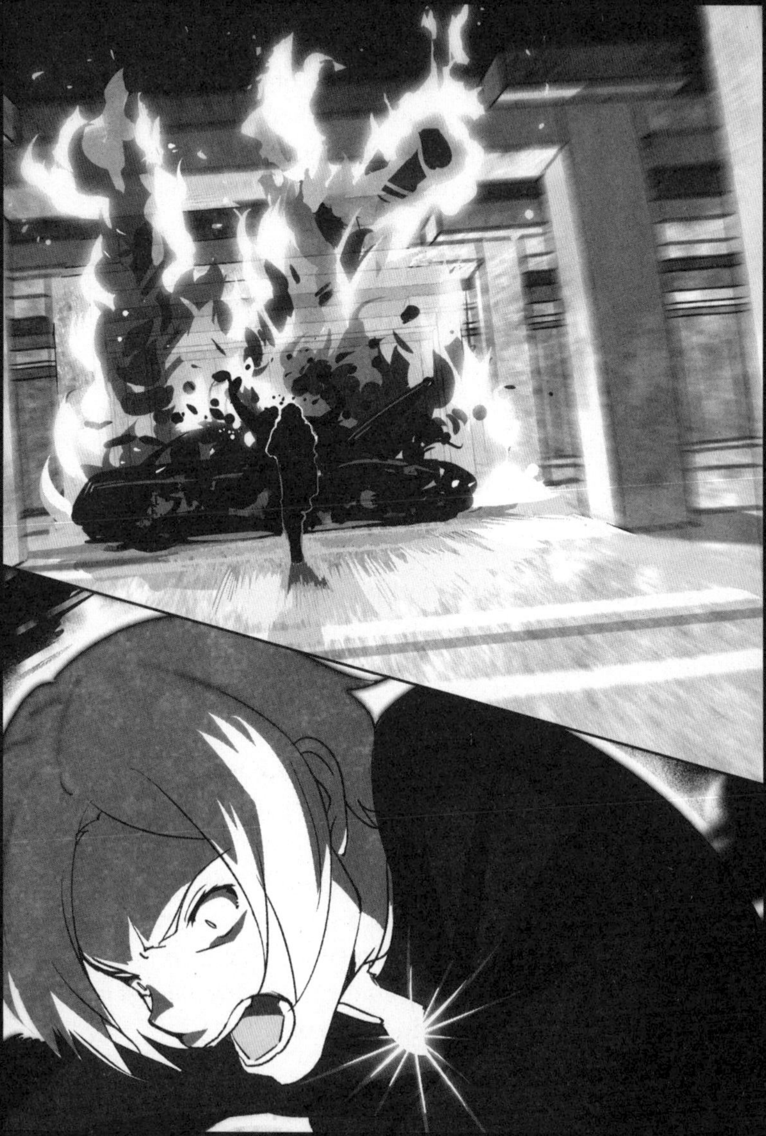

every floor of Saitama Super Arena and through the steel roof, the red light climbed and climbed.

...Is this...a Third Eye disengaging...?

At almost the same time as he thought this blankly...

Underneath him, a thousand black scraps of the flesh of a man who had been human just like Minoru were crushed and scattered.

Just as if they had been waiting for this, the ceiling sprinklers turned on and water rained down hard, washing away without a trace the soot and ash piled up on the protective shell.

9

Raising his face at the faint sound of soles rubbing against the linoleum flooring, Minoru saw Yumiko walking toward him, her long black hair swaying.

Minoru began to rise from the bench where he was sitting, but Yumiko held up her right hand to stop him.

"...How is your sister feeling?" she asked quietly.

"She woke up a little while ago and was able to talk. She's sleeping again now...," he answered in the same hushed tone.

"I see. That's a relief."

Nodding slowly, Yumiko arranged the hem of her skirt as she took a seat next to Minoru. He straightened his back unconsciously and continued to explain.

"As far as external injuries, she apparently just has some light scratches. She didn't see the Biter, either... That is to say, she doesn't really remember what happened. I explained things to her like DD told me to... That a burglar broke into the house and started to attack her, but I came home right then and he ran off..."

"Oh."

As she touched the fingertips of her right hand to her mouth, Yumiko said with a preoccupied expression, "In that case, we might not have to go so far as to do a memory block. That's up to the chief to decide, though. He'll be here really soon. You weren't hurt?"

"No, I wasn't... Are you okay, Yumiko? You should probably get someone to take a look at your wounds quickly."

On Yumiko's blazer, the fabric on the right arm, where the runaway Biter had raked her, and on the back, where she'd collided with the pillar, was shredded. At best, it would've been no surprise if she'd gotten some bumps or broken a bone—that's what Minoru had been thinking when he said that, but for some reason Yumiko stayed silent, her mouth locked in a frown.

"Um, did I...say something...?"

"No, not really. Just wondering what you should call me...," she said in a curt tone.

Hearing that, he finally realized that he'd casually called her by her first name, but even so, there was no helping it, since he didn't know her last name.

After a sidelong glance at Minoru, who was worrying over whether to apologize or get irritated himself, Yumiko gave a little shrug and answered again.

"I'm fine, just some light internal bleeding where I got hit. This level of damage is usual."

"Usual...?"

Minoru inadvertently turned his eyes away, but Yumiko went on speaking calmly.

"DD doesn't have anything wrong with his bones or organs, but he hit his head so he's being examined just in case. God, he's always making some excuse or other to skip practice, so he doesn't know even a single way to take a hit. Starting tomorrow, I'm going to have to get tough on him..."

Yumiko was talking about DD, who was probably the older of the two, like a big sister with a useless little brother. Minoru's mouth relaxed unconsciously. He'd thought she might be mad, but Yumiko only snorted.

After clearing his throat, he asked one more thing he was curious about.

"Um... So with the car on fire and the Third Eye making holes all the way up to the top floor, a lot of problematic things happened at the arena parking lot. How are you going to cover all that up...?"

"Easy. We say a meteor came down, cut through the building, and hit a car in the underground parking lot, which exploded and caught fire," Yumiko answered with a serious expression.

Minoru stared at her without meaning to.

"...B-but that's crazy..."

"The Third Eye came from space anyway. The only difference is whether it fell down or went back up."

"...O-oh, is that it..."

Three hours had passed since the fierce battle with the Biter.

The two of them were now on the top floor of a university medical hospital on the eastern side of the Omiya district in Saitama. Possibly because it was five o'clock in the morning, no other people could be seen on the dimly lit floor.

After the Ruby Eye had disengaged from the runaway Biter, Minoru and Norie had been driven to the hospital with DD behind the wheel. Just as if they'd discussed it beforehand, Norie was put on a stretcher at the emergency intake entrance and given a thorough examination right away. Luckily, she didn't have any injuries that seemed to be hurting her, but since the Biter had made her take powerful sleep medication, they put her in a private room on the top floor just to be safe.

A while ago, she had woken up for just a few minutes, spoken to Minoru a bit, and gone to sleep again. She'd probably have to take the day off from the prefectural office today.

Saying she and whoever the chief was would process the scene and keep information from leaking, Yumiko stayed behind in the arena parking lot. Minoru had worried in his own way about her injuries as he waited for Yumiko on a bench nearby Norie's private room, but after seeing how she walked just now, it seemed she wasn't seriously injured.

Judging from what she had said, she had probably been able to take the hits well. For her, even that extraordinary fight really was "usual."

But of course, for Minoru, all those things were still like events from a dream. There was a mountain of things he wanted to ask Yumiko, but he was still in a daze and couldn't even decide where to start.

As he was gazing vacantly at the predawn sky from the front

window, words that even he hadn't expected came pouring out of his mouth.

"That time... When the runaway Biter tried to kill Norie and me...," Minoru muttered.

Yumiko gazed at him hard as if encouraging him.

"...He looked at Norie and, how should I put it...seemed to hesitate. I thought there was absolutely no way he could communicate, but just for that moment, it felt like his thoughts came through. I felt like he... didn't want to kill Norie. And he actually did stop attacking... Why would he do something like..."

"..."

When Yumiko turned to face forward again, the silence continued for a few seconds, but finally she answered in a small voice.

"...It's believed that, to a certain extent, Third Eyes copy the memories and personalities of their hosts."

"Huh? ...Their m-memories...?"

"That's right. The two cases of runaway Ruby Eyes before the Biter also made repeated attacks that were mechanical and instinctual, but they said things that seemed to originate in the memories of their hosts. And that was despite the fact that the brains of their hosts were mostly destroyed at that point."

"...!"

He inhaled sharply. With his mind finally working as it considered the meaning of Yumiko's words, Minoru muttered in a hoarse voice, "...So... The reason it hesitated to attack Norie was because the memories and intentions of that man...the Biter, still remained in the Ruby Eye... Is that it...?"

"—That's the most logical way to think about it, yeah."

"But... I mean, the Biter's the absolute worst kind of person, and he's attacked and killed several people before now, right? He tried to bite and kill Minowa three days ago and all... Why would that kind of person let only Norie...?"

Having managed to say that much, Minoru bit his lip hard.

The reason that monster hadn't killed Norie was because it had copied the memories of the Biter? He felt like that hypothesis was just hard to accept.

Yumiko turned her upper body back to Minoru, who was silent.

Her dark eyes reflecting some inner hesitation, she wavered for a brief moment. But after blinking just once, the Jet Eye girl started speaking in a quiet tone.

"We've just now discovered the real name of Confirmed Ruby Eye Possession No. 29, code name Biter. He didn't have any IDs on him and his vehicle registration burned with the car. We put in an inquiry about the plate number and finally heard back...but seeing the name, both the chief and I were surprised. It was a huge shock for DD. Seems like he was a fan of the guy."

"Uh...a fan...? Was he a performer or something...?"

"Something like that. Apparently, he was a relatively famous gourmet food critic who wrote articles about restaurants for magazines and occasionally appeared on TV. Full name's Hikaru Takaesu."

"Hikaru...Takaesu...," he repeated in a whisper.

That name did sound familiar. Minoru didn't know much at all about actors or cultured people. Still, he guessed it hadn't been his imagination when he thought he'd seen the Biter somewhere before when confronting the man for the first time with his untransformed face on the roof of Saitama Super Arena.

As he was wondering why someone with that kind of social status would do those things, Yumiko started speaking again.

"Takaesu's mother was also a famous education commentator. But she died six years ago in a car accident. It's not clear whether it was really an accident or if her death was suspicious, but from a quick Internet search, it seems like Takaesu had been active in the entertainment industry with his mom since he was a kid."

"...Do you think he liked his mom...?" Minoru murmured.

Yumiko neither confirmed nor denied it. Instead, speaking in an even quieter voice that neared a whisper, she said, "I don't know. That's why I'm just stating the facts. The women we think were victims of the Biter...of Takaesu, were all unmarried regardless of their age. In other words, he never went after a housewife. These are just my completely baseless assumptions but...if the Biter projected his own mother onto your sister in her apron and kidnapped her without doing her any harm because of that...then those feelings were copied to the Third Eye, too, and that's why he didn't attack your sister even when he was in a runaway state..."

"But... If so, it's just like..."

Minoru hung his head low and forced his voice out from the back of his throat.

"It's just like the Biter's a victim, too. Are you saying he couldn't help killing people because the Third Eye was giving him orders? It's too late for something like that. He was the absolute worst sort of person who attacked and bit to death innocent people by his own choice, wasn't he? He was absolute evil, and it was natural for him to die, wasn't it...?"

After briefly falling silent at Minoru's words, Yumiko answered him in the most gentle-sounding voice she had used thus far.

"There's probably no such thing as absolute evil... Third Eyes produce many kinds of unique abilities, using the memories of the humans they enter as a template. On top of that, the Ruby Eyes give people the urge to kill others, and the Jet Eyes... Well, since I'm involved myself I'm probably not even aware of it, but I think we're definitely receiving some kind of orders, too. No one yet knows what meaning or purpose there is in that. What if...this isn't a natural phenomenon and the two colors of Third Eyes were sent to Earth by someone? If so, what the Ruby Eyes are doing might be considered good to them, and those of us getting in the way might be evil. But you know..."

Suddenly, Yumiko gently touched her fingers to Minoru's right hand, which he was clenching tightly on his lap.

"At the very least, I'm grateful for what you did, and I'm sure your sister and that girl from the track team are, too. You saved my life, DD's, your sister's, that girl's, and the lives of all the people the Biter might have killed next. No matter what anyone says, that's a good thing... Even if I question the existence of absolute evil, I also believe the opposite. There are things you should do and must do in this world, no matter what. For me, that's knocking all the Ruby Eyes all over the world back into space and decreasing the number of victims as much as I can, even if it's just by one person. Even if those actions go against the will of something in space."

"That's exactly right. There's no doubt that that, at least, is the reason we Jet Eyes exist," said a voice suddenly, full of dignity and strength.

Yumiko pulled her hand back at incredible speed, but Minoru quickly lifted his face without noticing.

A tall, thin man was walking down the hallway toward them, his shoes clicking against the floor. Although he was dressed plainly in a dark suit with a maroon tie, his sharply pointed eyes above the high bridge of his nose gave off a strong light. He might've been in his late thirties. Faint furrows were carved at both sides of his mouth and on his brow, but his pitch-black hair was neatly smoothed down, giving him a youthful look.

Was this man the chief whose name he had heard so many times?

His image was far from the managerial one associated with such a title; he looked like a warrior who would appear in a period novel. Usually, Minoru would be intimidated in front of a dignified person like this. But now, he stood up naturally without averting his eyes. Maybe it was because he was so exhausted or because he was aware that this was a Jet Eye, one of his own kind.

Yumiko stood up next to him at the same time. Putting both hands behind her back, she spoke first to Minoru.

"This is our chief. He has the dangerous ability of being able to manipulate the memories of other people. And, Chief, this is probably the final Jet Eye in the Kanto region. His ability—"

"I've heard. Should I call it a…complete defensive shield? It really is quite interesting. You're a professor's dream," he said in a voice that was smooth yet carried well.

The man gave a faint smile as he held out his right hand to Minoru.

"Good to meet you. I'm Himi, in charge of the Special Section of the Health and Safety Department in the Ministry of Health, Labor, and Welfare. Special Sec for short."

Minoru rushed to shake the hand that had been offered.

"Oh, I'm U-Utsugi."

"You don't have to be so formal. My ability isn't as dangerous as Yumiko here says. I can't do anything unless a person cooperates with me."

"No…I'm sure it's…"

The man named Himi had a huge hand that was both tough and pliant, likely honed by martial arts; Minoru felt just as if it were enveloping his whole body. After zoning out for a moment, he hurriedly released the hand.

"Uh, my own ability isn't a very powerful one. It can't protect anyone but me... Yumiko and DD were both injured fighting the Biter, and only I was unhurt...," Minoru somehow managed to say in an indistinct voice, his eyes still down.

But Himi's quiet yet clear voice overlapped the end of his sentence, which trailed off weakly.

"Yet you didn't run away."

Minoru's body tensed with a start, and Himi gently placed a large hand on his shoulder.

"To save your sister and Yumiko and DD, you made the best possible use of your ability and your surroundings to fight a huge enemy instead of running away. Even among Jet Eyes, there aren't many people who can do that. Let me be direct. You're the kind of person we need. Minoru Utsugi, please work with us to—"

"Please don't." Minoru cut Himi off, shaking his head with his eyes still down.

He looked up at the tall man's bold features for just a moment, then dropped his gaze immediately.

"If you know my name, then you've already looked into the incident eight years ago anyway. If so, you should know. I'm someone who runs, someone who hides. The only thing that's important to me is to have a peaceful everyday life. Even the reason I tried to save Minowa or Norie or Yumiko and DD was because I would feel bad if I couldn't save them... That's all there was to it."

"What's wrong with that?" Yumiko said from behind him, her tone unexpectedly soft.

Minoru just stood there, unable to turn around. He was even more surprised as he listened to what she said next.

"I'm sorry. I said a lot of things to you in the park that were unfair."

"...No... It's totally natural that someone would want to say those things to me..."

"That's not true. I...was probably jealous of your ability. It's because I thought...if I'd had your ability, I might have been able to save people that I failed to save before..."

"..."

"But it really was just my ego after all. I thought all that because I wanted to make things easier on myself... But...I want to save people when I'm able to do so, even if I'm only doing it for me. People don't even know why they really do things themselves, so I don't think it matters what your motivation is. What matters is what you do. That's all. I'm repeating myself, but...you saved my life. Whatever reason you had for doing that doesn't change how grateful I am. —What is it, Chief?"

Her last comment was directed to Himi over Minoru's shoulder. Minoru kept his eyes down as, in front of him, Himi spoke with a slight smile in his voice.

"Well...it's just that I was surprised. This is the first time I've heard you talk like this, Yumiko."

"Stop that... Anyway, I'm done talking."

Yumiko flung herself down onto the bench with a *thud*.

Biting his lip hard, Minoru replayed a part of what Yumiko had said in his mind.

What matters is what you do.

So is she saying someone like me would be able to do something?

Since discovering the nature of the protective shell, Minoru had thought that the orb had given this ability to him so he could cut himself off from the world. He had thought that it heard his never-ending prayers to be alone and was granting that wish through physical means.

But was that wrong?

Was this power given to him so that he could atone? Was somebody saying that by protecting more people he could make up for the sin of hiding alone in a dark hole while watching his father and mother and sister die...?

There's no way I can make up for it. Even if I saved dozens or hundreds of people, I doubt the stake of guilt driven deep into my chest would come out.

...But—but.

...If someday I lost my life in the process of fighting to save someone...

...Would you forgive me the next time we meet... Waka...?

Minoru didn't know how long he'd been silent. But when he slowly lifted his gaze, Himi was there, waiting for Minoru's response, his expression completely unchanged.

Minoru turned around just for a moment. After looking into Yumiko's eyes, who seemed like she wanted to give him a push, he turned to face Himi again.

"I'd like to ask you to surgically remove my Third Eye and erase all my memories related to it…but it would be no use, would it?"

"My apologies, but the answer is no."

"If I do work with your organization, do I get some kind of reward someday when everything with the Ruby Eyes has been settled?"

"Yes. When Special Sec is dissolved, the members will be given a bonus for their services. I can't tell you the amount here, however."

"Is that so? …It's only been three months since the Third Eyes came down, but you're so well prepared."

Himi smiled enigmatically at Minoru's comment.

"Well, there's a lot behind that. If you like, it would be possible for us to pay part of the bonus upfront…"

"I don't need a single yen," he said plainly, continuing. "But when everything is over, I want to use your ability."

Hearing this, Himi raised his eyebrows just slightly but encouraged Minoru to continue with a wave of his hand. After taking a deep breath, Minoru told him the rest.

"Use your ability to…erase all the memories related to me from everyone who knows me. From you guys as well."

Complete silence stretched on for a few seconds. As dawn gradually approached outside the window, an ambulance siren wailed faintly.

"—But realistically, wouldn't that be impossible?" Himi asked in an appropriately surprised voice.

Minoru gave his head a little shake.

"To be precise, you can just erase the memories of people who I'm aware know me relatively well. There shouldn't be that many, even in the neighborhood around my house and my school."

"…I don't understand what you'd gain from that, but…but if that's what you want, I'll make that promise. As long as I'm alive then, that is."

"Thank you. Then…if you want me, I'd like to join Special Sec and…"

"Your sister, too? You'd erase her memories of you, too?"

The one who cut Minoru off was Yumiko. Her tone itself was calm, but her voice had an edge of severity similar to when he'd first met her. Minoru turned around again and nodded.

"If I wasn't around, Norie could build her own family and live for herself."

"...I don't think even you know if that's what she wants, but... So what would you do, then, in a world where no one knows you?"

Yumiko's eyes gave off a challenging light, and Minoru stared right back into them.

"Who knows... Maybe...I just want to find out. Find out what a world where no one knows me is like."

Yumiko didn't attempt to make a single sharp comment in response. A little way away from her, Minoru listened to Chief Himi as he explained the details. It was decided that Minoru would visit the Special Sec headquarters in Tokyo the day after tomorrow when school let out. As they shook hands once more, Himi added something as if he'd just remembered it.

"Oh... While we're on the subject, I'm now headed for a meeting with the girl you saved...Tomomi Minowa."

"Oh...is Minowa in this hospital?"

"Uh-huh. Special Sec has what you might call a special arrangement with this hospital. At any other hospital, a detective from the precinct would come charging in immediately if we said someone was injured after being attacked by a burglar."

"That's...true. But why has Minowa been hospitalized for three whole days? Was she hurt...?"

"No, luckily she has almost no injuries, but she saw the Biter while he had his ability activated... After she regained consciousness, it took quite a while to give her careful counseling, explain the situation to her, and request that she cooperate with the memory block."

"...You're going to erase her memory...?"

"That's the standard procedure and also the best way to handle things. Even without being injured, the fear from being attacked by a Ruby Eye puts a huge burden on a victim's heart," Himi said frankly. He continued in a quiet voice, "To be absolutely sure, we'll seal all memories going back several hours before being attacked by the Biter. She's given her consent but says she would like to see you once before then. It seems she'd like to thank you. What will you do?"

"Oh... But isn't she just going to have her memory erased anyway...?" Minoru muttered, inclining his head.

Yumiko, who was leaning against the wall with her arms folded, said in a slightly harsh voice, "You really don't understand people's feelings, do you? Even if she forgets, you'll still have the memory, right? That's waaay more important, at least for her."

"..."

But for me—

For me, memories are always heavy, painful, sad things, Minoru repeated to himself as he recalled all the things that had happened after he ran across Tomomi Minowa on the embankment of the Arakawa River in the early morning.

He definitely did wonder what would have happened if he hadn't said or done the things he did then.

But it was surprising even for Minoru that that wasn't all he felt. Tomomi smiling in front of a backdrop of pure white fog. Tomomi as they walked next to each other down the hallway at school. Even Tomomi shedding tears on the bench in Akigase Park. Inside him, these images gave Minoru a feeling of sweet pain that was not at all unpleasant.

"...Let me see Minowa," Minoru said softly.

Himi nodded, smiling.

Tomomi Minowa's hospital room was also on the highest floor, not too far from the private room Norie was in.

When Himi knocked on the door, a voice from inside answered right away, saying, "Come on in."

With Yumiko prodding him in the back, Minoru steeled himself and pulled open the sliding door. When he stepped into the private room, the thing he sensed before anything else was not the smell of fresh flowers beside the bed, but the scent of Tomomi herself that he had smelled countless times. It reminded him of the sun.

"What're you just standing there for?" a voice from behind him said quietly.

208 THE ISOLATOR Sect. 001 - The Biter

Minoru stepped forward as he thought, *And what're you doing following me?*

Going around the white curtain, he saw Tomomi Minowa sitting upright serenely in the middle of the large bed.

Over her yellow pajamas, she was wearing an ivory cardigan. She seemed better than he had expected. The moment she saw Minoru, she broke into a big grin and waved her right hand.

"Mornin'! I'm glad you came, Utsugi. Don't just stand over there; c'mere."

Having already been told that earlier, he couldn't help but walk over to the bedside. Luckily—if luck was the right word for it—Yumiko and Himi stayed on the other side of the curtain.

"G…good morning, Minowa. How are you feeling…?"

He felt embarrassed about looking directly at Tomomi in her pajamas while he asked, but he managed to keep eye contact as she looked straight at him.

"I'm *completely* fine. From the start, I was only a little scratched up. Wanting to run is really driving me crazy."

After bouncing her feet up and down under the covers and laughing, Tomomi suddenly fell silent.

After a few seconds of silence, she asked him quietly, "…What happened to him…?"

He knew instantly that she was talking about the Biter. So Tomomi really had seen the Ruby Eye with his grotesquely transformed face, and she remembered it well, too.

Taking a big breath, Minoru spoke each word clearly.

"…Everything's fine now. He's gone."

"Really?! Did you crush him for me, Utsugi?!"

"…"

Of course, it wasn't like Minoru had taken down—no, killed—the Biter on his own. But if he tried to be modest and hold back in front of Tomomi now, it would only be for his own sake.

Minoru nodded with a soft yet certain motion and said, "Yeah. I have a power that lets me fight guys like that. So if any more bad guys come around, it's fine. Because I…"

Minoru stopped to take a breath and said in a louder voice, "Because I'll protect you, Minowa."

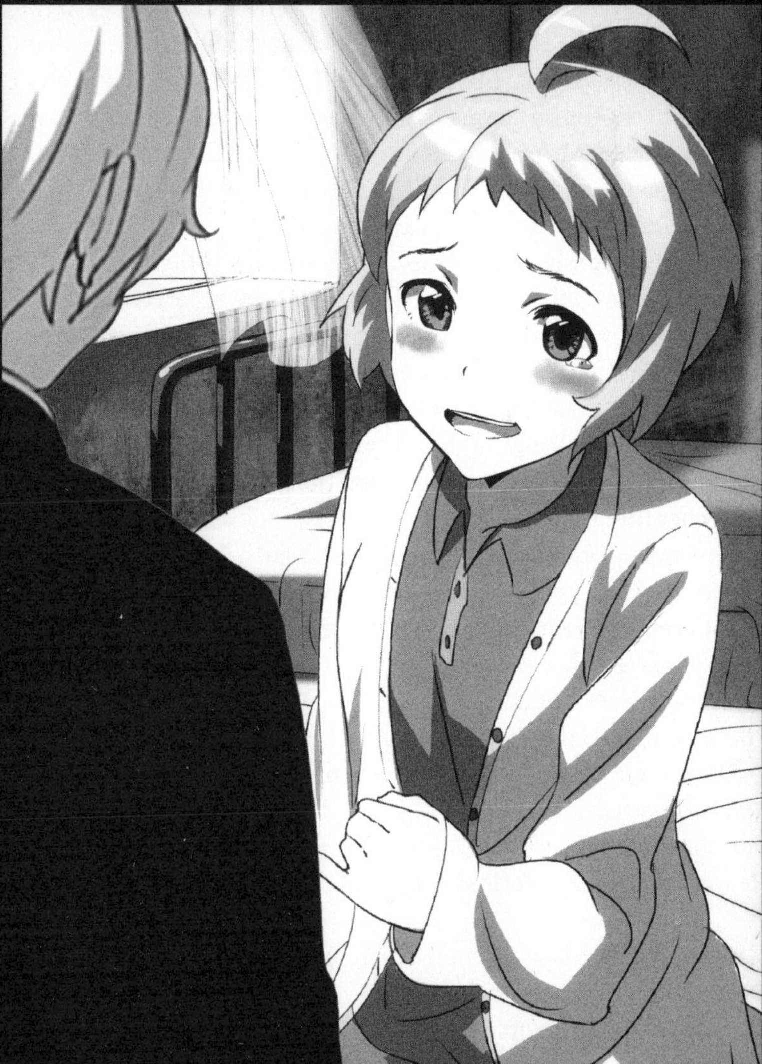

At this, Tomomi's eyes grew even wider, glittering like a starry sky. The stars gathered together and spilled from her eyes as pale, twinkling drops of water.

Minoru had seen Tomomi's tears three days ago in the twilight of Akigase Park as well. But now, he felt like the tears that wetted her white cheeks were a completely different color and temperature.

Even as the teardrops spilled from her eyes, Tomomi gave him another big smile and said, "Okay," in a shaking voice.

After taking a few deep breaths and getting her trembling breathing under control, she wiped her cheeks and went on talking.

"Um, you know…they've been telling me I have to forget what happened in the park. I don't mind forgetting about that scary guy, but… it's too bad that I'll forget you protected me, Utsugi."

"…Mm…"

With Minoru unable to say anything else, Tomomi leaned forward in bed and put out her right hand. From the clenched hand, she stuck out only her thin pinkie.

"Hey, Utsugi, promise me something. Even if I forget what happened in the park or all the times I talked to you before then…promise you'll still be my friend again when we meet on the embankment of the Arakawa River."

"…Okay." Minoru nodded.

Putting out his right hand, he wrapped his pinkie around Tomomi's.

As they said, "Pinkie swear," in unison, Minoru realized that he would at least keep this promise, even if this was a relationship he would someday lose.

He was just a little surprised at himself for thinking that way.

Minoru and Yumiko went out, leaving Himi in the hospital room to perform Tomomi's memory block.

They cut through the hallways and stood in front of a window. In the eastern sky, the morning star shone white amid the gradient created by night turning to morning.

The red and black Third Eyes had come from a much farther place than that star and descended to Earth. And then they changed the fates of those humans they encountered.

What meaning was there in that? Or was there no meaning at all?

"—Do you still feel like you want that girl…and everyone around you to forget about you?" Yumiko said quietly as she, too, looked up at the stars from beside him.

Minoru nodded, dropping his gaze to the city lights on the surface of the Earth.

"Well, then, I guess we'll only be knowing each other for a limited amount of time. For the time being, I'll introduce myself. Face this way."

Minoru turned. As she faced him and stuck her right hand straight out, she spoke in a dignified voice.

"—My name is Yumiko Azu, code name Accelerator. Let's work well together until I forget you."

So we never actually gave each other our names, he thought as he gently gripped Yumiko's scratched-up hand.

"I'm Minoru Utsugi. Let's work well together for as long as you remember me."

The End

AFTERWORD

Nice to meet you, or long time no see. This is Reki Kawahara. Thank you for reading the first volume of *Isolator*.

This is my first new series in the five years since my debut in 2009, but just like another of my works, *Sword Art Online*, this book is based on a work that was serialized on the Internet. I'd like to start off by writing about why the book was released at this point, when both *SAO* and *Accel World* are still being published.

There are two major reasons. The first is that, although I put *Isolator* (the title of the Web version is slightly different: *Isolation*) on hiatus while it was still incomplete, it's been stuck in the corner of my mind ever since my pro debut. If I had to say one way or the other, I tend to be the type who writes stories under pressure, so I was always concerned that I might never start writing it again if I abandoned it at this point.

The second reason is an issue of capacity.

For these past five years, I've basically published books at a rate of six books a year, putting one out every even month. This wasn't really something I decided from the start. When the end of the year approaches and my editor and I discuss the next year's schedule, it concludes with me declaring my intentions by saying something vague like, "Well…let's do things the same way we did this year I guess…"

That's why I didn't think much of it when, at the end of last year, my editor and I agreed to do one less book in 2014 for a total of five books. This was because the time it takes me to work on one book has gone up in comparison to the start of my debut and because it seems like my work outside of publishing will be increasing. However, afterward, a feeling of doubt or maybe hesitation bubbled up inside me. I wondered, *Is it okay to mess up my pace this easily? Before I decrease the number of books I publish, shouldn't I do my best for as long as I can?*

Even I don't really understand what point there is in getting hung up on six books. Maybe it's just that I'm randomly afraid of having something or other change when I do five books. In any case, that's when I thought of taking the existing manuscript of *Isolator*, doing the minimum amount of editing, and turning it into a book. I thought if

I did that, I could release one more book without putting pressure on my schedule.

Of course, before that, I had to get my editor to read the manuscript and look into whether it would be right for publishing. Luckily I received the okay, so I dove right into the editing.

However, the portion that seemed suitable for the first book was a draft from ten years ago, so parts that bothered me just kept coming up... I tried to fix everything that I could within reason, from small things like sentence composition and phrasing all the way up to big things like establishing characters, but before I knew it I'd rewritten more than 90 percent of the manuscript.

Naturally this took more time than either *SAO* or *AW*. It put intense pressure on my schedule, and I got to hear things like, "I knew this would happen..." from my editor. Still, I have no regrets. I feel that I poured every last drop of the light novel skills I currently have into this book, so now the only thing left is to hope that you all will enjoy it.

I'll end the discussion of the publishing process here and talk about the content a bit as well.

If we were to summarize *Isolator* by genre, would it go into the "supernatural battling" category? I'm both surprised and impressed by myself from ten years ago; he allowed himself to just write using the twist-free premise of "young men and women with mysterious abilities battling evil and powerful people." However, when I think about it, my other two works don't have any big twists, either, so instead of giving up on this book as being just that...I plan to be positive and move forward like I'm pitching a fastball as hard as I can.

If there was a part that could somehow be thought of as a twist, would it be the main character Minoru's ability? It's called a "protective shell" in the book, but more simply, it's the embodiment of something else: Who didn't, as a child, cross their arms in front of themselves and shout, "Force field"?

...I apologize, I guess that's not really a twist after all...

It's a complete protective ability that might seem a little strange for a main character. However, for me this was a rare series where I also wrote quite a bit from the enemy's point of view, so this adds the element of powerful enemies trying to figure out how to conquer Minoru's complete protective barrier. I'm working so hard to accumulate ideas that I even asked all of you to let me know through Twitter or letters if you had any great ideas about how to conquer it. Still, since the publication of *Zettai Naru Kodokusha* originally started from coincidence, it still hasn't been decided when the second book will come out. Before that, the publisher is still undecided about whether or not to put out the second book... But for now I'll say that all I can do as the author is try my hardest! With that, I hope to see you for the second book that will (probably) come out someday. The subtitle for this one will be "The Igniter."

To my editor Miki, who went through so much trouble and concern and annoyance because of the process I explained earlier, thank you for taking such great care of me! To Shimeji, who again took on a variety of difficult tasks involved in illustrating a light novel and who provided cool, beautiful, and impactful illustrations, thank you so very much! And just one more time here at the end, I'd like to ask all of you to cheer me on!

A certain day in April 2014
Reki Kawahara